NINE

ZACH HINES

WITHDRAWN

NINE

HARPER TEEN
An Imprint of HarperCollinsPublishers

Nine
Copyright © 2018 by Zach Hines
All rights reserved. Printed in the United States of America.
No part of this book may be used or reproduced in any manner whatsoever without written
permission except in the case of brief quotations embodied in critical articles and reviews.
For information address HarperCollins Children's Books, a division of HarperCollins
Publishers, 195 Broadway, New York, NY 10007.
www.epicreads.com

Library of Congress Control Number: 2018933340
ISBN 978-0-06-256726-0 (trade bdg.)

18 19 20 21 22 PC/LSCH 10 9 8 7 6 5 4 3 2 1
❖
First Edition

For all those who feel like they've already given up more lives than they even knew they had

IN THE SUMMER OF 1808, IN A WORLD PARALLEL TO OUR own, the sun flared, the sky turned orange, and the clouds gathered. It rained torrentially for months straight. After this "summer of storms," society emerged forever changed.

People discovered they had not one life, but nine. In order to avoid overpopulation and famine, governments devised a system of elimination in which people are rewarded for shedding their extra lives, bit by bit . . .

. . . until they are left with one.

PART ONE

CHAPTER 1

JULIAN HAD NO IDEA WHAT IT MEANT TO DIE.

Of course he didn't. How could he?

And yet, here he was.

Molly had to practically drag him to this party. To this beautiful house up on the hill, which was, tonight only, filled with teenagers. Apparently it was Gloria Merriweather's second house. Her parents never left their primary home in Magnolia Crescent, so it was all theirs tonight.

It really was the perfect place to die. It was isolated. There was a pool. There was a good breeze. You could see stars.

The party was a few hours old, and everyone, apart from Julian, was a few drinks deep; loose enough to get on with the main event. The Burners—dressed in white, as always—organized everyone into stations. One of them, a pudgy-faced boy in a white blazer with a red streak in his otherwise jet-black hair, directed Molly to the fireplace, where they were playing Kiss or Cap.

"Your last chance," Molly said to Julian. "Are you sure you're not going to join me?"

Molly was a good friend—Julian's only friend, really. He looked at the Two tattooed on her neck, and unconsciously touched the One on his. He dreaded the thought of having to navigate the party on his own, but he was definitely not going to join her at Kiss or Cap. He was even more certain of that now that he could see the unrestrained, perverse glee in every Burner eye.

"I'm sure," Julian said. "I don't even know why I came. And now I'm just making it weird for you."

"It's all right," Molly said.

Julian knew Molly wouldn't push. She got it. She got *him*, or at least Julian always assumed she did. Even so, he felt a sliver of shame at leaving her like this.

"Just promise to pick me up, okay?" Molly said.

"I'll be there," Julian said as the red-streak boy led Molly away to the fireplace. Julian waited a moment, then followed a few steps behind them. He found a quiet spot in the back of the room. He watched as Molly joined a group of six or seven kids in front of the fireplace. They were sitting on a thin plastic sheet spread out on the white carpet.

A beautiful Burner girl in a sharp white blazer—Constance—looked Molly up and down. "You're just in time for the next spin." She lit a stick of incense and put oddly serene electronic music on the stereo. She brushed her long, black hair over her shoulder in an unnecessary theatrical flourish, and then led Molly to a spot among her disciples.

4

"This is my circle, which means my rules," Constance explained. "Fortunately, I only have one: leave your inhibitions behind. Because no matter how dark your secret desires are, I want you to face them and embrace them. That's the way I host Kiss or Cap." Her red lips curled into a smile.

Constance's audience was arranged as if for spin the bottle, but instead of a bottle sitting between them, it was a 9mm handgun. Constance picked up the gun. She produced a full clip of bullets from her handbag, then slid it into the magazine well. In sure, confident movements, she cocked the gun to chamber a bullet, turned off the safety, and handed it to Molly. "Your turn."

Julian watched as Molly gingerly sat the gun on the floor in front of her, took a nervous breath, and spun it. It landed on Constance. A sly grin snaked across her face.

"Well, well," Constance said. The kids in the circle suppressed nervous chuckles. "Your first spin, and you've landed on the mistress. So . . . ," she said, staring Molly down.

"Will you kiss me? Or are you going to cap me?"

Molly picked up the gun and put it to the center of Constance's forehead. Molly closed her eyes. She swallowed, and the corners of her mouth twitched, betraying her nervousness in that Molly way that Julian instantly recognized.

Molly, he thought. You know you want to kiss her. So what are you doing?

Julian was suddenly struck with the feeling that, somehow in the last five minutes, Molly had become capable of social grandstanding.

He watched as Molly bit her lip, blushing. Her hand on the pistol was trembling.

5

Julian found himself holding his breath. He did not want to see what happened next. He left for the bathroom down the hall.

Inside, sitting in a full bathtub, he found Clayton Maxwell, from the back row of the calculus classroom. He was wearing goggles, a swim cap, and was drinking his own bathwater from a long straw.

"Don't worry," Clayton said. "It's just vodka. I'm drinking until I drown! Want a shot?" He laughed and sucked down a gulp of bathwater.

"No thanks," Julian said, and he backed out of the room.

What a complete and utter waste of time this was. What a waste of life. Of course, Julian understood that stupidity was the entire point of the evening; this was, after all, a Burners party, which by definition meant lives were to be wasted. But no matter how he looked at it, he could not see the humor. How is it even a joke when there is no one left at the end of the night to laugh at it?

So why not leave? he asked himself. Then he decided—

Yes, I should leave. I gave it a fair shot, and it was even worse than I expected.

Julian pulled his collar up to hide his One and weaved through the house full of giddy kids. They were all drunk, high, and ready to do something incredibly, ridiculously dumb. A junior in a white T-shirt, his hair dyed black in the Burners style, limped into the living room with a machete proudly sticking out of his stomach. Everyone cheered. He fist-bumped his bros, and two girls in short shorts reached for the blade, but he playfully slapped their hands away. His eyes were large and delirious, his pupils dilated.

"Careful now," Julian heard him say. "If this falls, I'm gonna

bleed out. It slid in real smooth and easy too, just like . . . butter."
He winked. The girls giggled. The kid's face was turning pale,
and he was covered in a shiny film of sweat. A ring of blood had
oozed out around the puncture wound, darkening the hole in his
white shirt. He must have been heavily anesthetized.

Julian winced and slipped through the crowd for the exit.

At the door to the porch, he got cornered by a kid in glasses—
Logan—who was hopped up on some kind of amphetamine. He
intensely ranted to Julian about his plan to hire a hot-air balloon
to perform the ultimate high dive into the Lake. "From. One.
Mile. High!" he said, practically shouting the last word into
Julian's face. The kid's eyes bulged from behind his glasses to
emphasize his cleverness.

"Uh, cool," Julian said flatly. "Good luck with that." He
slipped away when Logan found another person to inflict his
genius upon.

Julian crossed the yard, heading for his car parked in the
driveway. But he lingered for a moment in the garden by the
pool. Strung up above the water, dangling threateningly from
extension cords, were dozens of toaster ovens, blenders, and
other electronics.

Boys in trunks and girls in bikinis were standing on the roof,
ready to jump. They were shivering in the night air, all of them
holding a part of a long cable that kept the electronics aloft above
the water.

In the middle of them stood their signal-master, their conductor, Nicholas Hawksley. His jet-black hair was slick in a perfect
swoop, the number tattoo on his neck—a Five—bold against his
pale flesh.

Julian felt a shiver go up his spine. The painful lengths that some people will go to for a DeadLinks post. . . .

On the roof, shots were passed down the line. The kids were becoming heavily drunk—as they would need to be. Even as they tilted their heads back, finishing their drinks, their eyes never drifted from Nicholas. He paced before them with a twisted smirk on his face—angelic but shifting and dangerous—his white jacket flapping stiffly in the wind. His audience awaited his word, rapt.

Julian just wanted to disappear behind the hedges, head down the driveway to his car, and get out of there. But something about Nicholas commanded even his attention.

Nicholas shouted so everyone could hear, inside and out.

"And so, we come to the centerpiece of the *Night of the Terrible Twos*! Being Twos, you've already popped your death cherry. So that's a start. Good for you!"

Cheers rippled through the crowd.

"But Three is a much bigger milestone," he said. "When you hit Three, you will have proven yourself worthy of the Burners. And the first thing you need to learn . . . is how to burn with style."

Bang!

A gunshot rang out from the house. Everyone flinched at the noise, and Julian grimaced, thinking of Molly. Nicholas let the ring of the gunshot settle into silence, and then continued.

"We embrace death, and we make a mockery of it," he said. "Death. She is our bitch!" The crowd roared in approval.

Nicholas then held a hand in the air until the cheers died down.

"On my mark," he said, surveying his audience. He balled

8

his hand into a fist and looked into each and every nervous face. Then he brought his arm down with a swift, strong motion. "Banzai!"

Everyone shouted "Banzai!" in return and leaped into the pool, the electronics plunging in with them, electricity dancing over the water in skeletal blue fingers.

Screams of horror, gasps of pain, the hiss of extermination. Julian watched from the shadows, his pulse quickening, his mouth becoming dry.

Bang, bang, bang, bang, bang!

Staccato gunshots erupted from the house like firecrackers. Julian covered his ears. There was a pause, and then another, final *bang* from the pistol.

After that, a silence descended upon the house and the yard. Only moments before, it was alive with activity, with stupidity. Now it was still and motionless.

Then a moaning gurgled up from behind the pool.

Julian crept from his spot in the shadows. Dead kids bobbed to the surface of the pool as Julian approached the source of the sound.

A kid in board shorts missed the target—Jeffrey from World History. He had cracked his head on the concrete ledge beside the pool and lay like a crumpled doll. Julian caught a slimy glint of something he should never see, and quickly turned away. Jeffrey was moaning, choking on himself, struggling to get out some final words. Words of regret? Some kind of dark, unspeakable ecstasy? Julian couldn't tell, and he didn't want to know.

He caught a whiff of the metallic smell of blood and felt nauseous, but he resisted the urge to vomit.

Molly.

Maybe she didn't go through with it. Maybe she said, *Julian is right, this Burning thing is stupid.* Maybe she was waiting for him to come back and get her.

Julian hurried across the yard back toward the parlor. A cloud of smoke, a mixture of incense and gunpowder, escaped as he opened the door. Everyone around the Kiss or Cap ring was on the floor now, eyes closed, lights out. The backs of some heads were missing. Julian quickly looked away, but his eyes landed on the dark blood pooling on the plastic sheet. The blood was everywhere he looked. Inescapable. The oddly chill electronic music was still playing.

He crept over the bodies. He saw Constance in the middle of the circle, lying faceup, her eyes wide open, a gunshot through her temple, a fan of blood spread out on the opposite side. The pistol was still clutched in her hand.

He turned away from her and caught sight of Molly but quickly looked away. She was lying on a beanbag.

Julian couldn't make himself look at her again. He closed his eyes and stood for a moment, just feeling his heart thudding in his chest. "Molly?" he said, his eyes still closed. There was no answer.

You have to see, he thought.

Why else have you not left yet?

Just look.

Julian opened his eyes.

There was a red dot in the center of Molly's forehead leaking a thin stream of blood. Julian breathed a sigh of relief. It could have been much worse. Thank god he didn't have to see it from the back.

Julian turned off the music and sat down on the floor beside Molly's body. After a moment, the death rattle of the kids outside subsided, and utter silence fell over the room.

There was no one left to laugh at anything.

Just like that, the party was dead.

CHAPTER 2

MOLLY TERRA FELT THE MOST AMAZING MOMENT OF PER-fect, incandescent bliss. She was floating in a soft, cleansing jelly, suspended and separated from who she used to be. Ecstasy radiated through her in waves. Then her eyes snapped open and filled with water. The pleasure vanished instantly, replaced with animal instinct. With terror.

She thrashed around. By reflex, her mouth opened to scream, but water rushed into her, filling her lungs. She choked, panicked. Then she realized: she was in the Lake.

Calm down—you know what to do. You've been through this before.

Molly started kicking, clawing her way up. She broke the surface and spat out water, replacing it with huge gulps of air. She centered herself, treading. The pleasure that had been coursing through her had already faded into a strange emptiness. Molly wiped her eyes and looked around.

An eerie mist cloaked the Lake. Up ahead, a bright light in the fog strobed twice, followed by a heavily amplified signal tone, like a foghorn. Molly remembered—*Follow the light, follow the signal.* As her faculties returned, she tried to reach back into her memory for what had happened—to find the grim turn of events that had delivered her here. But there was nothing specific. Her last memory was Julian picking her up for a party. What was it? How did she go from there to here?

This gap in her memory frightened her, but she had her wits enough to recall the rebirth sickness phenomenon. Few very rarely remember the moments leading up to their demise. A fog shrouded any recollection of the actual moment.

That moment didn't matter now, anyway.

What mattered was that she was reborn in the Lake. The same as it was the first time, and the same as it would be for each time afterward: trudging, wet and disoriented, through luke-warm water toward the shore, toward higher life numbers, and, inexorably, toward the future.

Molly was growing up.

Eventually, her toes reached the silky mud of the lake bottom. She was able to stand, her neck and shoulders rising out of the water. She pushed the rest of the way to shore, more and more of her naked body emerging. She tried to hide herself, but it was difficult. Soon she gave up on the idea totally. Naked was fine, she decided. She was being reborn, after all.

Other people emerged from the mist around her. There was Constance. Molly caught her eye, but Constance looked away from her. Molly felt ashamed. Did she do something wrong? Molly could feel her face flush, but she kept steady. Kept trudging toward the shore.

When she reached the beach, Molly was met by the nurses in their distinctive powder blue robes. Their movements were clinical and professional. Saying nothing, a nurse handed Molly a towel and a paper gown.

"Is it crowded?" Molly asked as she wiped her face. The nurse didn't respond. She just directed Molly toward an imposing white brick facility. Inside was a throng of people organized into lines. Some were young, some were old, but they were all clad in paper gowns—all newly reborn. Processing.

Molly could feel herself slowly returning, like an image on a TV resolving from static. Officers read instructions: "Stay in your line. Please be patient. Be considerate of your fellow citizens."

Molly looked at the wet faces around her. Many of them, she was starting to realize, were fellow students. They were chatting, laughing—

The party. *Terrible Twos*. They all had to be coming from there. Watching the others laugh, Molly was suddenly struck with the feeling she'd missed out on something.

She rolled her eyes at herself. FOMO because you're dead. That's a new one, Moll.

The line snaked back and forth across the floor like the security line at a busy airport. A podium was raised above the crowd at the front of the room, where a man stood in a purple robe, his head covered in the ceremonial wrap that bunched around his face in thick folds of fabric. Over his eyes, a set of intimidating black goggles protruded.

The Prelate of the Lake.

The head nurse, who, by tradition, always remained anonymous. The nurses in blue kept everyone in line, and the Prelate kept them in line, tapping orders into his tablet that lit up signal lights around the room in an obscure pattern that only the nurses could understand.

After about half an hour, Molly reached the front and was led into a booth. The nurse there pulled a privacy curtain closed, then gestured for her arm. She held it out to him, and he took a small device that looked like a pen and placed it just below her elbow. The pen was hot, and it pricked her like a bee sting. She flinched.

"Ow. That hurt. How about a heads-up?"

"Just relax," the official said, his voice laced with bureaucratic impatience.

He then plugged the pen into his tablet and checked the readout. Molly stole a glance: the Genetic Verification Scan displayed her name, her age, and her life number ("previous: 2; current: 3"). The officer then took a handheld device from his belt. It was shaped like a smartphone. The numbering gun. A tiny blue light blinked as the device turned on.

"New number and new chip," he said. Molly remembered—a tiny electronic tag was implanted with every tattoo to ensure the authenticity of the life number. "Relax again."

He pressed the device against Molly's neck. She felt another burning sting, then caught a glimpse of herself in the mirror as the officer removed the gun.

There was now a black Three branded on her neck.

She was a Three.

She suppressed a tiny squeal of delight.

Decorum, please.

She was a Three now, after all.

Molly found her way out to the bus terminal. She checked the time on the clock tower: 5:30 a.m. Rebirth almost always occurred within thirty to forty minutes of death in the nearest Lake (though sometimes it could happen as quickly as ten minutes). Why? As with most things having to do with the scientific mechanism of rebirth, all anyone had was a good theory. Still, this was a useful feature of the process that she could rely on. Subtracting three hours for processing, this meant she died around 2:00 a.m.

The bus ride from here would be about two hours. She could remember asking Julian on the drive to the party to pick her up this morning around seven thirty.

Good. The timing should work.

Julian. He was another thing she could rely on.

The hills that surrounded the Lake channeled the valley wind into a swirl that moved across the terminal, picking up pieces of litter. At least it was still warm, even though it was already September. The wind rustled Molly's gown, and she pressed it against her legs as she found the line for her bus back to Lakeshore with a group of newly reborn Threes, Fours, Fives. . . .

They were gorgeous. At least, to Molly's eyes. The best physical versions of who they could be. Receiving a new body was the part of rebirth Molly had been most looking forward to; you returned at the same age as when you died, but you returned a *perfect* expression of yourself, in pristine physical condition—except, of course, for the "Wrinkle" you were likely to develop.

16

But those were usually small: an allergy, a rebirthmark, or a subtle shift in interests or mood.

Molly stroked her chin and felt a thrill of excitement: that small layer of fat she had hated so much had melted away. Take that, gym. Where's all your regular exercise and a balanced diet now?

Molly sipped from a Lake-issued juice box and looked out the window as the bus rattled along the route. Lake Road wound through the dense elm forests that separated the city of Lakeshore and the suburbs from the Lake itself. The trees were larger and thicker the closer the forest got to the Lake—their knotty branches entangling with each other, blocking out the sunlight and creating an inky, primal black space in the underbrush.

But Molly's attention was elsewhere. She was looking at her own reflection: at her chin, at her Three, at her newly lustrous, shiny brown hair. At how her chest now amply filled out the paper gown. She was admiring herself, but the way she would admire a beautiful stranger who passed her on the street.

So you burned that Two, and this is who you are now, Molly. You're the girl in the reflection. Nice to meet you. You have great hair, and you're a Three. Make this one count. She repeated that last part quietly to herself, like a mantra. "Make this one count."

Finally, the bus pulled into the Lake Road terminal and Molly climbed off, still in her paper gown. Standing there, leaning against his beat-up old car, was good old Julian. The One on his neck was more obvious to her than it had ever been before. She was surprised at how taken aback she was by the sight of it.

But still: there he was. Like he promised. She smiled, crossed the road, and walked to meet him.

CHAPTER 3

"*WEIRD?* YOU FEEL 'WEIRD'? THAT'S ALL I GET?"

Sure, Julian had learned at school how rebirth worked, and what you're supposed to do when you wake up in the Lake. But what he wanted to know is how it *felt*.

"Yeah, weird. At first, it feels like . . . like every part of your body is coming. Simultaneously," Molly said.

"What?" Julian looked over at her while still trying to keep his eyes on the road. "Wait, you mean like . . . like an *orgasm*?" He whispered the word.

"Yes. A full-body orgasm," Molly said. "It felt so good it actually kind of hurt. And when it stopped, I just sort of felt like . . . like I wasn't myself anymore. And I still don't feel *right*. It's like I've been having an out-of-body experience that's just now kind of settling down. It's hard to describe."

"Wow, that does not sound fun to me," Julian said. "Overwhelming pain. Paranoid confusion . . . the opposite of fun. What do you call it? Oh yeah. Torture."

Molly looked at her reflection in Julian's rearview mirror. She fluffed her thick hair. "No pain, no gain, I guess."

"Call me crazy, but I prefer the continuous physical persistence of being," Julian said.

Molly ignored this. She stroked her face and asked, "Hey . . . do I look fat?"

"Really? That's what you're thinking about?"

"I'm serious. Do I?"

"No. But you were never that fat to begin with."

Molly cocked an eyebrow at Julian. "Never 'that fat'?"

"Sorry, I don't mean it like that. I guess you do look . . . fitter? Good muscle definition. That kind of thing. You know, gymnastics is still taking tryouts."

Molly punched him on the arm. "You just want to see me in Lycra."

"Getting a little carried away with your new body there, I think," Julian said.

Although . . . the image of Molly and her fit, new body in a skintight outfit . . . It flashed into his mind—but he pushed it away.

Molly snorted a half laugh.

At some point last week, Molly became convinced that she needed to pop her Two.

Julian and Molly were among the tiny handful of students who were on scholarships at the academy, lower-class kids thrust into the finest educational institution that the upper crust of

Lakeshore could provide. That was how they'd met, in the head-master's office, completing scholarship forms on the first day of freshman year. But what they really bonded over was that, until a little over a year ago, Julian and Molly were the only Ones in the entire academy.

Though he never told her, Julian took a secret, silent pride in their defiant solidarity. He imagined they were two against the world, watching, above it all, as their classmates fell obliviously into the traps that society had set out for them: Homework. Foot-ball. Pep Club. Burning.

Such self-importance. . . . To think of those times now filled Julian with a deep, shameful sense of foolishness.

When Molly popped her One, she did it in secret. When Julian saw her Two on that otherwise ordinary morning in homeroom last year, as she slipped through the crowd toward her desk, her eyes looking anywhere but at him, he realized in an instant that he was utterly alone in this world. He lost his temper after school that day. "How can you be so stupid?" he yelled at her.

Molly opened her mouth in response but said nothing. It was like she was trying to find an explanation, but there were no words in existence that could capture why she had turned her back on everything they had spent so much time railing against. Instead, she closed her mouth, turned, and walked away toward the parking lot. They didn't speak for a week after that.

So, this time, Molly told Julian her plans as soon as she had decided to pop her Two. She leaned over to him in homeroom before Headmaster Denton started class. She watched him expec-tantly for his reaction as she explained how she was going to the *Night of the Terrible Twos*.

This time, Julian had vowed to be more mature. More adult. He closed his eyes and mustered a smile with only somewhat feigned serenity. There was no sense of betrayal this time. There was no anger. There was just that now familiar stirring of aloneness. He told Molly, "Don't worry, it's cool."

Everything was cool.

But that night, after Molly had made her announcement, Julian stared at the ceiling of his bedroom in the dark, a terrible loneliness grasping at him with long, sorrowful tendrils. He would've cried, but he had already decided that was not something he was ever going to do again. He lay awake, staring, until the tendrils gave up and retreated.

And so he went to the *Terrible Twos* party with Molly for moral support . . . but also for a kernel of hope that, maybe, he would give in and join the ranks of functioning high school society like Molly. That he might slip into the smooth flow of the world with her, the two of them again; no longer against the world, but a functioning part of it.

That sure as shit didn't happen.

Julian pulled up at Molly's house.

"Sorry, I'm spacing. I feel like I'm chasing my own echo here," she said. "I just need some time to sync up my mind and body. But thanks for the ride. You're the real deal, Jules. I know you didn't even want to come with me in the first place."

"Don't mention it," Julian said. "It's all part of the BFF Code. You know, be the plus one when they need it. Pick them up after they're dead. Etcetera."

Molly smiled at Julian and hopped out. She started to walk away but stopped and leaned back in through the passenger window.

"Hey, so did the Burners clean it all up afterward?"

"That's what I heard," Julian said. "But I left before that."

"So there's no funeral party or anything. . . ."

"Gross. You wanted to see yourself?" he asked.

"No. Um . . . I just . . . want to know what happened exactly?"

Julian's face soured as the image of her dead body popped back into his mind. He shook it off.

"You played Kiss or Cap with Constance," Julian said. "But I don't know what happened. I came back in and everyone was dead."

Molly was quiet for a moment as she thought. "Did you happen to pic anything?" she finally asked.

"You know," Julian said, trying to suppress his disgust, "it just didn't occur to me."

Molly sighed. "That's okay, you're right. I don't want to see that stuff, anyway." She took off for her house, and Julian watched her walk away and disappear inside.

For a long moment, Julian sat in the car in her driveway, in the lingering cloud of Molly's new-life scent: it was the musty smell of the Lake—sort of like rain-fresh mud—mixed with the faint chlorine whiff of the sanitizer from her decontaminated gown. He studied his hands gripping the wheel. They were thin and pasty. His thumbs were awkward, too small in proportion to his fingers. He looked out the window. Sunlight gleamed off the concrete sidewalk, so bright it stung his eyes. Motes of dust floated in the air like sad, errant confetti.

He was definitely not crying.

CHAPTER 4

JULIAN'S HOME SAT ON A SMALL HILL OVERLOOKING A scrapyard of mangled cars. The yard was built about ten years ago and significantly dragged down the property prices for everyone on the hill.

Most of the neighbors moved out during the yard's first year of operation. Julian's family was also once in the process of moving out, after his mother received a promotion at the Lake. The promotion meant she was able to secure Julian's enrollment at the academy. But this was a different time. The idea of moving was never discussed anymore.

The front door creaked on rusty hinges as Julian entered and tossed his bag on the chair. At the kitchen table, his little brother, Rocky, was working on his third-grade homework.

"Is Molly coming over?" Rocky asked.

"Not today, Rock. She's not feeling well."

"Did you kiss her or something?" Rocky said.

Julian playfully flipped his eight-year-old brother the finger. "Molly doesn't like me like that. She doesn't like any boy like that," Julian said.

Rocky shrugged. "She could swing both ways."

Julian rolled his eyes, wondering how his kid brother was staying on top of his friends' sexual preferences. He took out the pots to cook supper.

Rocky went back to his homework. "I think Molly would be a cool mom," he said.

Julian put the pots down with a clatter.

Mom.

Rocky always had a way of catching him off guard.

When Rocky was born, their mother was on Life Five. She was a senior official at the Lake, and was constantly brimming with energy, keeping Julian and Rocky and their father on the move to school, to parties, to sports. She was the engine of the family.

But just a few years later—it seemed to Julian to have happened overnight—she was on Life Seven. The change in her was so swift and so dramatic, it was as if she had been replaced with an entirely new person. Which, since she was in a new version of her body, was technically true.

Not long after she came home as a Seven, it became apparent that retrogression had bitten her. Bad. The doctors hadn't seen anything like it. She missed work frequently. She forgot entire chunks of her life. She lost a core aspect of her personality—her laugh, her sunniness. She forgot where they lived. Forgot she had a toddler at home who needed her. . . .

"Was Mom cool like Molly?" Rocky asked.

"Yeah," Julian said. "Mom was cool."

When she was on Life Eight, his mother disappeared for over a week. When Julian asked his father where she went, he clammed up. "It'll be all right. She'll come back," he said, not looking up from his workbench. Not looking Julian in the eye. "Let's not talk about this."

Right, Dad, let's never talk about this. Let's forget about this, forget about her like she forgot about us.

There was another incident that was permanently etched in Julian's mind, down to every awful detail. It was the middle of the night and his mother had been missing for days. The sound of breaking glass woke him up. He slipped down the hall and peeked around the corner. Instead of an intruder, he found his mother, ghostly, clad only in a paper gown, a Nine tattooed on her neck. Julian remembered creeping into the room, hoping she would recognize him, hug him, become his mother again. Instead, she looked at him and screamed, "You! It's because of you! You *bastard!*"

She charged toward him. His father, appearing out of nowhere, grabbed hold of her before she could reach him.

"Go to your room and lock the door!" he yelled at Julian.

Julian ran back to his room and slammed the door shut. From behind it, he heard the deep, muffled shouts of his father. He heard the front door slam. He heard the slap of flesh on flesh outside on the porch. He heard his mother's anguished screams tear through the night until, finally, there was silence, deafening in its suddenness.

When Julian worked up the courage to look out the window, he saw his mother running away from the house toward the scrapyard. But about a dozen yards out, she suddenly stopped. She turned and looked over at his window. Over at *him*. He could feel her eyes burrow into him. There was a connection to her bright green eyes that night that felt real and heavy, almost like it was gripping him by his soul. He could never forget that feeling. But then the connection was severed. The moment ended. His mother slipped away into a shadow.

That was his last memory of her alive.

After that night, a new word entered Julian's adolescent vocabulary. A word he had only read before in textbooks and Lake-issued warning signs. A word he rarely heard spoken aloud, and when it was, always in a whisper, always spoken by grave and worried adults.

Permadeath.

"Jules, can you help me finish this?" Rocky said. "Mrs. Landon is all on my case about math. She says she doesn't like 'my attitude.'" Rocky made air quotes with his fingers.

"Well, being a sarcastic jerk isn't going to help you. Neither will cutting corners," Julian said. "You don't need me to help you with multiplication tables. You know those. Besides, I have to put dinner on."

"Really? It's already so late. Let's just have a sandwich."

"Sorry, but I promised Dad. Even though he works doubles, he insists on having a family dinner."

"It will be way past my bedtime," Rocky said. "Dad would want me to get some sleep. He's all about early rising."

"What, and just leave me alone with him after he's worked a

twelve-hour shift? How about some brotherly solidarity here?"

Rocky groaned. "All right, but you owe me one."

"I'm indebted to an eight-year-old. . . ." Julian shook his head.

"So get over here and help me with these multiplication tables."

"Okay, okay," Julian said. He poured a can of soup into the pot and went over to his brother.

"See? Brotherly solidarity," Rocky said. Julian rolled his eyes.

Julian's father made it home even later than expected. It was almost nine thirty. "Damn traffic coming in through Retro Row was backed up all the way to Lake Road," he said as he dropped his work bag by the door.

They sat down dutifully for a now cold family dinner of bland tofu stew. The television was on quietly in the background—a report on how martial law was declared near the lake region in the Ukraine to restore order after a series of food riots. But then the anchor switched to a local report that made Julian sit up in his seat. The segment was about a video on DeadLinks that "apparently showed dozens of dead minors at a house party in Lakeshore."

The *Night of the Terrible Twos*, Julian realized as he saw shots of the scene. Julian was stunned for a moment that the party could've made so much noise it ended up on TV, but then he worried that he might somehow appear in the broadcast. Did someone catch him in their lens, wandering around the house? Julian turned the TV off before his father could notice. The last thing he wanted was another conversation about his One.

Dinner progressed as usual: Dad had little to say unless it was about work, school, or discipline—the holy trinity of unpleasant conversation. "Julian," he said, "I was talking to Marcus today at the shop." His voice was full of the familiar stern, logical tone that he adopted before delivering truths, particularly harsh ones. "Friend of his runs the Tasty's that's just south of the Row."

Julian swallowed his food and closed his eyes. He knew where this was going.

"Says they're hiring, and he can make accommodations for your . . . situation. He can interview you tomorrow after school."

"What?" Julian asked, flustered. "Fast food?"

"Well, it beats temp work at the dust house, doesn't it?" Julian's father said.

"B-but I . . . ," Julian stammered. He had a vision of himself wearing a fast-food uniform, manning a register, doling out pre-packaged orders . . . a vision of himself slipping into the mindless churn of the world. If he let it happen soon enough, he'd probably be burning, too.

"You what?" his father asked.

"It's just . . . shouldn't I concentrate on college applications this year?"

His father looked at him with narrow eyes as he chewed. He held Julian's attention until he swallowed.

"Applications?" he asked, as if considering alien life on a distant planet. "Son, I know it's been hard without . . ." He glanced toward Rocky. "Without your mother. But it's time you start seriously thinking about where your life is heading."

Julian looked down at his bowl. A rubbery skin had formed on his stew.

"I know there are some progressive colleges out there these days," Julian's father continued. "But if you are serious about getting into a good school, you'll need to—"

"I get it, Dad," Julian said. "You need money." He punctured the soup skin with his spoon.

His father's brow furrowed angrily and his face doubled its usual assortment of creases. He set his spoon down with a loud clink and took a deep breath. He leaned in toward Julian, his face a grave mask of lines. "*We.* We need money." He said each word slowly and carefully. "If you have a better idea, I'm all ears."

Julian looked away from his father's gaze. He knew where this was heading: the life score, the number assigned to your family based on the total number of lives extinguished among everyone in your household. The better the score, the more credits you got.

Their family score was terrible—even with the bonuses awarded for his mother's early extinguishments—and Julian, the One well past the schedule, was to blame.

"Okay," he said, looking at his bowl. "Job interview tomorrow. Thanks, Dad."

Julian's father's face softened. He leaned back in his chair and let out a long breath. "Can we go back to enjoying a family meal now, please?"

But Julian stood abruptly and took his plate to the sink.

"I'm finished," he said.

"Julian, you act like this is my doing," his dad said.

"It's okay," Julian replied. "Really. I'm just tired."

Julian locked the door to his tiny bedroom. Even calling it a bedroom was optimistic: it used to be the closet in the family room, but after his mother left, Julian had insisted on having a place in the house to call his own, and this was the only option. He had cleaned out the tools, removed the shelves, and set up his mattress on cinder blocks. He covered the walls in posters, mostly landscapes that were, importantly, devoid of people. Savannahs. Jungles. Long, wide views of oceans from cliffs. The goal was to create a haven of empty, intersecting geographics. A place to be alone.

He kept a shoebox under the bed with all of his most important possessions. Tonight, he pulled it out and sat with it on his lap, wondering if he should open it.

Finally, he decided he should.

Inside, on top of dog-eared comic books, a small collection of cash, and stacks of his old sketches of cartoon characters, sat his mother's Lake-issued ID card. She was smiling in the picture. Her eyes were big pools of green. This was his mom. The real Mom. Not the woman who struck out at him. Not the woman who burned her lives until she was nothing. This woman in the photo, she was his reminder.

His eyes itched. His throat felt like it was tightening.

Okay. Enough for now.

He closed the box and put it back under the bed. He lay down and stared at the flaking, chalky-white paint of the ceiling. He pushed all thoughts of his mother, of fast-food restaurants, and of life numbers out of his mind and checked his phone.

But it was filled with alerts from DeadLinks—mostly videos from the *Terrible Twos*. A carefully posed shot of Constance holding the pistol like a femme fatale, her piercing blue-gray eyes framed by two strands of impossibly black hair. It had 477 comments. He collapsed them—he didn't want to see what fawning drivel had been posted about her—and scrolled down further, past a series of shots of the kids from the roof with sharpened spikes of rebar torn through their stomachs.

And then, a shot of Molly.

His best friend, lying dead on a beanbag.

One of *them* now.

His eyes became hot, and he felt some hard thing forming in his throat.

He x-ed out of DeadLinks, revealing a tab beneath it that was always open on his phone. It was a satellite shot of a green island. It sat alone in a vast expanse of pristine blue water. The African island of Mauritius.

Julian zoomed in closer to the island. As more of the landscape resolved into focus, he scrolled away from the built-up city areas toward a remote mountaintop. He zoomed in further still until he found what he was looking for—a small one-room structure on the top of the mountain. Alone and isolated on an island that was itself alone and isolated in the ocean. It calmed him.

He zoomed out and out until the island once again was but a tiny speck on the vast blue expanse. Julian tried to put himself to scale against the pool of blue: he imagined he was a tiny, insignificant dot smaller than a pinprick. Less than a grain of sand.

Through the thin walls, he could hear his father putting Rocky to bed and locking up the house, but Julian remained focused on his map—zooming in and out on the island, trying to imagine what a conscious experience of emptiness, of nothingness, might feel like—until his phone eventually died, the screen abruptly cutting to black.

He plugged his phone in and turned off the lights. He closed his eyes. The lump that had been forming in his throat had dissipated. Soon he fell into the emptiness of a dreamless sleep.

CHAPTER 5

FRANKLIN ABSOLUTELY HATED MORNINGS. A MORE NATU-ral way of being was to rise when your body wanted to rise, and sleep when your body wanted to sleep. But school, the Burners, death—all that crap kept getting in the way of what was natural.

And the one thing Franklin hated more than just any ordinary morning was a morning like today's: spent listening to the pompous spin of the Burners' Gold Star, Nicholas Hawksley.

Boy, was Nicholas in his element this morning. From his Silver Star seat, Franklin watched Nicholas pace back and forth across the school's orchestra room—his hair already perfect at 7:30 a.m., his coffee-hyped energy percolating.

"Embrace your absurdity," Nicholas said. His voice was firm and poised as he gazed out at his crowd of white-clad disciples— a mix of boys and girls, the children of the ultrarich and well-connected, everyone in the academy who wanted to be cool and was willing to do whatever it took to achieve it.

All Burners were required to don the white blazer. The Lakeshore Academy dress code provided for a choice between blazers in either one of the school colors—navy or white. Although theoretically a student was free to choose white if they wished, in practice, only the Burners wore the white jackets. To complete the outfit, Burners were also required to don one visible but subtle accent of red ("a stain of blood on the veneer," as it was described in the Burners' Bible)—most opted for a red badge on the backpack or a red pin on the lapel. Franklin preferred a red ribbon bracelet. It ticked the box but was understated enough. He despised ostentation.

The meeting was larger than usual this morning. It was the influx of pledges in the back, newly minted Threes inspired by their recent deaths during the *Night of the Terrible Twos*. They were coming to observe, perhaps hoping one day to don the white jackets themselves, or maybe even stand up on the conductor's platform with Nicholas.

"Now, I know many of you out there are interested in joining our storied little society," Nicholas said as he gestured to the back of the room. "You had a taste of what life as a Burner is like at the *Night of the Terrible Twos*, so graciously hosted by Gloria Merriweather." He nodded to a short, dark-haired girl in the front row.

"There were eighteen burns that night. It looked great on DeadLinks. We even made the local news. 'A Little House of Horrors,' they called it." Nicholas walked a tight path back and forth behind the podium as he spoke. "By the time the authorities

33

arrived in the morning, I had already pulled a few strings. All the bodies had been removed and destroyed."

Franklin shuddered as he recalled how he had spent the night pulling bodies from spikes and fishing them out of pools, and then setting them all ablaze at the landfill. He frowned, but he was aware he was onstage and tried to keep it as imperceptible as possible.

Franklin knew the *glamour* of the deaths was important to preserve. But the blood and bile, the smell and ooze, the back-breaking *work* of dragging a body by whatever part was most practical, and still mostly attached . . . no one needed those details.

Nicholas returned to the podium. "The night will live on forever on DeadLinks, but once again we walk away untouched by the authorities. This is the power of the Burners." He gripped the podium and scanned his crowd. "And one day we're going to hold a party *quadruple the size.*" He nodded vigorously to punctuate his pronouncement.

"Because the Burners deserve a big, absurd fireball of glory! *That,* my friends, is how we should be dying. Not in some extinguishment clinic with a waiting room and magazines and nurses who don't give two shits about who you are or what you stand for."

He then shifted his energy into a subdued, darker register.

"But I'm getting ahead of myself. Before you get the blaze of glory, you need to become a Burner first." He narrowed his eyes as he scanned the crowd. "To do that, you need to have two things. You need to have guts, and you need to have toughness of mind. Because we require your burns to be *daring.*

"And make no mistake, at some point or another, as a Burner, you will feel humiliated. Our burns are public, and it's a fact of life that you can't control what others think of you. What we believe is gloriously absurd, other people find stupid, delinquent, or criminal. If you aren't mentally strong, this will wear you down. You will be tempted to quit. But you must own your inherent absurdity. You must embrace it. Believe in it. That's how a Burner deals with everything, really. By embracing the absurdity of the world and standing up to it."

Franklin looked out over the crowd. The would-be pledges were rapt. But he had to stifle an impending yawn.

"Absurdity is at the core, the essence, of everything," Nicholas said, pausing a moment to let it sink in. "We live and die, nine times over. Why? Did some creator make it so? Who knows? But truly, who cares?

"What I *do* know is that you might, when you are old and in your later lives, forget who you are completely. Aggressive lentic retrogression. They say it's rare. You might think, 'Well, it can never hit *me*.' But you would be wrong, because it can strike down a precious little snowflake like you without a second glance. Yes, for many of us, retrogression lies in wait as we get older. This underscores the fact that we should be enjoying our lives—and deaths—while we have them. We are, all of us, not out there *killing ourselves*"—he overenunciated the words—"*for a trifle.*

"Because you know what's worse than burning your Six when you're fifty years old and riddled with retrogression?" Nicholas continued. "Having wasted all your other lives without having some . . . *merriment.*"

Nicholas craned his neck to the back rows of the auditorium, his Five clearly visible.

"The world forces us to extinguish ourselves on the joyless,

35

clockwork schedule that the actuaries have drawn up. That's not burning. That's just death," he said, shaking his head.

"In life, we are told to find a way to move 'up.' Study as if everything depends on it. Cram all night to pass our exams. Fight for that job, then fight for that promotion. But it's a trap. Once we're 'up,' we start worrying about making it even higher, then even higher than that. Everything about our lives *and* our deaths, all nine of them, is scheduled, commoditized, proscribed . . . and—"

Franklin mouthed the kicker along with Nicholas: "—so damn serious." He resisted the urge to roll his eyes.

"The Burners celebrate the absurdity of our multiple lives by embracing the absurdity of our multiple deaths."

He ran his hands through his hair, smoothing his perfect swoop. He licked his teeth under his lips and then grinned widely.

"We are Burners. We don't follow life schedules. We don't go to your extinguishment clinics.

"The world tells us to burn? Well then, we will. But on *our* terms. And every burn will be a middle finger at the world!" Nicholas looked over his crowd, pleased.

He ran his hand across a white, leather-bound book on the podium—the Burners' Bible—and nodded to Franklin, who rolled his chair over to the laptop and entered a few keystrokes.

A screen descended above the conductor's podium and a projector turned on. Franklin then clicked to a slideshow of dead students—they were screengrabs from DeadLinks. One featured a kid in white robes hanging from the old elm tree out front; another, a ball of flames with legs, streaking across the yard; in the next image, two students were submerged in the school fountain, tied together in an embrace. Nicholas watched the pledges' faces as Franklin clicked through the macabre lineup.

"If you become one of us, you will be expected to execute your burns with creativity, panache, and heart," Nicholas said, speaking to the pledges in the back. "But the most important thing we look for in a burn is the figure-skating quotient. That perverse little indefinable quality that just hits you right here." Nicholas tapped his chest. "I call it mort."

It was a safe bet that even the pledges had seen multiple times the DeadLinks videos that the images were grabbed from. They were always forwarded around the school and vigilantly reposted every time one was flagged for removal. Their titles became legendary: *Spencer's Spontaneous Combustion in Seventh Period. Felicity's Fun with Blenders* . . . Franklin shuddered, remembering a few of the . . . flakier bits of *Chuck's Cheese Grater Madness!!!* (Franklin had wisely chosen to remove that particular slide from this presentation. After all, it was seven thirty in the damn morning.)

"All burns are meticulously recorded into the Bible," Nicholas said, tapping the book as he spoke. "Of course, we also have a video record, but the Bible is the one thing that connects us back to the first generation of Burners, way back in 1910."

"As the Gold Star, it is my profound and sacred duty to log and record our absurdity for the ages. Eventually, all of us will have but one life left to our name. We'll all be Nines, maybe addled with retro, maybe having forgotten everything about who we are, and then . . . poof. We'll be gone. But here"—he laid his hand on the cover—"your burns will live forever." Nicholas ran his fingers across the old cracked leather of the book, scanning the faces of the crowd.

The room was silent save a nervous cough or two. Some of the more senior members sat cross-armed. They had heard this before. But it was obvious in their eyes that they were glued to Nicholas, drinking it in just the same as the newbies in the back.

Franklin found Constance in the front row, chewing gum, her face illuminated by the projection, smiling slightly. Dang, she had a cute smile.

Nicholas looked down at the Bible. "Just five years ago, the Gold Star was one Georgie Vander. You might have heard of him. Or seen his name in the trophy case, at least."

Franklin looked up.

Ah. So that's where he's heading with this. The whole Georgie Vander thing.

Nicholas Hawksley was the son of David Hawksley, the director of the local Lake. He was the man in charge of the Lake itself, the associated facilities, and the nurses for the entire region. Franklin figured Nicholas's obsessive race against Georgie was some kind of an attempt to impress the old man.

"Georgie Vander's class of Burners recorded forty-four burns in one year. That's the most ever," Nicholas said, letting the statement dangle in the auditorium like a fishhook. And then, again with the overenunciation: *"for-tee-four."* Franklin crinkled his brow as he studied Nicholas. This here was off the script. This here was a window into Nicholas's actual plans.

"Forty-four? We will beat the life out of that number," Nicholas said, now grinning widely. "We will beat the class of Georgie Vander, and we right here"—he gestured grandly across the room—"will be the most impressive class in the entire Bible, going all the way back to nineteen freaking ten. So, to all you wannabes in the back, all you newly minted Threes . . . if you want to become one of us, get creative. Because we are going to make history."

Nicholas nodded to Franklin again. Franklin took a stack of manila folders from his bag and walked through the room, passing them out.

Nicholas continued. "In that spirit, today we shall have the absurd honor of witnessing a burn from our newest initiate, Amit Sandoval."

There was a quiet murmur of surprise. Some turned to look at Amit, who sat with a frown on his pasty face, staring straight ahead, trying hard not to acknowledge anyone looking at him.

Amit was "the fat kid." No one had ever thought he would be a Burner, but he begged to get in, and so Nicholas created an infamously mortifying hazing to prove him worthy. It culminated in a rather unsavory evening involving a nude and oiled Amit, a table full of tofu bricks, and a cauldron of boiling water with a chair fixed inside . . . *Amit's Miso Special*. Amit persevered, and eventually Nicholas allowed him in.

And now he had apparently created this burn proposal titled *Escape the Asylum*. The Burners were leafing through and . . .

"Whoa."

"Shit."

Various other gasps and cries of surprise.

"Say what you will about Amit, but he has learned to embrace his absurdity," Nicholas said. "The burn Amit has proposed here for his third life is something I have never encountered. And I have studied every burn in the book, so I'm not easy to impress."

He smirked and raised an eyebrow.

Nicholas handed a small bag to Franklin. Inside was a stack of red ink pens. Franklin passed them down the line. "These are the pens called for in Amit's plan," Nicholas said. "You each get one. Your instructions are clear in the dossier. The burn culminates during Headmaster Denton's fall quarter address after lunch.

"Listen." Nicholas paused. His trademarked *Listen*. The word invariably signaled the final movement of all his big speeches.

"We all must die. Nine times, each of us. That's the way of it. But we are going to make each death *count*. All you pledges in the back? Pay close attention today. Dismissed."

The Burners got up and left, murmuring quietly to one another as they headed out into the halls. The pledges followed them out, their faces pale, rattled by Nicholas's intensity.

As the room emptied, Franklin tossed Amit's proposal on the table.

"Did the fat kid really come up with this?"

Nicholas looked up at Franklin as if he had just heard the dumbest question of his life.

"That moron?" Nicholas said. "Of course not. I wrote it." Nicholas collapsed theatrically into a chair in the wings.

"But the Bible says every burn must be of our own making," Franklin said. "You know, 'from our inner absurdity.' This isn't—"

Nicholas cut him off. "If people believe that big dumb Amit can conjure this, then they might pull their heads out of their asses and think of something interesting for once. Besides, Amit *believes* it was his idea. So, he's fully on board, and we're technically still following the rules."

40

Nicholas inspected the sleeve of his jacket and discovered a tiny dark spot and furrowed his brow.

"Our class is a group of pathetic, boring losers," he said. "I swear to God, if I have to read another autodefenestration proposal . . . And they can't even spell 'defenestration'!"

He licked his finger and thumb and furiously rubbed the dark spot on his jacket between them. "If it weren't for these parties I spend so much time organizing, who knows how many of them would actually be going through with their burns at all? And I tell you what, burn parties get old. We barely got a ninety-second segment on the news. We need something viral."

There was a loaded pause as Franklin watched Nicholas attempt to eliminate the stain on his sleeve.

"Maybe we need to do more as their leaders," Franklin said finally. "Inspire them."

Nicholas looked up from his sleeve, his brow scrunched severely.

"Franklin, please contribute something positive to this conversation, or shut your mouth."

Franklin frowned as Nicholas continued.

"Now, let's say Amit pulls off this grotesque miracle today. There is no guarantee he will, by the way. It could be another stupid farce like Clayton's whole car-parasailing thing," Nicholas said, shaking his head.

Franklin remembered how Clayton had managed to clip a telephone pole and break his back. He had to be put down unceremoniously behind closed doors in the hospital.

"But let's say Amit *at least* dies in front of the school without dragging it out," Nicholas said. "The question then becomes:

What's next? Have you considered that, Franklin? Do *you* have any thoughts?"

Chastened, Franklin folded up his laptop and put it in his bag, then he started packing up his desk. "We would just get on with burning everyone else," Franklin said, flat and quiet, looking down at his bag as he packed.

"No," Nicholas said. "You're thinking small. We would need to top ourselves. Really stir the mort quotient. With something big. Something huge."

There was a mad scheme of some kind rattling around in the kid's head. "I'm sure you'll come up with something," he said.

Nicholas looked at him with his big, searching eyes and blinked. "I already have."

He handed a folder to Franklin from his bag. His lips formed a thin smile, framing his perfectly straight, bone-white teeth.

Franklin opened the folder. It was titled *You Never Forget Your First Time.*

Below was a profile of the school's only One: Julian Dex.

CHAPTER 6

"I HAVEN'T NOTICED A WRINKLE YET," MOLLY SAID, PULLING the plastic off a chocolate pudding cup. "But they say sometimes it takes a while. My sister went on for a year in her fourth life before she realized she couldn't smell flowers anymore. Then on her fifth life, she woke up deaf. You just never know . . ."

Julian nodded. They were at a table in the back of the cafeteria.

"The main thing now is that I'm feeling more confident in myself," Molly said.

"Are we talking *that kind* of confidence?" Julian asked, looking toward the entrance.

Constance was entering through the security doors. She was hands down the hottest girl in the school. She was curvy in the right ways; her hair was long, black, and impossibly straight; she had a cute face that could turn devilish with the right circumstance; and she was always pushing the dress codes to the boundaries of acceptable. Julian understood her beauty on an objective level, but he just wasn't turned on by her. The thing was she was *too hot*—almost untouchable. Certainly for Julian, a One, she was an impossibility.

Today Constance was vamped out in red lipstick and pouting at anyone who gave her a second glance. She was carrying a red pen, which she put theatrically in her mouth when the school security guard, a middle-aged man with a sad, thin mustache—a Six—asked her to raise her arms to scan her with a metal detector wand.

"I *wish*," Molly said, looking at her. "Dang. There sure are a lot of pretty girls in the Burners."

Julian looked at Molly with a sudden mixture of sadness and frustration. "Yet another reason . . ."

"Reason for what?"

"Come on, Molly, why don't you pledge already?" Julian asked bluntly.

Molly bristled at the question. "Jules . . . ," she said weakly. "It's over. I did it. So just drop it, okay? My family gets another rebate, and that's that. I won't burn again until my life table comes up. Which is . . ." She calculated in her head. "Eight years from now. My twenty-fifth birthday."

"Yeah, yeah," Julian said with undisguised bitterness.

Molly frowned. "Julian," she said. "Are you all right?"

"I'm perfectly fine," he said. "I know what I believe in. I know what's right. And I live my life by that."

Molly blinked, momentarily stunned.

"Is this about my Three? I'm a senior this year. I'm trying to put my life together," she said.

"Yeah, put your life together by killing yourself. Funny how that works."

"That's how the world works, Julian. What's your plan?"

"For what?" Julian turned a page.

"For life. We're graduating in the spring," Molly said, exasperated. "You need a plan."

Julian looked up.

"Yeah, okay," he said. "Here's a plan. There's this island in the Indian Ocean. It's called Mauritius. It has white beaches, a volcano . . . and no Lake at all."

"No Lake? Where is everyone reborn?"

"The nearest Lake is twelve hundred miles away in Africa. So rebirth isn't really a thing there. They just don't do it."

"Come on, that sounds like some urban legend bullshit."

Julian sharpened his eyes at Molly. "Mauritius," he said with finality. "You asked what my plan is. Well, that's my plan." Julian went back to his notebook. He could feel Molly staring at him.

"That's your plan," Molly repeated. "Some island in the middle of nowhere?"

Julian did not look up.

"Don't be an asshole, Jules. You're seventeen years old. I'm asking a reasonable question."

"I'm just saying that this shithole isn't for me. And yeah, maybe I don't know what I'm going to do yet, but I'm sure as hell not going to stick around here any longer than I have to."

"You mean in Lakeshore?" Molly asked, confused.

"Yes," he said simply.

"Come on, you're not going to Mauritius or wherever. If it's true that they don't have any rebirths there, then they won't let anyone in. They won't be able to support that many lives. Not on an island."

"Maybe, but I won't know until I see for myself," he said.

Molly laughed. "You're going to be some sad-sack emo One moping around Lakeshore your whole life, chasing fantasies, pretending you're immune to the world."

"Wow, you really know how to make me feel good about myself, Molls," Julian said.

"I'm sorry, but you know, people are talking. Everyone thinks there's something wrong with you. . . . You're my friend, and sometimes even *I* think there is something wrong with you," she added quietly.

Julian closed his notebook and looked up at Molly.

"Yeah, well, what if I just didn't do it? Like, ever?" he said softly.

"Didn't do what? Didn't follow the score?"

"Yeah, what if I just didn't follow it?"

"You have to be on Life Two when you graduate," Molly said. "There's no college out there that would accept a One. That's how the real world works."

"That's not how *I* want to work, though," Julian said.

Molly furrowed her brow. "Julian, think about it—if we all lived our nine lives any which way we wanted, the world would starve to death. You know what happened in India. The whole country is closed off now. It's hell on Earth."

"How do you *know* that? You haven't been there. All you know is what they tell you on TV," Julian said.

Molly looked at him sharply. She caught his eyes lingering on her neck.

"Admit it. You're jealous."

"Jealous?!"

"Yes, jealous that you don't have the guts to do it."

Julian choked out a sarcastic laugh. "I'm not jealous. It's just . . . I'm disappointed. I never thought you would turn out to be one of the idiots."

"You asshole," Molly said, standing up. She glared at him, a storm brewing in her eyes.

Julian shook his head. "I'm sorry. Hey, really. I didn't mean it. It's just . . . I hated seeing you dead like that, on the floor of Gloria's house. It . . . I don't know. It just made me realize that . . ."

"That this is the real world?" Molly asked. She didn't wait for an answer. "Well, it is. Whether you like it or not. You can't be a One forever. It's not legal, it's not normal, and it's not even right. For your own sake, *grow up*."

For the second time in as many years, Julian watched Molly walk away.

He snapped his notebook shut and looked out across the students gathered in the cafeteria, chewing their prepackaged soy protein nuggets, slurping down their saccharine pudding, chatting, laughing, all of them racking up their numbers, waiting to get out of school and start climbing their way up in the world.

Maybe she was right. Maybe he'd be stuck in Lakeshore. Nine lives, and all of them drained out in this shithole.

As he stewed, Julian caught sight of Constance in the back of the cafeteria, talking to Headmaster Denton. Denton was signing a form for her, using her red pen. Constance was smiling her sexy, red, twisted smile.

He watched her as she left Denton to find a seat among the row of white-clad students at the Burners' table in the back. It suddenly struck Julian why exactly he was never into Constance. It was because she had a kind of beauty that the world demanded he desire. It required him to want it, *to need it*—even though the rules were designed to keep people like him as far away from it as possible.

Well . . . he refused to be one of the idiots.

CHAPTER 7

THE CENTERPIECE OF THE LAKESHORE ACADEMY GROUNDS
was the sprawling, religiously manicured lawn that separated
the academic building from the gymnasium. An old stone wall
enclosed the yard, and a two-hundred-year-old elm tree anchored
the center of it. This afternoon, the old elm stood resolute as the
entire student body parted and flowed around it on the way to
the gymnasium.

Unlike the academic building, which was built of red brick and
lined with ivy-trimmed trellises, the gymnasium, a new addition
to the school, was built with the same kind of drab architecture
as the Lake receiving centers: white and gray brick, floor to ceiling, as blank and stark and boring as possible. That is, with one
notable exception. The north wall was an ever-growing mural
of graffiti. It was an unofficial tradition for the student body to

fill the wall throughout the year and wipe it at the start of the next. But not, rumors had it, before some of the art was stenciled, copied, and sold among a certain class of high-numbered connoisseurs. "Creative destruction," it was said to be called, capturing the vibrant imagination that high-numbered people lost with multiple rebirths. If true, this was perhaps an explanation for why some of the more controversial tags—"Piss in the Lake ☺" was one notable example—were allowed to remain for far longer than anyone expected they would.

Students were finding seats for the fall quarter opening address. Two security guards were stationed at the entrance to the gym, acting like they were in an action movie, thumbs hooked through their belts, scanning the incoming crowd.

Julian walked through the bleachers looking for Molly. He hoped maybe she might apologize to him—she knew burning was a sensitive issue, she'd even met his mother—and yet she had pressed that button.

Or maybe he should apologize to her? Was that being more mature about it?

Julian couldn't find her, but he did find the Burners all sitting together in the front row, a chorus of white. He took a seat behind them. They were oddly quiet. Many were scanning the crowd, looking for something. Julian noticed legs bouncing up and down, and hands being wrung, and knuckles cracked—and every single Burner was fiddling with a red pen. In the front row, Franklin was tapping his leg distractedly. Beside him sat Nicholas: as calm and cool and collected as always.

"Attention," Headmaster Denton rasped into the microphone. The fluorescent lights gave his bald head a sickly gleam.

The crowd slowly settled down.

"All of you here . . ."

Denton stopped, cleared his throat, and continued.

"*Nearly* all of you here have begun down that most sacred path of advancing your life number, of gaining the maturity and wisdom through rebirth that you will need to succeed in this world."

Julian felt a hot flash of embarrassment bloom across his face. Did Denton just single him out? He slid into his seat, shrugging in an attempt to hide the One on his neck.

"For those of you who are sufficiently advanced in life number, I have an announcement today." Denton turned a page in his notebook. "As of next month, those of you who have already achieved three lives now qualify for AP classes that carry early college credits. Those who qualify can . . ." Denton trailed off. He noticed an odd red drip falling on his notebook from the ceiling.

He looked up. Everyone looked up.

Standing on top of the scoreboard that hung over the center of the gym was . . . Amit? He was wearing a white straitjacket with two armholes cut into it, his arms jutting out of it like he had burst from his confines. He was holding a pile of white cloth. He looked pale and unsteady, a tourniquet wrapped tightly below his elbow. He let go of the cloth, which unfurled into a massive banner, covering the scoreboard.

It read: "Escape the Asylum! Embrace the Absurd!" written in smeared red blood.

Amit yelled, "Attention! This banner has been written in my blood!"

The crowd was silent, confused. There was a squelch from the microphone as Denton leaned over the podium to peer up.

"And your leave of absence has been signed in my blood!"

Just then, all the Burners stood and held up red pens and pieces of paper—leave of absence forms. Oh god, Julian realized, the red pens . . .

Amit's blood.

"Tomorrow!" Amit yelled. "I declare it Burners' Day!"

Amit tore the tourniquet off his arm. It released a few sickly pent-up spurts of blood from a black cut deep in his artery. The blood dripped down onto the podium in globs. Denton stumbled clumsily out of the way, barely dodging a splattering.

Exclamations rippled through the crowd.

As the blood from his arm quickly slowed to a trickle—was he expecting it to jet out theatrically?—the color drained from Amit's face, his eyes rolled back into his head, and he fell forward, plunging into the stage with a wet *thwack*.

For a moment, the room was silent.

Then it exploded into cheers.

The guards rushed to Denton, but he pushed his way through them back to the microphone, struggling to regain control of the room. He was screaming, "Order! Order!" But no one could hear him over the thundering cheers.

Julian stood among the screaming, thumping crowd. But he did not join them. He'd only ever seen Amit in history class. He was always silent, the kid who didn't raise his hand.

But now Amit was capable of . . . this? Whatever *this* was? Was this supposed to be cool? Was this supposed to be . . . *fun*? Some kind of statement? It looked more like a miserable way to waste a life.

Julian looked around at the hysterical crowd, but he could

see only one other person besides himself who was not cheering: standing in the front row, among his Burner cohorts, was Nicholas.

He was filming everything on his phone. He wasn't cheering. But he was smiling.

CHAPTER 8

THE TRAFFIC IN RETRO ROW WAS AT A DEAD STOP. FROM behind a bend up ahead, a cloud of smoke rose into the sky. The smell of acrid flaming tire seeped into Julian's car, even with the windows rolled up. It was a familiar scent on this road: a burned-out car—an accident, maybe, or an inconsiderate suicide gone wrong. . . . It could be any number of things. Maybe, Julian thought, it could be excuse enough to turn around and skip the job interview at Tasty's. Julian considered it, calculating the possible outcomes, but he was hemmed in by the traffic, and, anyway, on balance it would be worse to have to face his father than to just suck it up and go through with it.

Julian looked out the window at the buildings lining the street, which snaked along the foot of the hill. Retro Row, the bad part of Lakeshore, was formally known as Cypress Flats, a narrow valley that lay in a watershed that fed away from the Lake. It became swampy in the heat of the summer, an ideal breeding ground for mosquitoes. But one of Retro Row's most infamous products was the cicadas, unique to the area and, unlike any other species of cicada, able to thrive in the cold winter weather. They bred in the elm forests around the Lake and then hibernated, burrowed into the valley in eighteen-year cycles. Every eighteen years, after winter had descended, the ground would tremble with tens of thousands of pupae as they crawled out, took flight, and filled the valley with a cacophonous scratching sound. Residents sealed their doors and windows—the last thing anyone wanted was their floor writhing with three-inch-long insects.

Even considering that vile pedigree, Retro Row was best known for something else: it was home for the many who were so severely addled by retrogression that they could no longer function in proper society. They gathered in makeshift encampments by the river, or some of the luckier ones squatted in the buildings left empty by a decade of economic neglect. There was something about the retrograde attitude here that compounded in aggregate—every community outreach effort over the years had failed. Any attempt to rehabilitate or reintegrate the retrogrades here was met with obstinacy and, above all, a deep-seated fear of the Lakes, of nurses, of burning. . . .

In time, most people respected this and were happy to stop the failing rehab efforts. After all, these retrogrades were the people most ravaged by rebirth glitches—the ones who had lost everything. Let them have their space, Lakeshore had collectively decided. Let them have this Retro Row, as long as it was

clearly delineated, borders drawn, a place where respectable society didn't need to venture unless it absolutely had to.

Today, Julian absolutely had to.

As he sat in traffic, he watched as dozens of cats crowded
around a ditch near a convenience store. They were circling,
mewling loudly, jockeying around the hole. They were large, fat
animals with thick, matted fur—"Lake cats." Ferals who came
from the dark elm forests near the Lake, they were wilder, and
more erratic, than the typical house cat. They were digging in
the hole, pulling out little bone-white bits of something, and eating them.

Julian looked closely, trying to understand what those little
white morsels were. Pupae, he realized with disgust. Cicada
pupae, dug up from the ground. Pale white wings and legs pressed
tight against tiny, unformed bodies. Julian felt his stomach lurch
watching the cats fight to devour them. Julian noticed one cat in
particular, sitting above the scrum on an old wooden box. It was
all black with a white patch over its right eye. It had no interest in
the meal of bugs below him, or in the other cats scrambling with
one another to feed. Unnervingly, the cat was only interested in
Julian. It seemed to stare at him as he sat in traffic. The tip of its
tail twitched in rhythm like a menacing metronome.

A car horn sounded angrily behind him. Finally, the traffic
started to move, and Julian pulled away from the cat, keeping an
eye on it in his rearview mirror. Even as he drove away, its white-
splotched face continued to follow him.

Julian pulled up at the Tasty's just on the other side of the Row,
where the lower-rent suburb of Elmwood began to sprawl. He
hiked his collar up to cover his One and headed inside. A cashier

showed him a seat at a Formica table while he went to fetch the manager, a Mr. Mitchell. Julian watched as a couple in a booth across from him unpacked their food—the man was stirring a brown paste into a creamy white milk shake, while the woman was unwrapping an extremely pungent sausage sandwich. She leaned in close to it and inhaled the smell deeply before taking a bite.

"You're Miles Dex's boy?" a scratchy voice said from behind him. Julian turned to find a middle-aged man with a comb-over and a paunch poking through his red and white Tasty's vest.

"Yes, I'm Julian," he said, deciding he had better try his best to go through with this interview as properly as possible.

Mr. Mitchell shook Julian's hand with a single firm pump and sat down next to him.

"I heard you're a good kid looking for some part-time work."

Julian put his hands together and set them on the table. "Yes, sir," he said in an inflection that mirrored his father's "serious" voice.

"Tasty's is not just a fast-food restaurant," Mr. Mitchell said with outsized importance. "We specialize in compassion."

Julian nodded. "What do you mean?"

"No one's taste stays the same as they get older and higher in life number. We at Tasty's know that lentic retrogression manifests in different ways, but even if you can no longer taste salty, or sweet, or even anything at all, you have the same right to nutritious food, as flavorful as we can get it for you."

Julian nodded, sadness stirring inside him as he listened to the rehearsed speech.

"Do you have compassion, Julian?" Mr. Mitchell asked.

Julian suppressed a shudder.

How about I just say no?

Nope, no compassion. Only care about myself. Interview over?

Instead, he said, "I do, sir."

Mr. Mitchell asked for Julian's résumé. Julian slid a single folded piece of paper across the table to him. Mr. Mitchell studied it for a moment too long. Julian watched as he read—he noticed the number on the man's neck: Seven. He wondered what flavors he had lost in spending his many lives.

Mr. Mitchell folded the paper closed and looked up at Julian. His wet eyes scanned Julian's neck, but he couldn't find what he was looking for. He scrunched his brow in confusion.

"Forgive me the formality, but I have to ask you what your number is, if you don't mind, Julian."

Julian's face became hot and itchy. He swallowed. "I'm a One, sir."

Mr. Mitchell's eyes widened in surprise. "A One?" he said, exhaling with a quiet whistle. "A One . . . ," he repeated. He looked down at the table and said, "Gosh, I am really sorry, son."

Julian swallowed and looked down at his hands. He did not want to say anything else, but an uncomfortable silence had descended between them. The conversation demanded he ask: "Why?"

"Had I known," Mr. Mitchell said, "I wouldn't have asked you to come down so far. I heard you were low, but I assumed a Two at least. You see, I have this opening because I get a subsidy to hire low-numbered students, but it only applies to Twos and up. I'm really sorry, son, but those are the rules."

Hot anger bubbled in Julian's throat, but he closed his eyes and swallowed it. He said, "That's okay."

Mr. Mitchell slid the résumé back across the table to him. Julian put it in his pocket. Mr. Mitchell's mouth turned into a sad frown. He said, "I can't even remember being a One." He shook his head. "I really can't. But I wish I could."

Julian forced himself to smile politely. "Thanks for your time."

"Hey," Mr. Mitchell said, "dinner's on me."

Julian zipped up his jacket. There was a chilly wind on the top of the hill. He sat down on the hood of his car. The feel of the cold metal through his pants sent a shiver through him. He reached into his Tasty's bag to fish out a garlic soy protein nugget.

He looked down at the Lake. The moonlight sparkled off it. In the distance, he could see the beach and the receiving center. He strained hard through the darkness and could even make out a few people being reborn: dark spots breaking on the water, small figures trudging their way through the shallows toward the shore.

There was a fifteen-foot perimeter fence set off a few yards back from the shore and running the full length of the Lake, capped in barbed wire. Access to the Lake was strictly regulated. But down near the fence, there was a small bonfire. Two figures were walking around it. At first, Julian thought it was a couple of retrogrades, but he soon realized they were too put-together, too coherent in their movements. Eventually, as his eyes adjusted to the darkness, he could make out their clothes, and he realized that they were kids about his age.

A group of cats had gathered around their fire. One of the

kids—the bigger one—was feeding them little bits of something from his bag. The other kid—a girl with a ponytail—was writing something down in a notebook.

He briefly thought about saying hello but then decided it wasn't worth it—he'd have to make introductions, they would inevitably see his One, and they would surely ask questions. He could already hear them: Is that for real? How did you even manage? Aren't you even a little curious about what burning is like?

He checked his phone—10:00 p.m. He had to give it another hour until his dad went to sleep. He just couldn't bear to face him. Not tonight. He couldn't even get the god-awful fast-food job he didn't want and that his father, in his quiet, pressing desperation, needed him to get.

Instead, he leaned back on the cold hood and popped another nugget into his mouth. It exploded in a burst of overwhelming garlic flavor.

Am I so inferior? So useless? Because I don't want to do what they demand I do?

"Holy moly!"

Julian shot up in a start. It was a girl's voice, but it had a deeper, almost masculine register to it.

"Really hitting the garlic up here, aren't you?"

Julian found the two kids standing before him: a tall, heavyset boy and a girl with a gray hoodie pulled over her head and a pair of binoculars slung around her shoulder—the source of the voice. Had they walked up from the bonfire down by the fence?

"You gonna share the love or what?" the girl said as the two approached. Julian could make them out more clearly as they got closer—the boy was chunky, with big, frizzy hair. The girl pulled back her hood. Julian had never seen anyone as freckled as she was—her face was a universe of little dots on a pale white canvas. In the dark, her hair appeared burnt orange. Her eyes were large, dark, and deeply set. It was an odd face but also oddly compelling. He found it difficult to look away from her.

"Well?" she said. Julian snapped out of it and reached for the bag of nuggets. "Oh yeah, help yourself," he said. "They're garlic bombs, though."

They each popped a nugget and chewed.

"Cold up here, isn't it?" the girl said, her mouth full.

"Yeah."

"So, you're hanging out on a car—alone, freezing, eating garlic nuggets," she said. "One of those nights, eh?"

Julian snorted in disdain, but nugget bits got caught in his throat. He started to cough. Thankfully, he was able to suppress it before it got out of hand.

Not soon enough to stop the girl from shooting him a sly grin, though.

"Why don't you come down to the fire?" she asked.

Julian was surprised by the invitation, but he just couldn't go down there. Not tonight.

"I'm killing a bit of time before I head home," he said.

The girl nodded and then waved her hand in front of her mouth. "Damn, this is—blech," she said. "You have flavor issues?"

"No," Julian said, subconsciously hunching to hide his One.

The boy stepped forward. "I'm Glen," he said.

"Julian."

The girl stepped closer and held out her hand. Julian took it in his. Her fingers were long and delicate and warm.

"Cody," she said as they shook.

"You go to Lakeshore Academy or something?" Glen asked. "Never seen you around before."

"Yep."

"We're the Poplar Public High scum," Cody explained, gesturing over the elm forest in the general direction of Poplar Heights, the other city that shared the Lake with Lakeshore. "Our football teams might literally kill each other on the field, but there's no reason you can't share a bonfire with us," Cody said. "We're just feeding the cats. The winters are so cold around here, it gets tough for them."

"Thanks." Julian considered their offer. These people looked nice, but still . . . he could see Cody's number—Three—and Glen was a Four. Julian didn't have it in him tonight.

"But really, that's okay," Julian said as Cody stepped closer toward him, peering at his neck.

"Wait a minute, Mr. Julian, are you a One?" she said boldly.

Julian swallowed and stiffened his back. "Yes," he said quickly. There was a moment as everyone waited for follow-up elaboration, but Julian was not about to justify himself to these strangers.

"You're probably the oldest One I've ever seen," Cody said, breaking the silence.

Julian looked at her hard. He hoped she could pick up on the strong, uncomfortable vibes he was trying to broadcast.

Finally he said, "Yeah, well . . . I am what I am."

Where the hell did that come from?

"You are what you are," she said, chuckling quietly to herself.

Despite the cold, Julian could feel his hands dampen as she studied him.

"Well, if you don't want to join us, you don't have to," she said. "It's a free country. Except in regards to killing yourself."

She looked at him as if waiting for a response.

"Thanks," Julian said, puzzled and uncomfortable.

Cody cocked her head to the side. "You know," she said. "I have a real interest in people like you."

"You mean Ones?" Julian asked gruffly.

Cody nodded. "That's right. Ones. Abstainers. People who don't follow the life score."

Julian looked warily at this oddly compelling girl who was full of strange ideas.

"You sure you don't want to come down by the fire? We're also spotting." She tapped the binoculars hanging around her neck.

"Spotting what?" he said.

"You know, animals getting messed up with the Lakes. People trying to hop the fence. Weird stuff like that."

Yes. Lots of strange ideas.

"Thanks," Julian said. "But I should head home, actually."

"All right, then," she said, nodding.

He watched as Cody fished her phone out of her pocket.

"What's your number? There's a party on October first. Someone like you might be very interested in attending."

Julian looked at her for a long, dumbfounded moment. Was this girl actually inviting him to a party?

"Well?" she said impatiently.

"Yeah. Maybe I can make it," he said.

Julian took his phone out of his pocket and they exchanged

numbers. "October first. That's two Wednesdays from now," she said. "I'm trying to keep it somewhat quiet. So if you want to upgrade your 'yeah maybe' to a 'cool!,' then text me ahead of time. All right?"

"All right," Julian said, and slipped his phone back into his pocket.

"Thanks for the nuggets," Glen said.

"Yeah, thanks," Cody said. She looked at him curiously, as if she were studying some small, exotic animal. "Good luck being . . . whoever you are, Mr. Julian." She smiled, revealing slightly crooked teeth.

As he watched her descend the hill, Julian realized his heart had been beating rapidly, and his hands were clammy and moist.

Their figures became smaller and smaller as they returned to the bonfire, and as they receded, Julian felt a hot flush of regret under his skin. Why didn't he join her? What was holding him back?

Who are you, anyway, Mr. Julian?

CHAPTER 9

HEADMASTER DENTON WIPED THE PERSPIRATION FROM HIS scalp with a handkerchief, then licked his lips. Toweling his scalp was a routine, everyday occurrence—he sweated profusely, no doubt a function of being pent up in the academy with teenage Twos and Threes. But licking his lips was a peculiar habit reserved for those moments just before he was about to do his favorite thing: exercise authority.

Sitting across from Denton, calmly watching the old man working over his cracked, puckered lips, was Nicholas Hawksley. After the Amit stunt, Nicholas was apprehended by the guards. They called the cops. He was detained for hours, but he could not have been less worried about his situation. Nicholas was absolutely certain that Denton would drop the charges and have him released. It was all part of the plan. And as sure as death follows life and life again follows death, Denton had him released from the security room and escorted to his office after detention closed and the late-evening practice sessions ended.

"Hawksley, I am your savior today. The police wanted to hold you overnight," Denton said.

Nicholas inspected the dark spot on his sleeve from the morning. It was faded now, but the shadow of it was still there, faint and nearly imperceptible to any ordinary observer. But it was perceptible to Nicholas. He moistened his fingers and attacked the spot, waiting for Denton to get on with it.

"You know that all extinguishments must conform to the law," Denton said. "Conducted in licensed extinguishment clinics."

Extinguishments. Denton would not say the word "burn." He would not say the word "Burners" either. The Burners were not an official school club, though every ten years or so, some new Gold Star would apply to put them on the school's official register. But it was a lost cause—extinguishments simply had to be by the book, conducted in a monitored, clinical setting.

"Your *stunt*, if I can call it that . . ."

Nicholas interjected, speaking for the first time since Denton had sprung him. "I admit it looked more impressive on paper." He shook his head. "That straitjacket just doesn't *read* when you cut holes for the arms. Muddles the whole asylum/suicide theme."

Denton scrunched his face as if biting into a sour lemon. "Whatever it was, it flagrantly violated that central precept of the law, and it deliberately put me—a Six—at risk. That is a serious offense, Nicholas. I've already suspended Amit for a week, but he was clearly just a pawn."

"Was it that obvious?" Nicholas said, releasing a loud sigh. This was such a waste of his time.

Denton glowered. "The way I see it, you don't respect authority. That comes from your failure to understand what authority actually is."

Nicholas suppressed an urge to scoff. Denton couldn't have been more wrong. The one thing Nicholas did understand inside and out, the one thing he respected above all else, was authority. Namely, his own. Sometimes that put him in conflict with *other* authorities. That, perhaps, was where Denton's misconception came from.

As if to reinforce the point, Denton said, "I am in a position of authority over you. But authority is not just the exercise of power over others. True authority lies in the *management* of others. In steering people. In directing events toward your own goal. Tonight, I convinced the guards to release you, and in so doing I have steered you away from several weeks of community service. This means you are in a position in which you are now compelled to comply with my will, and contribute toward my goals."

"You're saying I owe you one," Nicholas said abruptly.

Denton licked his lips furiously.

"Your *organization* . . . ," Denton started, "though it is prohibited, serves an important function here in the school. Let me tell you why you are allowed to walk freely through these halls. Why you are allowed to commandeer the orchestra room every morning. It is not by your doing, but thanks to my . . . largesse."

Sure.

Nicholas leaned back in his chair and smirked. "Well, sir, let me say thank you. I mean that sincerely."

He put his hands behind his head, stretching his arms. Finally, Denton was getting to the point, which was that Denton *needed* him.

Denton frowned, his face drooping so severely it looked like it had been melted by some foul acid. "Today, Lakeshore Academy has the most pupils it has ever had," he said. "This is not just our issue. In general, the population in Lakeshore is rising rapidly, as is the case across the entire country."

"Yes," Nicholas said. "The lunch lines are becoming far too tedious."

"This is not a joke, Hawksley. Our traditional tools to manage this, our incentives and checks and such . . . they need to be updated to reflect this reality. This is what I have long said, but always to deaf ears. The proposals the board of supervisors are discussing are inadequate for the task, and I have submitted comments to this effect."

"So, sir, what exactly do I owe you?" Nicholas asked loudly.

Denton glared, his lip trembling as his tongue writhed inside his mouth.

"We need to push up the school's life score," he said. "We can do much, much better."

Push up the school's life score? That meant getting more kids to higher numbers faster. Get more kids burning. *This* was interesting.

"We can do much better. On that, we agree," Nicholas said, as relaxed and direct as if he had suddenly become Denton's peer. "So, you want to better the school's life score. And, at the same time, you say I owe you one."

"I think you can see where I am going with this," Denton said. "You may be many things, but you are not an idiot."

With some flourish, Nicholas placed his hand over his heart. "That's the nicest thing you have ever said to me."

"It's certainly not my intention to compliment you," Denton said. "And one more thing . . ." Denton leaned across the desk toward Nicholas, his tongue now working hungrily over his lips.

"I'm sure that if our score was up high enough, it would be impressive to many people in positions of greater power than mine. People like your father."

Nicholas glared at Denton, trying to channel all the anger that invoking his father brought into the mix. . . . Nicholas directed that bile back toward Denton through his fierce stare.

"I'll see what I can do to . . . repay your favor," Nicholas said flatly.

Denton leaned back in his seat and nodded.

"However," Nicholas said, leaning toward Denton and lacing his voice with conspiracy and intrigue—he wasn't about to let an opportunity this golden slip away, especially if he had to deal with Denton's trolling—"might I ask you, then, in the spirit of helping us both, if I might have a look at some of the student records? I'd like to find information on someone in particular."

Denton studied Nicholas for a long moment. And then he licked his lips and smiled.

CHAPTER 10

"ALL RIGHT, ROCK, GET A MOVE ON." ROCKY WAS SITTING AT the kitchen table, his math homework open beside him. Again.

"But breakfast is the most important meal of the day and I haven't had it yet!" Rocky protested.

"Wait, you're doing your homework *now*? You said you finished it last night."

"I . . . was exaggerating," Rocky said and laughed.

Julian picked up a slice of toast and placed it in his brother's laughing mouth.

"Try cramming, then."

Julian's father entered the kitchen and looked at him. "Can I speak to you for a moment, Julian?"

Julian sighed and pushed Rocky toward the door. "I'll meet you at the car in two minutes," he said to his little brother. Toast in mouth, Rocky gathered his homework and headed out to the car. Julian followed his father into the workshop.

"Didn't see you last night," his father said.

"Yeah, sorry, I came back late, didn't want to wake you up," Julian explained halfheartedly.

Julian's father nodded. "Well?"

"I didn't get the job, Dad," Julian said, clenching his jaw. "They can't hire Ones."

His father sat down on a stack of old tires with an air of exhaustion. "Goddammit," he muttered. He ran his hand through his thinning hair.

"Why are you still here?" Julian asked. "Aren't you going to work today?"

"They called me off," he said. "Too many mechanics, not enough work. Jules, we need to talk about you. We can't avoid it any longer."

A now familiar flush of anger pricked at Julian's skin. In the six years since his mother had died, Julian had to watch his father's sad, steady decline. Every year there was less and less money, and his father could never manage to pull them out of the spiral. And now, all the family's troubles were about to be pinned squarely on Julian. He did not want to hear it. Not today.

"Dad, I need to get to school," he said. He hiked his backpack onto his shoulders and headed for the door.

"Five minutes," his father said, his voice deep and grave. "This is hard for me to even bring up. But I need five minutes, Son. This affects all of us. It affects your little brother."

Julian stopped at the entrance and turned around. "What is it?" he said.

His father fixed his gaze at a random point on the wall. "The situation is worse than you know," he said. "We're going to lose the house unless I can make the next payment."

"The house? Dad . . ."

Julian's father turned to him, his face creased and serious.

"Now, there's a rebate we can get to cover the debt, but our life score is too low to qualify for it. I respect you, Son. God knows. I understand how you feel—what with everything that happened to your mother with the . . . the retrogression . . ."

"Please don't," Julian said, hoping he could somehow end this conversation before it got any further.

"I'm just saying that I want you to live your lives the way you want—when you want. But sometimes life isn't about what we want, and we need to make sacrifices for others."

"Dad, it's just . . . I just can't do it. I've tried. Believe me. I've stood on the edge. I've looked over it. I tried to take the step. But I just keep seeing . . . Mom." Julian exhaled.

His father frowned gravely. "I would do it all myself. But I'm a Six already. I'd have to burn up to Eight or maybe even Nine to get the money. I don't think that's a good idea . . . With Rocky being so young still."

Julian's heart was beating faster. His blood was pounding. He knew well how the life score worked. Being younger, being lower, his lives counted for so much more. They counted less the higher, the older, and the more damaged you got.

"I'm sorry, Son. I don't know what else to do," his dad said.

Julian closed his eyes, lost in the sudden shock of the moment.

"How many?" Julian asked quietly.

"Two," his father said. "You would need to be on Life Three in a month."

"There's no other way?"

His father shook his head. "I know you think that the world is messed up and the deck is stacked against you. I used to think the same way—that it's not fair. It's not right. And you know what, life has turned out to be a real hell sometimes for me these past few years. But one day, I decided to stop being angry about it. Instead, I decided to deal with it."

He stood, wiping his greasy hands on his coveralls.

"Great pep talk, Dad," Julian said, turning away. He didn't want to look at his father. Instead he glanced around the shop. There was no inspiration, no way out. Nothing but old tools and his old man.

"I have to get to school," Julian said.

His father looked at him, his face a mask of stone, but Julian knew he was waiting for an answer, a clarification, a reaction, anything. . . . But Julian did not have anything to say. He just turned and walked out.

He sat down in the car. Rocky was in the passenger seat, still working through his homework. "You're late," Rocky said.

"I know," Julian said.

He turned the car on and looked back at his house through the rearview mirror.

CHAPTER **11**

THE SELF-PROCLAIMED BURNERS' DAY BEGAN UNEVENT-
fully. It was business as usual in the morning, except there was a
decided lack of white in class or in the halls. It wasn't until lunchtime that everyone realized what the Burners were up to with
their holiday. Constance had entered, stood on a table in the cafeteria, and announced that Amit's dead man's party was being
held that very evening in the old farmhouse out past the practice
football field. Everyone was invited.

Julian had noticed Molly talking to Constance after lunch. It
looked like Molly was pledging: she was huddled with Constance
in the corner of the cafeteria in a whisper, her face intense and
conspiratorial. There was also one undeniable, irrefutable piece
of evidence: Molly was now wearing the white blazer. Surely, she

would be at the party. Whether or not she was a Burner now, he needed someone to talk to.

Julian arrived that evening to find the farmhouse decked out in a kind of disco asylum vibe, sticking with the theme of Amit's burn. Food and drinks were served on gurneys. Monitors had been installed in the ceiling, showing Amit's DeadLinks video on loop. Over and over, he fell splat onto Denton's podium. There was a special red punch. Julian sniffed a glass of it—cherry and strongly alcoholic—and then put it back down.

Around 8:00 p.m., Amit himself arrived, in his newly minted Four body. Franklin had driven him there. Amit stepped out of the car unsteadily, and the crowd erupted into a chant of "Amit! Amit!"

No longer the fat kid, Amit had been reborn in a slender frame. He returned high fives and fist bumps as he entered, but he was stumbling and his eyes were unfocused and searching, almost as if he wasn't sure where he was.

The centerpiece of the living room was Amit's Three corpse laid out on a gurney. A sign hung from it that read, "Here lies Amit. He gave his life so that we may have a day off." Not long after Amit's arrival, Nicholas organized the Burners into a line and one by one they paid "respects" to the corpse, in the form of jocular insults. The final Burner was Amit himself. But he said nothing when he saw his corpse. He just looked at it, breathing heavily.

When Nicholas began a toast to Amit, Julian slipped out the back of the room into the yard. At the keg, a group of bros was helping one of their own stand on his head as they chanted,

"Death by keg stand! Death by keg stand!" Others were turning the nozzles on a group of girls, who ran from the spray, squealing.

Watching the stupidity, Julian felt empty, sad for the waste of it all. Not just for the waste of life, but for the waste of synthetic beer. For the water wasted on it, soaking into the dirt. He could feel something bubbling up from somewhere deep inside him.

He searched through the entire party twice until he finally found Molly at the fire ring, drinking with Constance and a few other girl pledges.

"Julian?" Molly said, surprised at seeing him approach. "I didn't expect to see you here."

"I know, it's not exactly my scene."

"Yeah, people *having fun*," Constance interjected. "This must be so novel for you."

Julian looked to Molly questioningly. "Is she, like, literally mocking me right to my face?"

Molly took him by the arm and said, "Let's go over here."

She walked them out of earshot of the pledges.

"What's going on, Moll? Am I embarrassing you in front of your new friends?"

"You're starting to, yeah. Why are you even here, anyway?"

Julian wanted to say, *Because I don't know what to do. Because I need a friend. Because I am afraid of becoming exactly like all these people.*

Instead, he said, "There's just . . . There's been some shit happening, and now you're burning like everyone else, and . . ."

"Julian, please don't get into another argument with me

about this. It's not the time, all right?" Molly looked back over her shoulder at Constance.

Julian suddenly felt a heavy, dark pain inside his chest. He could feel it course through him, crawling inside him.

"Yeah, it's not the time, is it?" Julian said. He turned to walk away.

"Wait, Jules, tell me what's going on, okay? But let's not make this about me," Molly said. She grabbed him by the shoulder.

He shrugged her off.

"No. You have a good time. With your *friends*," Julian said, and walked off.

He was almost gone, almost out of there, almost to his car—when Franklin appeared and tapped his shoulder.

"Nicholas Hawksley wants to talk to you," Franklin said.

"Me?" Julian asked, surprised.

"You."

For a moment, Julian was frozen, unthinking. All he could do was absorb Franklin's presence before him: His hair was militant, closely cropped. His face was stern and severe, with a single crease bisecting his forehead.

"But I'm leaving," he said.

"You should hear what he has to say," Franklin replied flatly.

Julian knew he didn't need to go with Franklin. He knew he could leave. But something stopped him there, some new, powerful feeling inside him. Something compelled him to find out whatever the hell Nicholas Hawksley would want with *him*. It was a mysterious force just like at the *Terrible Twos* . . .

You need to look at what this is.

"All right," Julian said after a long moment.

Franklin led him into the farmhouse. A group of Burner girls was watching him from the porch as they passed a joint around. Julian suddenly had the feeling that he had stepped outside his body. That he was watching himself from afar, watching as he was being led to some kind of setup.

"The infamous Julian Dex," Nicholas said as Julian entered the room. "The only One in the academy." Nicholas stood sipping a drink beside Amit's dead body.

"There's an ice luge outside, ladies and gentlemen," Franklin announced to the revelers still in the room. "Enjoy yourselves. A tribute to Amit!"

Slowly, the room emptied. Franklin followed the last person out and shut the door softly behind him, leaving Julian and Nicholas alone. Nicholas approached Julian and handed him a glass of the red alcoholic beverage, which Julian held awkwardly. Nicholas then settled into a sofa beside Amit's corpse and beckoned for him. Julian sat down beside Nicholas, hesitant. Nicholas was so close to him, Julian could feel his warmth, a dull, ambient presence in the air that also smelled strangely floral.

"We've been going to school together for what, four years now," Nicholas said. "And we haven't spoken a word."

"We've said a few," Julian said.

Nicholas smiled at him dimly. "Well. First, it can't be avoided, I want to give you my deepest condolences about your mother."

Julian became hot all over. His face flushed.

What?

"I'm so very sorry," Nicholas said. "With nine deaths, we tend to become immune to real horror. But what happened to her all those years ago . . ." Nicholas shook his head, as if full of pity. "It's incomprehensible."

How did Nicholas even find out? Did everyone know?

"How did you . . . ? *How*?" he stammered.

"Well, I am a curious person by nature. And quite often I find myself in a position of great access," Nicholas said calmly. "I'm particularly interested in discovering truths. Such as in the case of your poor mother, for instance."

"What do you mean?" Julian said quickly, almost frantically. "Do you know something about what happened to her?"

"I just know that there has to be something more to the story. More than what was said officially. An upstanding Lake employee who became retrograde so quickly? It is simply too . . . aberrant."

More to the story. Julian swallowed, his throat hard and tight. "What do you want from me?"

"Now, please," Nicholas said gently. "Don't be angry with me. I don't mean to open old wounds. I just want you to know that I understand." Nicholas's eyes searched Julian's for a connection.

"Understand what?" Julian asked.

"Why you are the way you are. People might talk about you. 'Oh, he's the only One in the school, blah blah, he's afraid of death, blah blah, he doesn't get the joke, he's so boring.' But that's bullshit. Quite obviously. Indeed, I respect you," Nicholas said.

"You . . . *respect* me," Julian repeated, incredulous.

"Oh, very much so," Nicholas said. "You *get it*. You get the absurdity of the world. How could you not? After all you've been through . . ."

A memory of his mother burst into his mind. It was during her final days on Life Eight. Julian was grabbing at her hospital gown, begging her to remember him. But she could only look down at him, her green eyes ghostly, empty. He pushed the image from his mind and noticed that his hands ached—he was clenching them, his too-small thumbs turning white. Julian wanted to run, he wanted to flee. But he had already come too far. He knew he had to see this situation to its conclusion.

He had to look at what this was.

"You get it better than most of the kids here who claim to be Burners," Nicholas continued. "The point of the club, all along, was to make a statement. A protest against this ridiculous way we have to live our lives. But somewhere along the line it just became a big party." Nicholas gestured to the gurney containing Amit's Three corpse.

Julian tried to swallow, tried to loosen his stiffening throat.

"Listen," Nicholas said. "There is something I want you to know, Julian. And please don't take this the wrong way. Understand this is coming from a place of deep respect."

"All right," Julian muttered.

"Like I said, I have certain access to information that I get in my position. So, trust that I know what I'm talking about when I say this."

Nicholas leaned in close and put his hand on Julian's shoulder.

"Burning, Julian, is not optional, as much as you may hate to hear that. There is no question about it."

Julian finally managed to swallow. "I know," he said.

Nicholas smiled. "I have a personal motto I swear by . . ." He put his arm around Julian. Julian could feel his warmth, his scent, which was now heady and dizzyingly botanic, like overly ripe roses that were about to die on the vine.

Nicholas lowered his voice. "You must seize your life by its neck, and choke it to death. It's the only way to win."

Julian suddenly felt hot all over. His head started throbbing. His mother's blank face manifested in his mind again, strobing in and out to the rhythm of his pounding blood. Her face was a hollow mask. Her eyes were cloudy and unseeing. Julian had to leave. Now. He stood up.

"Thanks for your advice. But I have to go," Julian said.

Nicholas rose from the sofa to look him in the face.

"That's fine, but I want you to understand something before you go. Anyone who remains a One as long as you have . . . that's not luck, or stupidity, or fear. Julian, in my world, you could be big. You could be bigger than me."

Julian sucked in a hard breath. His head throbbed.

"What are you saying?"

"I'm saying that the Burners need someone like you, Julian. And someone like you, who is out there wondering about things you can never know . . . well, you might need the Burners in return. We have a way of making things happen." Nicholas turned to Amit's Three corpse.

"For example, this body should be in the morgue warehouse or processed in the dust house. But here it sits. Why? Because I have connections. Those connections might just help me find out more about what happened to your mother, Julian."

Julian was frozen to the floor.

Nicholas stepped close to him. "You don't need to prove anything to me. I know you're ready. Just come see me whenever *you* know you are." Nicholas tipped his glass to Julian as if to toast, and then walked away.

Julian was overwhelmed. He felt that heavy black ooze inside his stomach roil with heat, like a surge of magma boiling out of the earth. He felt the fire of it rise in his chest until his breath became short. He had to get out of there. Now. He willed his legs to move.

He went to exit through the back door, through the kitchen.

There he encountered Amit, alone. He was eating a plate of cake. Not a slice, but the entire cake. He was shoveling it into his mouth with his bare hands. At first, Julian thought maybe Amit was trying to burn by overeating. But no, that's not what this was. Tears streaked Amit's cheeks. Amit was crying as he ate, the frosting smeared over his glistening face.

He noticed Julian watching and looked up. After a moment, he said, through sobs, "I can't . . . I can't taste anything." Watching Amit stupidly stuff cake into his mouth, Julian felt a terrible, palpable sadness. He pushed out the kitchen door, letting it slam behind him.

When he turned the lights on in his car, he discovered a cat sitting calmly in the dirt in front of it. That same cat from the Row. Entirely black, except for a white spot around its right eye. It just sat, still and unbothered, in Julian's headlights. It cocked its head at Julian, studying him. Almost like it pitied him.

Julian laid into the horn, but the cat barely registered the noise. He honked again and again, and finally the cat stirred and slunk away into the shadows. As he watched it disappear into the dark elm forest, that hot black ooze that had been coursing through him all night filled him up completely with heat, permeating every inch of his being. It was a burning fire of despair, he realized—despair for this disposable world.

It flowed through him that night as he drove home. It flowed through him as he lay awake. As he sat at his window looking out over the fence to the scrapyard, at the burned-out husks of cars, at the aimless arcs of old tire tracks in the dirt.

It flowed through him as he looked in on his father's room, at his father and Rocky sleeping in the same bed, his father's arm around the boy.

Watching his brother sleep, he felt the despair finally began to dissipate. As it cooled and faded, Julian discovered a simple, sudden understanding left behind in its place. He embraced it as if it were a revelation. Growing up, like burning, wasn't a choice. It was always there, waiting to happen to you.

There was only one thing you could do about it.

Nicholas's voice rang in his head.

You must seize your life by the neck and choke it to death.

The next morning, Julian found himself standing in front of a school poster. It was hanging in the hallway outside the orchestra room: *Rebirth is a natural part of life. If you are worried or have questions, please see your guidance counselor.*

It was 7:00 in the morning. Julian had not slept at all last night.

"Good morning," a voice said from behind him.

Julian turned. It was Nicholas.

"Well. I'm here," Julian said.

Nicholas grinned.

"Come on in, then. I have some fresh coffee."

CHAPTER 12

AS HE SAT IN THE BACK SEAT OF A VAN TRUNDLING THROUGH downtown Lakeshore, Julian leaned his head on the window and calmed himself by focusing on the streetlights. They cast pools of sickly yellow, pockmarking the empty city roads. It was nearly 11:00 p.m., and they would be approaching Lake Tower any moment now. The streetlights became long, blurry lines in Julian's vision.

The streaks of light shimmered as if oscillating between reality and unreality, and as Julian focused and unfocused on them, he escaped from the tiny, suffocating space of the van and these kids he didn't know at all—kids he had total contempt for until a little over one week ago, when he met Nicholas outside the orchestra room and joined the Burners.

The lights jarred a memory: he was a child, perhaps eight or nine years old, together with his mother in the garage, the hazy afternoon light leaking in through the windows. A rattan chair came into focus. A large black cat sat upon it. The image of this cat resolved in his memory, becoming clearer . . .

It had a distinct patch of white surrounding its right eye. . . .

Wait. Was this the same cat Julian had seen in the Row? The same cat that seemed to be waiting for him outside Amit's party?

In his memory, it sat on the chair, looking at young Julian inquisitively, its tail flicking back and forth.

His mother said she had found him wandering around outside. "This is the smartest cat I've ever had the pleasure to meet," she said, stroking his head. "He hangs around the Lake all the time. Everyone on my team slips him food. But how the heck did he end up here? We live twenty miles away."

Julian knew that she must have continued talking, that the moment must have led somewhere else, to something else, but he had long ago lost where it went. The only clear substance left behind from that memory was the cat with the white eye patch, sitting atop a chair. Intense and imperious, it watched almost as if it knew that, years later, he would be all that remained of this memory.

That cat . . .

It couldn't be the same cat.

Could it?

Julian rubbed his eyes and pushed it from his mind. More recent images were quick to flood into its place. First was the moment from last week, when Nicholas had led Julian into the orchestra room for his first Burners meeting.

He could feel his heart thudding in his chest even now, the

same way it did when Nicholas had escorted him inside and sat him in the front row. He could feel again the pinpricks of anxiety on his face when Nicholas had looked at him slyly during his speech that morning. Nicholas talked about the power of the spectacle found in a well-executed burn.

It felt like the sweat was still damp on Julian's forehead, the same as it was when Nicholas had put his hand on his shoulder and led him over to Franklin, and the three of them had spoken about how Julian was special, being the only One in the academy, and how they were going to plan the biggest burn anyone had ever seen. "After this," Nicholas had said, grinning, "everyone will want to be a burner."

It wasn't long until Nicholas and Franklin were discussing with conspiratorial glee the most dramatic way to execute *You Never Forget Your First Time*—the most outrageous way to pop Julian's One. When they had hit upon the idea of the Tower, Julian initially had objected. He'd tried to say no because this seemed risky—the Tower was in downtown Lakeshore. It was home to the Lake Department headquarters for the three counties that shared this particular Lake, a population of almost two million—but Nicholas said that was why it was such a compelling stage.

Fine, Julian had argued, but the downtown district was full of Sevens, Eights, Nines. . . . All crimes in high-numbered areas were compounded, punishments exponentially harsher.

But to this, Nicholas had snaked his arm around Julian's shoulder and spoken with a calming, quiet poise. "Just put your trust in me," he'd said. "Everything will work out."

Julian didn't have much choice after that.

Because in the midst of all his excitement about Julian's burn, Nicholas had promised to help him discover what had happened to his mother. He had promised Julian access to the truth saying, "You buy truth with trust."

That was the bargain. And so Julian had accepted.

Soon enough, these dark plans, these hushed conversations, these morning Burners meetings and evening sessions out on the bleachers all conspired together to deliver Julian to this moment. To this very seat in this van, to this position, with his head on his arm, watching the lights blur past him, wondering how he got here, how he could have possibly traveled so far from the boy who would not burn to become the boy who would make the most spectacular burn the school would ever know.

The van pulled to a stop in an alley sandwiched between the Tower and the Adirondack Bank building. Franklin was driving, Nicholas was in the front seat. Clayton was beside Julian in the back. All of them dressed in black. The two back-seat benches in the van had been removed, forcing Julian and Clayton to sit awkwardly for the ride, bracing against the windows or holding on to the door handles.

Julian looked at the empty floor where the seats used to be—soon enough, that was where his lifeless body would lie. He stared at the floor unblinking, rubbing his chest. This was the only chest he had ever known. The only body. Soon it would be . . . shattered. Exploded. Nothing at all recognizable as what it was—what *he* was—right now.

How could he do this?

Was the first one the hardest?

Did it get easier to throw them away?

The group pulled on ski masks, and the plan conjured on the bleachers was finally set into motion. As Nicholas suited up, he looked Julian in the eye and smiled. "My," he said. "Subterfuge certainly is exciting, isn't it?"

Julian opened his mouth to respond, but nothing came out.

Nicholas used the map on his phone to review with Clayton where to place the cameras in the park across the street. Once he was satisfied, he turned to the rest of the group and smirked. "It's banzai time."

Nicholas, Franklin, and Clayton hopped out into the alley. Julian hesitated for a moment, but Nicholas flashed him a reassuring smile as he beckoned Julian out of the van. Julian complied.

The stench of trash and stale oil hit Julian with a smack. With the inescapable feeling that this would be his last few moments inside this body, all of his senses became heightened. The shadows of the downtown buildings loomed over him. The distant wash of traffic filled his head with static. As the group moved through the alley toward a back entrance to the Tower, they passed through panels of moonlight that shone through gaps between the buildings. Julian's focus caught the individual motes of dust floating through them.

Clayton hid in a shadow near the main road until the coast was clear, then he dashed across the street to the park, a bag of cameras slung over his shoulder.

Then Nicholas produced the linchpin for the entire plan from his back pocket: an official Department of the Lakes keycard. Nicholas's father, of course, was the director of the Lake in Lakeshore, so no one asked questions. With Nicholas, everything seemed possible.

He swiped the card at the back door. A pneumatic lock hissed, and the door swung open to a bright, fluorescent stairwell. It was like looking into the sun: Julian had to turn away. Suddenly, two rough hands—Franklin's—gripped his shoulders and pushed him into the stairwell, behind Nicholas.

The three of them took the stairs up thirty flights. At first, they took them two steps at a time, in a light jog, but after fifteen flights, they slowed considerably. Julian's calves ached, and a sour smell of sweat clung to the crew as it made its way surely and determinedly to the top. Julian panted like a tired dog, to which Nicholas responded through wheezing breaths, "No one said it would be easy, huh?"

Finally, the door to the roof swung open, and Julian and the two other boys limped out, exhausted and sucking in huge breaths of the bracing night air. Julian felt a familiar arm wrap around him, and he was gently turned around.

Nicholas's face was cut with a long grin, his teeth gleaming white against the night sky. His bangs were matted against his forehead by the wind. He said four words to Julian in a small, gentle voice: "Don't think. Just jump."

Time slowed as Nicholas led Julian to the ledge of the biggest, most iconic building in the state. It slowed until all Julian could feel was his chest, rising and falling in rhythm as he stepped toward the precipice. As he peered over the drop, time became a viscous matter that surrounded him like jelly—delaying the cheers and calls from Nicholas and Franklin, which arrived at his ears as muffled booms.

He closed his eyes and tried to think of his mother, but she came to him abstractly. She was just a word. "Mother." Just letters. He tried to summon her image, but instead, what came to him was that damn cat: it sat, perched on a chair in their garage, lost somewhere in the past but still watching him even now, as if through time and space.

Julian shook the cat from his mind. How on earth could that cat be his last thought in this body? He wanted a last thought that was momentous—something deep and meaningful. As he peered over the edge, as his head spun from the height, Julian reached inside himself, searching for anything. But there was only that cat with its white eye patch and its piercing gaze and its flicking tail.

Nicholas's hand was tighter on his back now. Pressing him. He had to do this.

Oh well.

Julian held his breath. He leaned forward.

His body slipped into weightlessness, and his mind retreated into a blank as the rush of wind whipped against his face, forcing his eyes closed. He could sense his feet tumbling over his head, his guts lurching inside him. All he could hear was the whistling sound of his plunge.

Then a brief, terrible explosion of shattering pain. A torture of enormous depth; a cosmic rending of reality. A tearing of his self from his sanity. One last, piercing "fuck you" from the world.

But, in an instant, the moment ended.

And just like that, he was gone.

CHAPTER 13

JULIAN OPENED HIS EYES, AND THEY STUNG. HE OPENED his mouth, and his throat filled with water. He kicked his legs frantically as he looked up with burning eyes—it was blurry, but there was light above him, darkness below. He reached for the light, pulling his arms down in hard jerks. After several thrusts, he burst to the surface of the Lake.

He spat out gulps of water. While struggling to tread, he touched his chest. It was still there, his heart wild inside it like a trapped bird. His arms—still there. His legs—there. He checked other important areas. Everything, *everything* in its right place.

He was here. In a new body.

A giddy thrill coursed through him.

Fuck me, I did it!

He had died and come back—this was a thing that people did every day, and now, finally, he had done it, too.

A loud tone sounded from far ahead. A yellow light on the beach strobed on and off. Julian knew, like everyone knew from elementary school lessons, that the light and the tone guided you home. He started swimming toward it, his arms moving with increasing confidence as the knowledge set in that they were, in fact, his arms. His *new* arms.

On the beach, Julian hid his nakedness—he felt embarrassed, but less embarrassed than he imagined he would be, given that everyone else was naked, too. He surveyed the beach—it seemed normal, apart from nurses wrapping naked rebirths of every age and type up in pale blue paper gowns. The paint was peeling on the receiving center up on the hill, revealing large splotches of bare concrete. An American flag shifted weakly in a small breeze. This was the place he had spent so much time dreading? It was . . . pretty innocuous. Pretty lame.

A hand grabbed his shoulder and turned him around. It was a grim-faced nurse, offering him a gown in latex-gloved hands. "I would hustle up now to beat the crowd," she said, gesturing toward a large group of about twenty confused older people. Food poisoning at an early bird special? Gas leak at a retirement home? He put his gown on and headed up the hill.

There was a tickling, cottony feeling inside his mouth. He ran his tongue over his front teeth. He used to have a slightly chipped tooth from a fall he took one Halloween when he was three. But now it was whole again. He ran his tongue over it repeatedly. It felt alien.

He touched his arms, his chest, and ran his hands along his

stomach. It was firm and hard, whereas in his previous body, he had begun to develop a thin but noticeable layer of cushioning fat around his belly. He squeezed the muscles together in his butt. He touched it when no one was looking—it was taut and hard.

The nurses, dour and serious all of them, herded Julian to the shortest line inside the receiving center, behind a young man with red hair and a twitching eye. A massive American flag hung from the ceiling at the head of the room. The bureaucratic sanitization of this place filled Julian with reassurance. This was *normal*. A *normal* thing to do.

But then he saw the nurse in purple at the podium under the flag.

It was the Prelate, Julian recalled as his memories came back.

He stood stiffly, surveying the proceedings from behind a purple cowl and menacing black goggles. If the bureaucracy was vaguely comforting in its promise of order, the Prelate was a grim reminder that order also meant repercussions. It meant punishments for those who veered off course. Feeling the familiar tendrils of anxiety prick at him even in this new body, Julian turned away from him.

A nurse approached him with a clipboard. "Would you complete this survey for us?" she asked. "Your answers are for statistical purposes only."

Julian took the clipboard and looked at the survey of about ten multiple-choice questions.

What best describes the feeling you have inside your new body?

Julian stared at the answers. For a moment, they blurred together into an indistinct jumble of letters. He blinked several times until the words came into focus. He gripped his pencil and circled "(A) Disconnected—it does not yet feel this is the real me."

What best describes your current mental state?

(A)   "At peace. You feel whole and/or contented."
(B)   "Happy. You feel a sense of joy or elation."
(C)   "Distressed. You feel that something is wrong."
(D)   "Lost. You feel uncertain about your circumstances."

Julian circled "At peace." But he immediately second-guessed himself.

His head spun. He handed the survey back to the girl and rubbed his eyes, trying to push away his confusion.

A male nurse in thick glasses waved him into a numbering booth. Wanting to appear adult and experienced, Julian answered his questions—name, address, ID number—simply and directly, in as few words as possible. The nurse turned Julian around, and he soon felt the cold steel of a stethoscope through his thin gown. Two minutes passed as the nurse studied Julian's breathing. Julian looked away, toward the long hallways and closed doors of the administrative wing.

This is the Lake receiving center in Lakeshore, he told himself. Those were the hallways your mother walked.

What was behind those doors? What was in those rooms? She had known.

"Well," the nurse said, turning Julian back around. "It seems your heart skips a beat every minute."

Julian blinked. "Is that a problem?"

"It's a pretty common Wrinkle. Nothing to worry about."

Nothing to worry about?

Julian closed his eyes when the numbering gun was put to his neck. He felt a quick, prickly stab. His new number. The punctuation to his new life.

In the bathroom, standing in his gown, Julian stared at the number Two on his neck. He touched it. This was all so easy, he realized. Except for a vague sense of unreality that was already starting to fade, everything about this seemed relatively painless. Well . . .

Except, of course, that he could recall nothing about the final moments of his death. He remembered the van, and the memories of that cat . . . But what had transpired exactly once they arrived at Lake Tower? Did he actually jump? He must have. But was it willingly? Did he *feel* the impact? He pushed the thoughts from his mind before he could consider the grim possibilities.

He stood in another line outside, this one for the bus back to Lakeshore. He watched with his new eyes as the driver stubbed out a cigarette, a small spark leaping out from under his boot. The bus rocked as the driver pulled himself up the steps to his seat. He turned it on and it rumbled to life, kicking up a cloud of dust.

Julian got home late. His father and brother were already asleep. He walked quietly through the house to his room, took off his gown, and put on clean underwear. "If you're feeling bad, always put on clean underwear." This was one of his mom's favorite pieces of advice.

He lay down in his bed and stared at the ceiling. You're a Two now, he thought. All those days as a One . . . all that time spent saying no. All that time spent pushing back, hiding away . . . it was gone.

You are someone new now, he thought. He held this thought in his mind for a few long minutes, turning it over carefully and examining it for hidden feelings and secret valences. He felt no disdain with being transformed, but he felt no comfort with the thought either. It was just there. A new fact he had to accept.

Lost?

At peace?

Did it matter?

He was new. This was the only fact that mattered. A new Julian.

Suddenly, he grabbed his phone from where it was charging on the bedside table. He opened a new message.

Recipient: Cody.

He typed: "Hey. So where is that party of yours?"

CHAPTER 14

THE NEXT MORNING, JULIAN FOUND HIS FATHER IN THE
workshop. It wasn't even 7:00 a.m., and he was already in his
dirty overalls, sifting through a pile of tools.

"Hey Dad, I'm a Two now," Julian said.

His dad turned around and upon seeing the Two on Julian's
neck, he let out a sigh of relief. "Is that where you were last night?"

"Twenty-four-hour extinguishment clinic," Julian lied. "Sorry
I didn't tell you. It was just—something I had to do myself."

He had spent the morning considering whether he should tell
his father about *You Never Forget Your First Time*. But then he might
also have to admit why he did it. That he was chasing the promise of finding out something about Mom.

And a promise from who? A kid running a high school suicide
club?

It would sound foolish and stupid and naive. And he didn't want that shot down—not now. He needed to believe in something right now.

"I'm sorry, Julian. But you're doing the right thing," his father said softly.

"I hope so," Julian replied. He hiked his backpack up on his shoulder and went to the kitchen to corral Rocky.

Rocky was strangely silent on the ride to school. But before he hopped out at the middle school, he turned to Julian and asked a question: "That was you, wasn't it? On DeadLinks?"

Julian looked back at his brother blankly.

Shit.

Of course. The Burners had made a video.

The knowledge that Rocky had seen the video brought it crashing home for him: he had leaped off the Tower. What he did was reckless. Risky. Dangerous. Actually: *wrong.* Breaking into the Tower . . . throwing himself off the top . . . in a high-numbered district, no less! This cold, hard reality somehow got lost in all the planning, excitement, and subterfuge.

And yet, it had happened. It was a thing he did, and a thing he didn't want his brother to ever look up to.

"They're supposed to be cool, right? The Burners," Rocky said.

"Supposed to be," Julian said blandly.

"So, you're cool now, too, I guess," Rocky said, a proud smile on his face. He hopped out of the car and made his way to middle school, laughing with a blond-haired kid who ran up to him.

Cool?

Shit. Shit. Shit.

What kind of example was this? Jumping off a thirty-story building, breaking the law, and losing a heartbeat?

Then another troubling realization hit him: if Rocky saw the video, then everyone saw it.

Julian's heart sank as the realization set in.

Of course everyone saw the video. That was the whole point. So much of their planning time for the jump was spent discussing the mechanics of recording it: camera placement, angles, lighting . . .

Julian always knew that his death was meant for public consumption, but some part of him kept putting off coming to terms with what that actually meant. Maybe, he thought, he would just come back on Life Two shameless and ready to accept the world's watching eyes.

But here he was, a Two, his old sense of shame still intact.

In homeroom, he could feel the eyes of everyone turn to him as soon as he walked through the door. He felt them stay on his back as he crossed the room to his seat. During his morning classes, yet more eyes tracked his every move. Even in the hallways, when he tried to stick to the shadows, the eyes would follow him. Compounding this were all the watchers on their phones, playing and replaying the video. Views stacking up higher and higher until they towered over him.

Julian's instinct was to shrink away, but of course Nicholas was there to greet Julian the moment he entered the cafeteria at lunchtime, his white jacket crisp and freshly pressed and his broad smile revealing a row of polished, expensive-looking teeth.

Nicholas started applauding, and Julian became hot with embarrassment. Soon, everyone in the cafeteria joined Nicholas in cheers, whistles, hoots, and shouts. The Burners banged their feet in a rhythm, like at a football game. The sound rose to a deafening roar and reverberated off the concrete walls. The din filled Julian's head, and he looked away from it, closing his eyes, trying to push his embarrassment down inside a black hole.

Finally, the befuddled teachers and guards tamped down the commotion and Nicholas, beaming, led Julian across the room to the Burners' table like a trophy kill. In a daze, Julian returned their fist bumps and high fives.

"Jules," Nicholas said, pulling him in close. "You make your plans and you hope for the best. But this . . . this is more than I could have ever hoped for. We have over five thousand views, and it's only been up since six a.m."

He studied Julian's face and scrunched his brows together in curiosity. "You *have* watched it, haven't you?"

Julian shook his head.

Nicholas's eyes bulged in surprise. "Aren't you wondering why everyone is cheering for you? My goodness, boy, let's embrace the good times here!"

"I-I just . . . ," Julian stammered. "I don't want to."

Nicholas clicked his tongue in a playful *tsk*. "Oh, I get it. This is about seeing your dead body," Nicholas said. "That's a perfectly normal response. Many people don't want to attend their funeral party, let alone watch the moment of . . . impact," he said, raising his brow to highlight his punning. "But you have got to see this. It has made a real impression."

"Because the loser One kid just popped his cherry?"

Nicholas frowned. "Julian," he said sharply. "Show some pride in yourself. People are watching this video because it is exactly what the Burners stand for. A powerful, impressive, undeniable moment when the system is burst open right in front of everyone, right at the pinnacle of society. You made this statement, Julian," Nicholas said, tapping the table furiously with his fingers. "People are listening."

Nicholas retrieved his phone from his pocket and queued up the video. He offered it to Julian like he was slipping him a drug.

"Take a look at the message you sent to the world," Nicholas said.

Julian took the phone.

He pushed play.

Titled *You Never Forget Your First Time*, the video was forty-eight seconds. It was a series of shots from different angles and at different speeds and in varying degrees of close-ups. It began with a body—his body, he realized intellectually; but emotionally, it was just a body here, a freaking *ragdoll* for all it mattered— plummeting thirty stories to the sidewalk and exploding into a cloud of red mist, spraying blood onto a hapless Lake employee standing outside the door, carrying a briefcase. This entire sequence was about eighteen seconds, all in. The other thirty seconds were various reprises from different angles and speeds. In all angles, Julian's face was pixelated and blurred—a crucial part of Nicholas's plan to protect his identity in case the authorities came snooping.

Watching it, Julian was surprised to find his reaction bordered more on relief than revulsion—it was difficult for him to link that exploding body with who he was now, but at least the pixelation on the face was so well done.

"So, no one can unscramble my face? Not even the police?"

"No way in hell," Nicholas said, sounding mildly offended.

"And the body?"

"We picked it up within minutes of impact. All the little pieces." Nicholas smirked. "Bleached the hell out of the sidewalk, too. Not a scrap of DNA left behind."

Julian exhaled. "But everyone at school knows it was me. Even my little brother in middle school knows."

Nicholas rolled his eyes.

"Look, Julian. Worst case is if the police do somehow link the falling body back to you . . . this is, mind you, if they even *bother* to investigate it, and then someone at school squeals, despite the fact that they know *I am protecting you* . . . in this rare event, there are people I know who could make a problem like that go away very quickly."

Julian nodded. After the clip finished, he looked at the view counter, which was running up more views even as he watched.

"But come on, this is some impressively sick stuff right here. Who knew you could be such a sensation, right?" Nicholas asked.

"Not me," Julian said, handing the phone back to Nicholas.

"Jules, that was a leading question," Nicholas replied. "Because the answer is . . . *I knew*. I knew all along that there was someone important inside you who needed to be set free. Now meet me after school in the parking lot," Nicholas said. "There's something we need to do. It will make you feel much better about this whole thing."

The rest of the day, Julian still found himself wanting to shrink away from all the attention. But at the same time, he couldn't help but marvel at Nicholas's power: he had managed to open up this entirely new world—a world where people looked at you, cheered for you, thought about you. . . . It was disorienting, but impressive.

If Julian wanted to truly be this person Nicholas had given him the opportunity to become, then he would have to embrace a version of himself that Nicholas wanted him to be. He would need to own it. The kid in white who watched his own Dead-Links videos.

But it all seemed impossible to Julian. He was going to end up a huge faker. A hack. A pretender.

This worry ate away at him bit by bit all afternoon. He wondered absently if maybe he was actually starting to experience some kind of disassociation—a delayed-onset retrogression maybe?

After school that day, Julian met Nicholas in the parking lot. He led him to the Burners' van parked behind the gymnasium. Julian took the passenger seat as Nicholas drove it out of the school lot and up a winding dirt road that stretched into a tree-lined bluff that overlooked the Lake. Julian's One body lay in a garbage bag where the back seat was supposed to be.

"Trust me," Nicholas said. "This is like a closing ritual. For your One, I recommend it."

From the top of the bluff, the road wound into a thick grove of evergreens. The afternoon sun was an orange glow on the horizon by the time they came to a stop in a small clearing. In a quick flash, Julian saw an image of his mother, superimposed in the hazy light, looking at him with ghostly green eyes. The image made his skin rise up in goose bumps. He tried to shake it from his mind, but he couldn't. Her face lingered for a moment behind his eyelids, slowly fading as he rubbed them.

She was the reason he was doing all this. Why he flung himself from a rooftop. Why he was thrust into the spotlight. Why he hadn't just gone to an ex clinic for a doctor-assisted extinguishment like a normal person. If there was some secret truth out there about her, Nicholas was going to find it. If he could get them into Lake Tower, he could surely get Julian anything else he wanted.

"Hey," Julian said as Nicholas pulled the van to a stop in the shadow of a pine tree. "So, I did this ridiculous burn the way you wanted . . ."

Nicholas cocked a curious eyebrow.

"And . . ." He looked down at his hands. "You promised you could find out what happened to my mother."

Nicholas looked over sharply at Julian from behind the wheel, his brow suddenly furrowed. "What, you think I've forgotten?"

"No, I'm not saying that," Julian said. "But I mean, that's why I'm here. I want to find out what happened to her."

Nicholas nodded as he pulled the lever on the van's parking brake. "Of course you do," he said, "and so do I."

"Well, I'm wondering when we're—"

"Never fear. I am working on it, Julian," Nicholas said with an eerily bright sunniness. "But you should know that it requires some . . . finesse."

"Finesse?"

"I need to call in a favor with a certain well-placed person. This kind of thing takes time, but I assure you it is moving forward."

Julian nodded to him. "Thank you. Sorry to press it. It's just . . . It's important to me is all."

"I gave you my word, and I assure you I shall provide,"

Nicholas said, opening the door and hopping out. He looked back through the van, toward Julian, his smile now taking on a crooked, conspiratorial bent. "I have big plans," he said. "For the Burners. For *us*. We are just getting started, my friend."

Julian rubbed his eyes until every little bit of the lingering image of his mother faded away. He hopped out of the van and together the two of them hoisted the garbage bag with his One body up onto their shoulders. It had an odd, sweet-sour, bacony odor. They carried it a short distance to an old fire pit and tossed it onto the coals with a crunch.

Nicholas and Julian stood beside each other for a moment, looking at the bag. "Think of this as a mental break between the old you and the new you," Nicholas said. He produced a can of lighter fluid from his backpack and doused the body. "To tomorrow," Nicholas said. He took a lighter from his pocket and handed it to Julian.

But before Julian struck the flame, something stopped him. Some strange, powerful urge. Like the feeling that overcame him at the *Terrible Twos*. An urge . . . *to look*.

He couldn't resist it. Using his keys, he cut a hole in the bag, just big enough to look in and catch a glimpse of his old One face. He saw an eye, blue-black and swollen shut, double its normal size, and then part of his face: purple and battered and ruined. That was enough. Julian had seen enough of his old life. He folded the plastic back over to cover it up.

He struck a flame on the lighter, and tossed it onto the body. "To tomorrow," Julian said. The flame caught the lighter fluid in a quick burst. The two boys watched the flames dance for a moment, and then Nicholas put his arm around Julian and they walked back to the van, the acrid scent of his old life wafting into the air.

On the ride back down the hill, Julian and Nicholas sat in a meditative silence, broken only when Julian's phone chimed.

It was a message from Cody.

"Glad you're coming. Party Wednesday night, 7:30 p.m. Bardo Books in Poplar. Be there. xx"

Julian exhaled, and all of the day's stress left him. He took in a breath of new life, in a new body.

He turned to Nicholas and allowed himself a small smile.

CHAPTER 15

IS THIS RIGHT? THIS CAN'T BE RIGHT.... CAN IT?

Julian sat in his car looking at Bardo Books across the street. It was a narrow shopfront with a door frame painted in a sort of kaleidoscopic tribal pattern of red, green, and blue.

It felt later than it was. It was only ten minutes after seven, but it had been dark since after five, now that it was October. This vague disconnect, combined with Julian's general unfamiliarity with the city of Poplar Heights, made him feel uneasy and anxious, like he had entered a foreign land without a compass.

He had been watching the door for over ten minutes, waiting for Cody, hoping he could follow her inside and minimize any awkward interactions that might occur if he had to go in alone and look for her. But not a single person had entered or left since he arrived.

What kind of party is this? he wondered.

At an old bookstore on a Wednesday night?

After a few more minutes of hesitation, Julian decided to get out of the car. He tucked his hands into his blazer pockets and walked through the brisk night toward the entrance. There shouldn't be any reason to sit and freak yourself out about going in alone—not anymore, he told himself. Not when you're a Two.

Sure enough, there was no sign of a party inside. It was just an ordinary bookstore—bright, warm, smelling of stale paper, and silent except for the creaking of floorboards. Julian walked up and down the rows looking for Cody, but the only person he saw was a hunched-over old woman, an Eight, who stood still in the back of a row of shelves, staring at a large book she had balanced daintily in her small hands.

"You looking for the girl?"

It was the woman behind the counter, peering at Julian from over rectangular glasses. She looked to be in her forties, her hair tied back in a bun. The proprietor, maybe.

"Yeah. Cody," Julian said.

"Try the alley around back."

This party was getting stranger and stranger.

Julian walked along a narrow passage beside the building, stepping gingerly over garbage bags. He listened for signs of a party, for signs of any kind of human activity, but all he could hear was the occasional odd scraping sound, like the scurry of a small animal. He pressed on, rounding the corner to the alley.

Julian froze in his steps. About a dozen large, rangy cats turned to look at him, and then, at once, they scattered, leaping into the shadows, climbing up scaffolding or scrambling behind garbage cans. Left standing where the cats had vacated, beside a scattered mess of metal pans half-filled with milk, was Cody.

"Very strange," she said, looking up at Julian from a notebook. "They're usually friendly."

She scribbled something, then looked up to the fire-escape scaffolding, where a row of cats stared down at Julian imperiously. "They're observing you from a distance." As soon as Julian looked at them, the cats leaped away, into the shadows.

"Weird," Julian said, feeling embarrassed at the feline attention.

Cody raised one finger to pause Julian and continued writing whatever it was she was writing in her notebook. Julian remembered the first and only time he had ever seen her before—on a cold night out near the Lake fence, feeding cats and writing in that notebook.

"Most biologists consider the Lake cat a subspecies of the common domesticated cat," she said. "But at this point, considering how much time they've spent at the Lakes and how that's warped them, they should be a totally separate taxon." Finally, she closed her notebook and walked toward Julian.

"So, Mr. Julian," she said. "You came."

"Yeah. Is this the . . . um, party?"

Cody stepped in close to him, so close he could smell apple-scented shampoo. She peered at his neck and furrowed her brow, her face tightening into a sour look.

"You're a Two now," she said, her voice laced in disappointment.

"Oh yeah . . . ," Julian said, nervously touching the Two on his neck.

Cody looked at him with big, questioning eyes.

"It's sort of a long story," Julian continued, struggling to fill the awkward silence.

As he stammered, Cody grabbed her backpack that was lying on a stoop and pulled out a small black device. She returned swiftly to Julian, and without another word, grabbed him by the neck. With her other hand, she pressed the device to his Two tattoo and held it there. Julian flinched and tried to pull away, but she squeezed his neck long enough to hold him in place. Finally, the device beeped, and she removed it.

"What the hell?" Julian asked, rubbing his neck.

Cody read the device. "This is an authenticator." She frowned, apparently disappointed with whatever it was telling her. "That Two is real. And it's fresh. Did you do it of your own accord, Mr. Julian?"

Julian, flummoxed, stepped away. "Do I need to explain myself to you?"

"Yes, you do. When I invited you here, I thought I was inviting a One. A very *old* One, who was special because most people who are Ones are just little kids. Except now it turns out you aren't as special as I thought. You're just some ordinary teenage Two."

Julian frowned, hot embarrassment flushing up his neck.

"And where did you invite me, anyway? To a back alley full of cats?"

Cody ignored his question and looked back up at the fire escape. The cats there kept their distance, still in the shadows, but eerily peering at Julian, their eyes iridescent alien dashes in the darkness. Cody scrunched up her face in thought, watching the cats watch Julian.

"Tell me," Cody said, and turned back to Julian. "Did you do it for a good reason?"

"Yes," Julian said. He forced himself to look her in the face, to be confident in his new Two body. "It was for my family."

Cody frowned severely. It dimpled the sides of her cheeks. She nodded to him, beckoning him to continue.

"Things have been seriously messed up since my mom . . . died," Julian said. "So I have to do certain things I don't want to do. But why am I going into this with you?"

"You mean, like, *Nine*-dead?" Cody asked matter-of-factly.

"Yes. Permadead."

Cody nodded. Her eyes softened, and something flickered in them—a small shimmer of empathy, perhaps?

"Let's go into the basement," she said, and led him down a small flight of steps to a cellar door.

That would certainly be an improvement on an alley, he thought.

But, actually, it wasn't much of one.

The basement was one large, open room. Several small groups of people were gathered among stacks of books. Most of the groups were four to five disheveled-looking young people ranging in age from middle school to maybe college age, sitting before an older, more clean-cut person standing at the head of the group—it looked vaguely like a Sunday school session at the Temple of the Nine.

"What is this place?"

"It's retro night," she said. "The retrograde population keeps growing. And the disease keeps getting worse. Look at all these kids," she said. "It's hitting people younger and younger now."

Julian puzzled at the sight—retro in teenagers? How had he never heard of this before?

Cody continued, "Between this and what I'm seeing with the cats, it seems something is changing at the Lake."

Julian had read the conspiracy theories on dark corners of DeadLinks—rebirth isn't always a guarantee; not everyone gets nine lives—but he never took them too seriously. He knew no one who had been touched by that kind of problem. Plus, there were too many people wrapped up in the Lake system. Too much process. Too much bureaucracy. How could it be failing and not a single person had said anything about it?

"Of course, the Lakes deny there's a problem and suppress any evidence of it," Cody said as if she were reading his mind. "Nonetheless, someone has to be the Good Samaritan. That's what these nice people here are doing. They're called Friends of the Lake."

"You're one of these Friends?"

"Not really. I do my own research," Cody said. "For example . . ." She looked around the room stealthily. "Recently, I've been studying the Lake fauna. Animals that have been changed by the Lakes. The electrified fish in Asia, for example, or the virulent cicada populations that bloom every eighteen years and somehow thrive in the cold winters around here. And then, there are the cats . . ."

"Yeah," Julian said. "What's up with them?"

"I developed a theory when I was working with my previous . . . partner," she said, choosing the word carefully. "The cats here at our Lake have begun coming back to life, just like people."

"Cats with nine lives," Julian said.

"Right." Cody nodded. "Cats having nine lives used to be common folklore. That was centuries ago, before the Summer of Storms, before the Lakes were formed."

"And now the legend has become reality," Julian said. "Why?" Her curiosity was infectious, worming its way into Julian's brain.

"I don't know. But Mr. Julian, I'll tell you what I do know. These cats here at our Lake . . . each time they come back, they come back smarter. They also become much more risk-averse, less independent, and more . . . *focused*. It's like they have some innate knowledge about the new multitudes of their lives. They seem to know that their lives tick down to the last one, just like we do."

Okay. . . .

It suddenly struck Julian that he was in a bookstore basement full of retros, listening to a stranger's conspiracy theory about creepy Lake cats.

He became paranoid—the last thing he wanted now was to end up on some watch list. Not after *You Never Forget Your First Time*.

Julian nodded absently, and looked out at the room: there must be thirty retros here.

"You said this was a party," Julian said.

Cody gestured to a folding table in the corner with a simple spread of snacks.

"There are pretzels right there," she said.

Pretzels.

Julian turned to her. "Why did you invite me here?"

"Well, I wouldn't have if I knew you were a Two."

"You mentioned," Julian said.

"There have been rumors of groups of people in the Lake Superior States who have refused to follow the life table. Who are forcing the hand of the Council of the Awakened. I thought, maybe . . . I knew it was a longshot, but I wondered if you might be one of them."

"I've never heard of them," Julian said. "I just didn't want to burn. And you didn't need to trick me into coming here."

She scrunched her face. "Cut me some slack. I mean, I hang out with a bunch of cats after school. Talking to boys isn't my strong suit."

Right.

He could relate. Well, the old version of him—the One— could, anyway. "So that's what this was about. You were looking for someone to, I guess, research?"

"I wouldn't put it that nakedly," she said.

A trophy in the academy cafeteria and a research subject in a bookstore basement. Julian wondered when he would get to be just Julian. No numbers, no subtitles.

He sighed and looked down at his hands. Even after he set his old life on fire, these were still his thumbs. Still too small, even in his new body.

"Actually," he said. "Since I'm here, there has been something weird happening to me that involves a cat."

Cody looked at him. "Really?"

"There's a specific cat I keep seeing. I've seen it in different times and places . . . and even in my memories. It's almost like it's been following me. Or . . . kind of haunting me."

Cody crinkled her brows and frowned. Those dimples returned to her cheek.

"Are you sure that it's always the same cat?" she asked.

"I'm sure," Julian replied.

She grinned. "I knew there was something about you, Mr. Julian."

Julian rolled his eyes. "But does it mean anything?"

"I can't say. I'd have to verify if it was in fact a Lake cat, for starters. If it was a Lake cat, then well . . . I'm not sure. But I can tell you those cats are aware of something that we can't sense directly. It's possible they have some primal insight that we lack. Have you heard of quantum entanglement?"

Julian shook his head.

"A function of the many-worlds theory?"

Julian just looked at her.

"The basic gist is that the universe is a multitude of worlds. Many dimensions. It's hard for the human mind to come to grips with this, but what if there were other minds out there that could understand this? Innately? Feline minds, for example."

"You're saying cats are more aware of the reality of the universe than we are?" He paused. "Who *are you* again?"

"I'm not saying that we're incapable of understanding the true nature of multitudes. It's just that, as people, we take the normalcy of the world for granted. No matter how you explain it, having nine lives is a strange twist of fate for our species, and a relatively recent one at that. And yet, now it's a basic fact of the world. An everyday thing. It's our life. Everything revolves around it. But accepting something as normal doesn't make it normal. The word 'normal' is just a mask. A shield.

"Because if you think about it for a moment, strange twists of fate are a daily occurrence. Everything we know about the world keeps changing. With every passing day, our world is revised into something new. Even before the Summer of Storms, our lives have always been in multitudes, if you realize that every morning is a new iteration. Every day we walk out into a different place. Every minute, every second is a crossroads. You can go this way or that way. The future is, literally, a multitude. Nothing is normal. Everyone needs a reminder of that. There is no normal."

That was for sure—this was *so* not normal.

Julian felt someone watching them from across the room. He turned to find a kid glancing over at him: a boy about his age, wearing a camo jacket. He had bright white hair and long, irregular splotches staining his neck. The kid's eyes were pale blue, and they weren't just watching—they were examining and evaluating. They reminded him of Nicholas's eyes. Eyes that were scheming to snuff out lives, one by one. The boy's left eye suddenly twitched erratically, and the kid shook his head with some kind of tremor.

Suddenly, he was pushing his way through the crowd, coming for Julian.

"What are you doing?" he shouted as he approached.

"What?" Julian said, bewildered.

Cody grabbed Julian's arm. "Let's get out of here."

"Who are you?" the kid shouted.

"I—I'm Julian. I go to Lakeshore Academy," Julian responded.

Two of the older people in the crowd stepped in front of the kid and gently held him back. As they redirected him toward the other side of the room, the kid kept glaring at Julian—a wicked look on his face.

Cody pulled Julian back to the exit.

"Who the hell was that?" Julian asked.

"Just a retrograde," Cody replied. "He calls himself Robbie. He's . . . particularly volatile."

A retrograde?

"He looks so young," Julian said.

Cody opened the door.

"Retrogression used to get worse as we got older, a compounding effect of multiple rebirths. But like I said, there are younger and younger people with it. It's highly disturbing."

Outside, the cats again scattered from the milk pans when Julian emerged from the basement door. They melted away from him into the shadows.

Julian's heart was racing, and he could feel it skipping a beat. His Wrinkle.

"Cody," he said, "I think I have to go."

Cody looked up at Julian, her cheeks still dimpled in a concentrated frown. "It's not always like this. Robbie, he—"

"I'm sorry, but I should get going," Julian said, stepping away from her, back toward the road.

Cody shouted at him: "Hey!"

Julian turned back around.

"The next time you see that cat that's been following you . . . take a picture."

Julian looked at her for a long moment.

"Okay," he said.

"Something is wrong with this world," Cody said. "The cats know it. And maybe they know you know it, too."

Julian couldn't think of any way to respond.

Cody made a gun with her thumb and forefinger and fired it with a wink.

"See you," she said.

Julian sat for a few minutes in his car, listening to the rhythmic hum of the engine. He looked out at the kaleidoscopic bookstore facade. Bardo Books.

Well, he thought. She sure knows how to throw a party.

CHAPTER 16

"GOD*DAMN*," MOLLY SAID QUIETLY AS SHE LOOKED AROUND the massive pink room. "This is the size of my entire house." The small, red-haired girl standing beside her, Anastasia, nodded.

"Check it out. Lake views," Molly said as she walked over to the enormous bay windows. Her eye was drawn to the Lake, maybe two or three miles down the hill, a slash of sparkling blue cutting through the dark elm forests like an open wound.

"This is kind of obscene," she whispered to Anastasia.

"Be quiet," Anastasia whispered back. "She can hear you."

"Ladies, please," a polished voice said from behind them. "If I could have you over here. We have an important lesson to go over."

Constance's hands were folded behind her back like a yoga instructor about to impart some Zen wisdom. Her perfect enunciation had always struck Molly not as ladylike per se, or high society, or whatever it was she was going for—Molly read it as just plain expensive. And now, having been given a tour of Constance's sprawling estate, Molly had confirmation that yes, it must indeed be very expensive.

"Being a Burner means you have to be willing to put yourself out there," Constance said. "So I want you to think of one secret you've never shared with anyone. A secret that you are most ashamed of."

Constance stood before a large aquarium that was built into the wall. It contained a single red fish that drifted lazily, its eyes tilting about, looking at nothing. A plush leather bench was set up before it, stacked with cheer outfits. Molly suddenly felt an acute longing for Julian. She wished he was here with her now.

Constance had brought Molly and Anastasia, her two "favorite" girl recruits, to her home, ostensibly to impart some kind of important piece of Burners wisdom. But having just toured Constance's cavernous lair of wealth and privilege, Molly realized something—Anastasia was the only other person in the school, besides her and Julian, on scholarship. Meaning poor. They were the only two poor girls, and now they were, apparently, Constance's "favorites."

"Write your shameful secret down on this notecard, please." Constance handed them each a pink notecard and pen.

Molly tapped the card with her pen, unsure of what to write. She couldn't immediately summon a shameful secret. She was, however, filled with shame of a different type.

Ever since her freshman days, Molly had been fixated on Constance and the Burners. Maybe emboldened by the Two she got junior year, Molly felt like she might finally be heading somewhere in her life. Beautiful, popular, successful Constance became the embodiment of her desperate aspirations. During *Kiss or Cap*, the gun had landed on Constance, and Molly had kissed her. Constance received the kiss, and even returned it with gusto. Molly knew it was just for show, but she let herself get her hopes up. She started her Three life the next day excited for the future. When Constance moved in and recruited Molly to pledge, Molly said yes without even thinking about it.

But every day since then, in every Burners' meeting, Constance barely gave her the slightest glance. And now, in this house with this Lake view, with its mazelike warren of plush rooms, Molly realized that she was on a hopeless mission. No matter how hard she tried, Molly would never be like Constance. Nor would she ever be with someone like Constance.

She didn't have a big, beautiful house. She was just a poor kid chasing life numbers.

Shame. That's what she felt.

Shame for her stupidity—for her belief that she had ever had a shot.

But she knew that wasn't the shame Constance was looking for today. Instead, Molly quickly dredged up an embarrassing confession and scribbled it onto the notecard.

Constance gestured to the aquarium behind her. "This is Xanadu," she said. "He's one of those electrical fish that live in the Lakes in China. My dad got him for me during a business trip.

121

He's kind of cute, don't you think?" The fish's mouth opened and closed dumbly.

"What we are going to do now is put our hands in his water, one at a time."

Molly looked to Anastasia—*what?*

"Come on now, don't be shy," Constance said, gathering the girls up beside the tank. "This won't hurt."

"It's gross," Molly said.

"Sometimes we have to do uncomfortable things in the Burners," Constance said placidly.

Constance helped the girls dunk their hand into the water for a few seconds each. Xanadu had sunken to the corner of the tank, huddled as far away from them as it could get. Once they both had wet their hands, Constance passed out a towel.

As Molly dried her hands, her fingertips began to tingle. Then her lips. She tried to speak, but she found her tongue wouldn't respond. The tingling spread from her lips to her chest. She looked down at her hands, but she could no longer feel the coarse fabric of the towel she was holding. She could no longer stand, either. She felt like her body was deflating. She found a spot on the floor next to the bed and slid down against it. In front of her, Anastasia was leaning against the bench with Constance's cheer clothes. She was also staring forward, her eyes searching the room, as paralyzed as Molly was. Constance walked between them.

"So," she said, turning the notecards over in her hands. "Xanadu is what they call a paralysis fish. They are only found in two or three tropical Lakes in Asia. He makes this kind of poisonous energy in the water that shuts down your body's systems one at a time. A real stunner." She winked and turned over the first card.

"So, Anastasia here," she said. "You went over to Mr. Alakhai's house to watch an art movie in sophomore year? Alone?" She grinned. Anastasia's mouth just gaped dumbly.

Constance continued, "It says here that 'nothing happened,' but still you were too scared to tell anyone." As Constance shook her head disapprovingly, Molly watched Anastasia's eyes, trapped in her unmoving body. "An *art movie*. How very naughty of you."

Constance flipped Molly's card over. "Molly," she said, "you had a crush on your best friend, Julian, in middle school. Julian? The one that jumped off the Tower?" She *tsk*ed, shaking her head.

Molly could not move. Couldn't say or do anything. Fear surged through her body. She gasped for breath, but it barely came, and this panicked her more.

"Here's your lesson for the day," Constance said. "I don't even know you girls. And yet you blindly followed me into my home. You told me your shameful secrets, and you stuck your hands into poisonous water. Why?" Constance tore up the cards and let them tumble from her hand into a trashcan beside the fish tank.

"Because of control," she said. "That's what I have and what you lack. The ability to control others is all that matters in this world. More so than wealth, or education, or even looks. That's what the Burners have taught me."

She checked her watch. "I'm curious if you'll come back on your next lives with this lesson under your belts. Now, pardon me. My cookies are almost ready."

Molly and Anastasia sat frozen as Constance padded down the stairs. Molly could hear the television turn on, its noise drifting faintly into the room. She looked at Anastasia across from her. She sat still, like Molly, her eyes able to move only tiny distances in their sockets.

The only coherent thought that could break through Molly's panic was—

No.

They can't *kill us*. That's against the rules. That's against the law. All deaths are voluntary. Whether they're extinguishments or burns, you must *decide* to do it!

Molly's fingertips began to heat, like they were being held to a stove. The feeling drifted up her arms, as if they were on fire. It spread into her chest and she could no longer breathe. It was as if all the air had been evaporated at once from her lungs. She could feel them collapse on themselves, sucking at each other. That terrible, painful feeling spread to her throat, closing it, and then, finally, it closed her eyes, too.

CHAPTER 17

THE FIRST STRANGE THING TO HAPPEN TO JULIAN THAT DAY occurred in the cafeteria, when Amit approached him.

"Hey Julian," he said. It was hard to imagine this was once the fat kid. When Amit came back in this new body, it really stuck. He was almost gaunt now, his cheeks hollowed and ghostly. The fact that he could no longer taste things probably had something to do with it.

"What's up, Amit?" Julian said.

"Have you seen Molly?"

"No," Julian replied, shaking his head.

He hadn't spoken to her since the confrontation during Amit's funeral party. He understood why she might not want to talk to him. They had been drifting apart for over a year, ever since the burning started. And then he lashed out at her for it, only for him to succumb himself to the same temptations. After he jumped from Lake Tower, she must have seen him as the ultimate hypocrite. No wonder she avoided him.

But he wished that was all behind them now. He wished they could be friends again.

Amit's question was worrying though—where *was* Molly? Julian had noticed that she missed the last few Burners meetings. He also didn't see her in the lunchroom anymore, but he had just assumed that she was off with Constance or other new friends. Did she quit the Burners?

Amit was concerned because they had calculus together, and she'd been absent the past few days. Molly had always been helpful, assisting him with his homework and such. He shook his head gloomily. "Do you think she dropped out or something?"

It was definitely not like Molly—the girl who was already planning a burn eight years from now, on her twenty-fifth birthday—to be missing classes . . .

Would she have left the academy without a word?

And that was just lunch.

In the afternoon, during the change from fourth to fifth period, a harsh shouting tore out over the usual din of the crowd. At first, Julian thought it might be some kids on the football team hazing. Or possibly . . . He cringed, trying to remember if there was a burn scheduled for today.

The shouting was vicious and angry—and coming closer. Someone was moving down the hall, pushing through the crowd, yelling at the top of his lungs. As the voice approached, the yelling became more intelligible.

"The Bardo!" he shouted. "The Bardo!"

Julian turned around and saw the crowd of students part, and the source of the voice emerged.

It was a kid in a camo jacket. He had white hair and a pale splotch stretching down his neck, so ghostly white it was luminous in the school's fluorescent light. Julian recognized him instantly. That retrograde from the bookstore. The one who had been staring at him and Cody.

Robbie, Cody had called him.

Well, Robbie was now in Julian's school somehow—how did he find him here?—and was screaming the name of the bookstore.

"You!" he shouted when he saw Julian. "The kid from Bardo Books."

"Who are you?" Julian asked.

Robbie charged at him. He grabbed Julian by the shirt and pushed his back up against a locker.

"You stay away," he snarled. "Stay away stay away stay away stay away!"

"What are you talking about?" Julian stammered as he struggled to pull out of Robbie's grip.

But before Robbie had any chance to respond, he was yanked off by the school guards.

Robbie grabbed one of the guards' arms and knocked him to the floor before he could reach for his baton. But the chubbier guard already had his baton out—he rapped Robbie on the back of the neck. Robbie spilled to the floor. He rolled over, his eyes floating in his head, untethered from any sense of sanity.

"You all stay away!" Robbie shouted.

The chubby guard helped his partner to his feet, barking, "Turn off less-lethal."

The guards flipped a switch and there was an audible hum as their batons electrified. Robbie pulled himself up and dodged a few of their swings, but finally one of the blows cracked him in the chest, and Robbie's eyes bulged, stunned.

He collapsed onto the floor. The guards, breathing heavily with exertion, dragged Robbie toward the detention room. Did they kill him?

Julian's heart was thudding in his chest.

Stay away from what? From Cody? From the Friends?

For the rest of the student body, a kind of vaguely shaken normalcy resumed. Some kid down—or extinguished, they couldn't even tell—nothing too new there. The only thing really of note was that he looked like a freak, and he was gunning for Julian.

Julian could hear their quiet chattering. Their eyes on him again.

And then, another now familiar feeling—Nicholas's arm snaking around his shoulder.

"Look how popular you've become," he said.

Julian, still breathing hard, didn't know how to respond. He didn't want to tell Nicholas that he recognized this kid—from a bookstore basement gathering for retrogrades, no less.

He turned to Nicholas, who was grinning madly. Julian could see the only concern in Nicholas's head right now was how to play this to the advantage of the Burners.

Julian's hand was shaking, residual fear still coursing in his blood. His heart skipped a beat. He didn't need this right now.

What he needed was Molly. Wherever she was.

He excused himself from Nicholas's grasp and went to the bathroom. He washed his face, trying to cool off his mounting disquiet.

He tried to call Molly, but the phone went straight to voice mail.

CHAPTER **18**

JULIAN WAS DRIVING HOME FROM SCHOOL WITH ROCKY
when he noticed a thin, dark line forming on the horizon.

He thought maybe it was an optical illusion, especially since it
appeared to expand and shrink as if it were pulsating. Sometimes
the dust house would fire up for an evening shift when the bodies
were backed up. The creepy wisps of gray cloud the incinerators
emitted would bleed into the sky, causing odd visual distortions.
Maybe this weird line was the last few rays of the setting sun
shimmering through a cloud of body ash.

As he watched the shimmer on the horizon, he thought about
when he was going to take his Two.

Julian had asked Nicholas again after school about the information he promised on Julian's mother, and again Nicholas
played it off, buying more time. He was working on it, Nicholas

assured him. He was in touch with people directly at the Lake, in fact, just last night, and he relayed the request, and now it's a waiting game. . . .

Nicholas had put his arm around Julian's shoulder on the yard that afternoon, as the last few stragglers drained out of the school. "As always, I'm in complete control of the situation," he said almost melodically into Julian's ear. Then Nicholas squeezed Julian's shoulder with two firm pumps and was gone, a white jacket drifting across the dead brown grass.

He was working on it. . . .

Sure, Julian could go to the extinguishment clinic tonight and burn his Two, let his dad know and be done with the whole thing. But he was certain that if he did that, he would not be able to force himself to die again for the Burners.

And if he didn't die again for them, there was no way Nicholas would deliver.

And he had to deliver.

Julian was going to get what he had been promised.

That realization was set in his mind as if it were chiseled into a stone tablet. He had decided it that morning when his father pulled him aside and put pressure on him to deliver his Two as soon as he could.

He remembered that painful conversation, watching the odd line on the horizon shift and mutate in the last rays of the sunset.

There was a foreign kind of intimacy in those moments with his father—neither of them had ever been the kind to sit down and share their struggles or hopes or fears. But in compelling Julian to burn, a long-stagnant pool must've stirred somewhere inside his father, some kind of alchemical pot of emotions. His father had even become misty-eyed this morning.

He wanted to talk. He wanted to share things.

"You are probably far too young to remember this," he had told Julian, "but there was always something your mother would say to you when you were little. She used to hold you and say, 'I don't need nine of you. I only need the one of you and I'd be happy forever.'" He shook his head.

"She came to hate the idea of extinguishing," he continued. "This is when you were about five or six years old, back when she was working at the Lake. Back before . . . she was let go. She would tell me that she never wanted you or your brother to extinguish. But she knew it was unrealistic. Just a pipe dream. She knew that you would have to do it one day. I mean, that's just the way of it. She knew it was an impossible wish, and . . . well, maybe that's why she wished it. Why she kept it between us. Why she didn't want to share it with you."

Julian looked away from his dad. He looked down at his hands spread on the kitchen table. His thumbs were still too small. They would always be, he realized, no matter which body he was in.

"Why are you telling me this, Dad?"

Julian's father rubbed his chin as he spoke. "It's why I've never put pressure on you to extinguish while you were growing up. You never wanted to. And she never wanted you to. But we all knew it was a fantasy that that kind of life could last forever."

"Yeah, I get that now," Julian said, looking up.

"So I want you to know that I don't take it lightly that I ask you to do this. After your Three, I will never ask anything like this of you again," his father said. He cleared his throat with a raspy cough and swallowed. "You will be your own man," he continued, speaking slowly to keep his voice even. "You can make your own decisions."

Julian nodded, not knowing how to respond to his father in this state.

"When your mother was let go . . ." His father took a lengthy pause. "That's when it all went wrong. That's when everything started with her sickness. When the money problems began." He wiped at his eyes, as if he could clean the sadness away like the residue of sleep.

"I still have no idea what happened at the Lake. Why she was let go. Or why they ended up finding her Nine body there. But I swear, if there were any way to find out what happened to her . . . that's all I would want. Some conclusion to all of this."

A conclusion.

That's what Julian was going to get.

He shook off the memory and returned to the road, to the strange line up in the sky.

It suddenly expanded, doubling in size, then it arced downward, forming a ragged S figure on the purplish-red backdrop of the sunset.

"What is that?" Rocky asked from the passenger seat.

Julian had no idea. He leaned in closer to the window, peering.

The S shifted again, now twisting unnaturally, as if it were a living thing. It turned, expanded again, and . . .

It started coming for their car.

The closer it came, the more it grew in size. As it got closer, he could make out that it was no solid cloud. It was actually a composite of tiny specks.

"Cicadas," Julian said.

A swarm coming up from Retro Row.

The cloud loomed over his car now, rattling overhead with an awful, horrible scratching sound. The millions of insects blotted out the last of the sunlight. Individual cicadas that strayed from the swarm pinged off his windows like hailstones. Julian flinched, holding his breath in the sudden eclipse. Rocky looked at him, his face stricken with worry.

"It's all right," Julian said. "They're not coming for us. They're just passing over."

Julian slowed and pulled to the side of the road as the swarm eclipsed them.

Plink, plink, plink . . . Errant cicadas lost from the storm bounced off the windshield.

He grabbed Rocky's hand to calm him.

And then . . .

It passed.

The awful clatter quieted as the dark cloud left, and the last few rays of the daylight returned. Julian leaned over and watched out the window as the cloud of insects twisted up and off toward the horizon. He exhaled, suddenly aware he had been holding his breath.

He looked over at Rocky and forced an off-kilter grin.

"See? They had somewhere else to be. Someone else to terrorize."

Rocky laughed a little, softening up. "That's freaking creepy, though."

"It's just as creepy as the dust house, really," Julian said.

The strong older brother. It was a role Julian was beginning to feel comfortable with.

He was going to own it, and he was going to bring a truth back to the family—the most important one. For his brother as much as for his father.

And so, as big brothers do, Julian had to shoo Rocky quickly into the house when they got home later that evening.

He wasn't going to let his little brother see the other bizarre twist of nature that day, which Julian had spotted in the headlights as they pulled up, crumpled under the window outside the living room.

Once Rocky was inside, Julian approached the strange animal form that lay under the window in the shrubs. It was on its back, unmoving.

It was a cat.

He turned it over.

It had a white patch over its right eye.

And it was dead as hell.

CHAPTER 19

JULIAN STOOD IN THE DARK ALLEY BEHIND BARDO BOOKS holding a garbage bag containing the dead cat. He watched, impatient, as Cody cleared a space on a concrete step leading down to the basement. "Put it here," she said.

He had sent her a picture the night before, and she had responded immediately—she had to inspect the body.

"Shouldn't we go inside?"

Julian could feel the eyes of other cats in the shadows, watching.

"Don't think that would go down well anymore." She looked up at him and blinked. "The Friends got a call from the Lakes. They were asking a lot of questions, so . . . Yeah. That was the end of that. Bookstore's just for books now."

"That Robbie kid came for me at school," Julian said as he brought the bag over to the step.

"He *what*?"

"He was running down the hall shouting for me. Telling me to stay away. The guards stunned him or maybe killed him, I don't know."

Cody frowned, dimpling her cheeks.

"Do you know what he meant?" he asked. "Stay away from what?"

"He's unhinged," Cody said. "Retrogression can be enormously destructive. It can really erode someone's mind."

Julian nodded. He understood that all too well. But still, between that incident and Cody saying that the Friends got a call from the Lake, something felt wrong. Ominous. It felt like there was something at play that he couldn't identify, that he maybe didn't even have the faculties to identify. But Julian didn't press it right now.

Cody extracted the cat from the bag with small, delicate motions, like she were handling a baby bird that had a future in front of it.

But this was no baby bird—it was just an inert heap of fur that used to be a cat. It had once been animated and alive. It had watched him. Studied him. Followed him. Julian had discovered scratch marks on the paneling outside the window where he found its dead body. He had no way of knowing how long those scratch marks were there, but he felt sure that the cat was trying to claw inside the day it died. Why? He had no idea.

But now it was just a body.

Julian thought about how things were phrased like that: now that the cat was gone, it was no longer a he or a she, even though it was still right there. It wasn't a being anymore. This "body" is

just a thing that was left behind. The little linguistic trick of calling dead things "bodies" reminded him of the Lakes, with their
orderly lines and complimentary towels and no-nonsense nurses
and watchful prelates. A deceptive and soothing system, keeping
people one solid, crucial step removed from the horror of death
and rebirth.

Cody crawled through the fur with her fingers, stopping to
examine the cat's head, leaning in close to its eyes. "Definitely a
Lake cat," she said. "You can tell by the markings on its face and
neck. Like this patch on its eye. It's very symmetrical and precise.
Telltale sign."

She carefully placed it back in the bag. "We need to take it to
Cat's Cradle. Do you have a car?"

Julian looked at her, puzzled. "What are you talking about?"

"Most Lake cats have been microchipped. Glen can check for
the chip and look it up at Cat's Cradle," she said.

"Glen? Cat's Cradle?" Julian asked.

Her mouth bent into an impatient frown. "Can you drive us
there or not?"

Cody sat in the front seat, the bag containing the cat body on her
lap. Julian tried to steal a glance at Cody's face, but it was hidden
in the shadow of her rusty coils of hair. Cody didn't look over at
him. Her eyes were always on the window, constantly scanning
outside for . . . something.

As they drove, she explained that as the retrograde population
continued to grow over the past few years, many of the retros left
children behind. Kids whose mothers and fathers had forgotten to
come home. Forgotten they had kids. These orphans often ended

up on the Row, searching for their parents. They mixed in with the rest of the retros. At some point, after the county of Lakeshore stopped providing aid to Retro Row and just cordoned it off, they also began rounding up these orphans and putting them in group homes. Quite often, children in these homes would disappear forever—the authorities explained that they were sent to other homes that were less crowded in different states, but no one knew for sure. That's when the Friends of the Lake intervened. One of the wealthier members donated an old house to the cause. It was off in the elm forest, halfway up a mountain. He named it Cat's Cradle, after Cody's propensity to befriend cats. It was full of the children left behind by retrogrades—and it was Cody's home.

That was where they were heading now.

Cody was insistent that Julian stay off Lake Road and the other main thoroughfares. She directed him down alleys through the main heart of town, and then led him out onto a winding two-lane country road. The elm forests were dark corridors on either side of them.

That's when Julian realized that there was a pair of headlights behind them in the distance, always there, taking every turn they took. Cody was aware of this too. She was nervously pulling on her hair.

Finally, after the headlights continued to tail them down two more unlikely turns, she looked over at him. "Mr. Julian, I was hoping we weren't being followed," she said. "But that looks increasingly like it's not the case. We're going to have to lose them."

"Lose them?!"

"There's a dead orchard up ahead," she said. "It's like a maze."

Julian turned to her with a snap. "If it's the cops, we should just pull over and deal with this."

"This is not the cops," Cody said. "If you don't take this turn, then I will."

She reached across him for the wheel. Julian swatted her hands away and slammed the brakes, throwing them forward against their seat belts. Cody clutched the bag with the dead cat to her chest to stop it from flying into the windshield. The car skidded along the road sideways. Julian pumped the brakes again, and they jerked to a stop facing the entrance to the orchard.

Cody looked at him with a wild look.

"Mr. Julian, we do not want to be caught by these people. Gun it!"

Julian swallowed a lump into his stomach that exploded in a burst of adrenaline. He slammed the gas, and they squealed into the orchard. Cody clutched the cat to her as they jostled over the tractor-hewn rows between shriveled apple trees. Behind them, there was a swish of lights as their pursuer followed.

Julian was nothing more than a racing pulse and two hands on the wheel. Cody called out turns to him, weaving him left and then right into different rows. Tree branches lashed the windshield. The lights of their pursuer grew more distant and finally disappeared behind a row heading the opposite direction.

"We lost them!" she shouted, elated.

Cody spotted an opening up ahead that spilled out into a field and a dirt road beyond it. "This field loops around and we can get back on the road."

When they rocked out onto the clearing, Cody collapsed back

into her seat and released a long whistle. "Boy! That was close, huh?"

Julian's heart was throbbing in his throat. He wanted to stop the car right where they were. Kick her out. Turn around and go home.

But he couldn't. He couldn't stop now. The pursuers could again appear behind them, or some other threat that Cody had failed to mention could pop out at them from nowhere. He gritted his teeth and kept driving.

Once they were back on the road, Julian turned to her with a nasty frown.

But Cody spoke first: "I know what you're thinking. *What the hell did she get me into? And why am I still in it, instead of just kicking her out right now?*"

Julian glared at her.

"The answer is, there's something wrong with this world. And we need to find out what it is. I know you feel it, too. I knew it the minute you showed up at the bookstore."

Julian didn't reply. He drove on in stony silence. But their pursuer did not return. Soon enough, they were following a winding road through the elms until they reached a small clearing of vegetation on the side of the road. It was easy to miss in a quick glance, but a narrow dirt trail was cut into the trees beyond the clearing.

"Told you this place was a real rustic getaway," she said.

They proceeded down this old trail, which was nothing more than a row of weeds running down the middle of two ruts. Eventually, they emerged at a ranch house that was half-hidden in the shadows of two towering elms.

Two old cars in various stages of disrepair were parked at the garage entrance, up on concrete blocks, the tires removed. Cody directed Julian to park beside the porch. As he turned the car off, Julian saw there was a large greenhouse behind the house with rows of browning, sorry-looking plants.

On the porch, two boys with dusty blond hair watched them warily. They looked about ten or eleven years old. Rocky's age. They both had a handkerchief tied around their neck.

"Why don't you come in and let the heat cool off a bit, huh?" Cody said. "You still look a little jumpy."

Julian had the same feeling that had driven him into trouble in the past: he needed to look. He had to see what this was.

He climbed out of the car and followed Cody inside.

"Welcome to Cat's Cradle."

There were about a half dozen kids in the living room, young ones who were six or seven and older teens who looked like they were in high school—but they certainly weren't enrolled in the academy. Maybe they went to Poplar Public High like Cody did?

The house was a mess. Clothes and stacks of books were everywhere. Musical instruments and toys for the younger ones were heaped in the corner. Cody explained that Friends volunteers visited them from time to time, but the visits had become increasingly erratic and so they were working at becoming self-sufficient. There was a rotation for the chores, which she described as an example of "emergent organizational principles."

She showed him out back to the greenhouse, where they were trying to grow vines of tomatoes, though the vines looked shriveled and brown-gray. Tiny, withered gourds were poking out of the soil in planter boxes. "We've been having a hard time getting these plants to take. I think it's the water table coming from under the Lake," she explained. "It's spreading to all the farmland and corrupting things."

The thing that struck Julian the most wasn't the controlled chaos of the house, or the vain attempt by a bunch of apparently orphaned kids to establish actual live crops—it was the fact that most of the kids had on scarves, or handkerchiefs, or wraps that otherwise hid their numbers.

"We don't talk about numbers, life scores, or burning," Cody said. "We just live like we're all Nines."

Julian shook his head in wonder as Cody led them through the living room to a hallway in the back. A world without life scores . . . an existence that Julian never dreamed was possible except, perhaps, on Mauritius.

Cody was right about one thing: the world did contain multitudes.

"You're an orphan?" he asked her.

Cody looked at him over her shoulder and winked.

"You don't go to Poplar High either, do you?"

Cody nodded. "Now you're getting it."

She took him down a hallway.

There was a red door that was open and Cody rushed for it, closing it before Julian got close.

"My room. And I'm a private person," she said, and then led him to a computer room at the end of the hall.

It was like an electronic junk shop filled with computer towers and monitors. Cabling ran across the floor like a swarm of stranded eels. A big black kid sat in the back, his hair a large frizz.

He turned to them when they entered, sipping chocolate soy from a jug with a straw.

"We don't knock now?"

Cody set the bag down on his desk and turned to Julian. "This, however, is not a private space, even if some people think it is."

The boy rolled his eyes.

"We like to think of it as the command center," Cody said.

The boy pushed his chair over to the desk and inspected the bag. "What's this? And who's that?" he asked. "The kid who freaks out the cats?"

"I'm Julian," Julian said.

"I remember you," the boy said, peering at him. "From the Lake a few weeks ago."

"That's right. Glen, isn't it?" Julian asked. It all came back to him. The bonfire that night with Cody.

"You sure it's a good idea to bring him here?" Glen asked.

Cody nodded. "He's got a good vibe."

Glen frowned and gave Cody a stern look. She just stared back, a wordless conversation between them. Then Glen sighed and put the straw back to his mouth. As he took a big sip, he opened the bag to peek inside.

He spat his milk out all over his shirt. "Goddammit! What the hell, Cody? There is a dead cat in this bag," he sputtered. "That is 100 percent gross."

"It's a Lake cat," Cody said. "Julian found it outside his house. It had apparently been following him around. Can you find the chip and look it up?"

Glen wiped the milk from his shirt. "Yeah, yeah. I'll run it. Give me a few days."

Glen looked over at Julian and blinked.

"You kill it?"

"No!" Julian exclaimed.

"Then what's your malfunction right now?" Glen asked.

Julian looked at him, puzzled.

"He's just rattled," Cody said. "We were followed. But Mr. Julian here is an ace driver. We lost them in the orchard."

Glen shook his head. "You're being followed, and now retro night is shut down, too. They're circling closer and closer."

"Who is circling?" Julian interjected.

Glen looked to Cody, obviously wondering if she was going to cut this stranger in.

"Who?" Julian said again, more demanding.

"The nurses," Cody said finally. "They don't like us. They don't like that the Friends are helping out the retrogrades. They don't like that I'm studying their cats. But really, what they don't like the most is that we're telling people that the Lake system is changing. Too bad."

Glen gave Cody a look as if to say, *Are you sure we should be talking to this kid?*

Cody turned back to Julian.

"Listen to me, Mr. Julian. I'm totally serious when I'm saying this."

"Okay," Julian said, worried.

"There are reports—"

"Rumors," Glen interrupted.

"—*from highly credible sources*," Cody barreled on, "that not everyone is getting all nine. Sometimes, people aren't coming back to life."

"What?" Julian said, incredulous. The very idea was unthinkable.

"It's rare, but the retros tell me they've seen it. People are permadying when they were on Seven, or Six, or even *Five*."

Julian closed his eyes. People were voluntarily extinguishing their lives. If they didn't know it could be their last, then—

Suddenly, this sounded a lot like one of those conspiracies passed around the darker corners of DeadLinks.

"Why are you bringing me into this?" he asked, skeptical.

"Seems like the cats chose you. Not me. And I trust the cats."

All right.

That was enough for one evening.

Everything inside Julian's being was telling him, *Stay away stay away stay away stay away* . . .

Julian stood. "I have to go home."

"Mr. Julian," Cody said, peering at him from under her curls. "Of course, you *can* go home now. Go to bed. Go to school. Burn your Two. Then your Three, and so on. But you're not going to escape the truth. *If* you come back to life at all : . ."

Julian eyed her for a long moment.

Finally, Glen laughed, breaking the silence. Julian headed for the door.

"You'll be back," Cody said. "Once we find out what this cat was trying to tell you."

Julian didn't take the bait. He walked out of the house, past the numberless kids who lived there, out to his car. He drove home—slowly, carefully, checking his rearview, but there were no pursuers this time.

He got home just before midnight. For some reason, he had to check on Rocky. He had to make sure his little brother was home, safe in his bed.

He was. Sleeping. A One.

A One, Julian knew, who would soon enough have to enroll in high school.

Who would, soon enough, have to burn.

Julian returned to his room and sat on the edge of his bed, but he couldn't lie down. His mind raced.

Cody was right about one thing.

He did go home.

But he couldn't escape.

CHAPTER 20

BY ABOUT SEVEN THIRTY THAT OCTOBER MORNING, IT WAS
clear that this was the first truly cold day of the year. Not just
chilly or brisk. But cold. Bone cold.

The air was still and windless. Just walking through it stung
Julian's skin, like he was wading through a pool of jellyfish. He
had to pull the collar on his white blazer tight against his neck as
he crossed the yard to the orchestra room.

The room was warm inside, but Julian couldn't shake the
cold, shifting in his seat as Nicholas presided over the Burners, a
lord before his court. He crowed about all the new members who
had joined, singling out Julian's great example as inspiration.

"Twenty new pledges since your big jump," he said, grinning.

Julian just slunk lower into his seat.

Nicholas then presented plans for an elaborate Halloween

party he was setting up for the entire senior class. Called *The Drop Dead Drop*, it would take place in an abandoned carnival in the Row on Halloween night, utilizing a derelict old roller coaster for the titular deadly drop. The party would, according to Nicholas, easily best the infamous Georgie Vander's score in one fell swoop. It was "the death blow" that he had been longing for.

But Julian couldn't keep his focus. Anxiety flowed through him like a drug. Cody had gotten to him last night. Her theories had wormed their way into his brain, and he had stayed up all night becoming obsessed with her worldview, which, he realized, she had been laying out for him in bits and pieces all along, like luring some little mammal into a trap.

If Julian believed her, then he would need to contend with a new reality: there was a chance that he wouldn't be coming back on his next burn. How big a chance? He had no idea. Of course, Cody could be delusional. But maybe she wasn't. Julian did watch his mother degrade and her sanity crumble, a victim of the Lake. The worst thing you could think of? It was definitely possible.

Either way, if Julian was going to risk it, he would be risking it for what his family really needed—information about his mother.

He had to pull Nicholas aside. He hung back after the meeting ended. Once everyone left the orchestra room, he approached the conductor's podium.

"Jules, my friend, I have a lot on my plate here," Nicholas said, leafing through a stack of documents. "Clayton's burn tonight at the football game had been scheduled for weeks, and now it's all going tits up. Our dear friend is absent today, and he hasn't been answering his phone or reading our texts. Seems he has cold feet all of a sudden. Add to that the fact that we need to find a generator *now* for *The Drop Dead Drop* because *of course* the three that are already at the fairgrounds are completely inoperable," he continued without pausing for breath. "So unless this is about how to get a generator, or you know where Clayton is presently, I just don't have time." Nicholas slid the documents into his bag, and looked up at Julian.

"*Is* this about a generator?"

"No," Julian said. "But—"

"Well, then, I must get to class or Denton is going to have my balls on top of everything. My god, I tell you that killing a whole class of kids is a whole lot of *work*! I should be getting extra credit for this."

Nicholas buckled up his bag and swiftly made his way to the exit. Just like that, he was out the door, and Julian was left standing alone in the empty orchestra room, no closer to any answers.

Nicholas didn't show up at the Burners' table during lunch. Franklin was missing, too. Constance explained to Julian that the two of them were in crisis mode, trying to fix the burn at tonight's football game.

"Why don't they just cancel it?" Julian asked.

Constance shook her head as if she were fielding a supremely basic question. "It seems you don't understand this burn tonight. Do you?"

"No," Julian said.

"Well, not everyone is privy," she said, smiling.

"Right," Julian said flatly.

Nevertheless, Constance continued, if for no other reason than to revel in withholding information from him.

"I can't tell you what it is exactly," she said. "But I will tell you there was a fair amount of preparation involved. At this point, it's better to just go through with this now, even without Clayton. I guess Nicholas is scrounging up a replacement."

"If you see Nicholas, tell him I'm looking for him," Julian said.

Constance tightened her lips into a smile. "Sure thing, cutie," she said, and gave him a little wink. Julian regarded Constance for a moment. A wink from the hottest girl in school?

Some kind of game. It had to be.

He spent the rest of his lunch period in the library. When the bell rang for the start of fifth, he texted Nicholas, "We need to talk. Meet after school?"

Nicholas never responded.

Julian sat through his afternoon classes beside himself, his leg involuntarily bouncing in his seat. He traced the lines on his notebook as the teachers droned on about algebra or the hunger crisis spreading across Eastern Europe.

He could not stop obsessing about what they might uncover on his mother. For some reason, he kept imagining this discovery appearing to him like the answer key in the back of a textbook, a thought that made him feel stupid and foolish. What if there was nothing to find? No answer? No special truth out there about how she had vanished? What if there was just a single, simple fact? She became addicted to death until all of her lives were gone. What if that was just . . . it?

After the last bell rang, Julian planted himself right outside the big oak doors at the exit of the academic building, waiting for Nicholas. The sky above the yard was a bright blue, so vivid it almost shimmered.

Finally, he found him, striding swiftly out the doors, deep in conversation with Franklin. Julian steeled himself and stepped forward. "Nicholas, we have to talk," Julian said.

Nicholas brushed past him. "I'm afraid I'm very busy," he replied. "We are T minus four hours from the game tonight, and Clayton is completely AWOL."

Julian shook his head and stepped in front of Nicholas as he tried to move around him. "I'm sorry, but this is important."

Nicholas studied Julian's eyes, then turned to Franklin. He nodded to the bigger boy. "I'll catch up," he said to Franklin, then turned back to Julian. "Jules. My friend. I apologize for being so busy, but I am here for you now. So, what the hell is so damn urgent?"

"It's . . ." Julian looked away as he gathered his thoughts. "You promised you would get information on my mother," he said.

Nicholas's eyebrows creased in annoyance. "I'm *working on it*, as I have said to you before. Now, is this why you pulled me aside while I'm extremely busy?"

"Nicholas," Julian said. "Don't delay this anymore. I need this now. This is what I'm saying to you."

Julian tried his best to glare at him, and judging by Nicholas's expression, it seemed to be working. The smirk dropped from his face, and he ran his tongue over his teeth. He looked back at Julian with a stony silence.

Julian continued, "You took me in and you gave me this chance and you spent all this time with me. And I appreciate that," Julian said. "So I have to be honest with you . . ."

Here comes that skipped heartbeat. One . . . two . . . *now.*

"I joined the Burners because I really have to burn two lives," he said. "It's not about status or anything like that. The fact is that I need to be on Three for my dad to get a tax refund to pay off our house. That's the truth of it. I have to burn one more life, and then that's it. After that, I'm done burning."

Nicholas narrowed his gaze at Julian. His eyes flicked back and forth as he listened. Listened and processed.

"And I could just go to an ex clinic, you know," Julian continued. "Just go in and get it over with and get the refund and move on with my life. But I joined the Burners because you said we could find out what happened. That's why I'm here."

Nicholas flattened his lips into a stern, grim line. "Julian, I'm . . . *shocked.* I'm utterly shocked to hear this." Nicholas glowered and shook his head, pissed.

Julian's veins were flooded with cold. His stomach lurched.

Did he just blow it?

"So not only am I working my ass off," Nicholas said in a kind of obviously mock wonder. "Putting in all this time and effort and social capital to hunt down the Lake office files on your mother, but you're also trying to get money from the state on top of it all? How convenient, really."

Nicholas frowned deeply, as if he had been personally, grievously injured.

"You act like I'm supposed to feel sorry for you, but it seems like you have it all figured out. Everyone is actually working for *you.* Why should I be helping you at all?"

"No," Julian said, feeling it all slip away from him. "No, no, no. Nicholas, that's not what this is about. I'm just—I'm trying to be honest with you."

Still shaking his head, Nicholas raised a hand to silence Julian. "You're gaming me," he said. "It was never about the Burners, was it? It was all about Julian all along."

"Well, n-no," Julian stammered. "I don't mean to disrespect the Burners. You've opened my eyes. I'm glad I joined."

As Julian stammered, Nicholas just stood there, watching him with those cold, calculating eyes.

"Are you *glad* you joined the Burners, Julian? Really?"

"Really," Julian said.

Nicholas shook his head. "All I have to go on is your word."

"I know, but I'm good for my word," Julian replied. "Trust me."

Nicholas rubbed his chin for a long moment as he thought. Finally, he said, "Well, the fact is that indeed, I do have some news about your mother."

Julian's heart raced. "Really? What is it?"

"My sources found something. But here's the thing. I don't totally understand its significance, so I wasn't sure if I was ready to present it to you."

"They *found* something? Is it like her employee records or something? What is it?"

"Composure, please," Nicholas said quickly. "I would have liked to find some context to put it in. A bigger picture. I promised you, after all, that we would get to the bottom of this. Because maybe this is just a clue, and not the whole story."

"Just tell me!"

"Listen, Julian," he said, raising his hand.

That "listen" . . .

"We have a little problem here, you and I. I went to all these lengths to obtain this information, but you are at this moment a bit of a loose cannon. I'm not sure what your game is. Are you exposing our club to some sort of risk I have yet to calculate? This is about trust, Julian. I need to trust you."

Nicholas stepped back.

"I like you, my friend. I really do. However, what you just told me now . . . about going to an *ex clinic?*" His face contorted like the words were rancid in his mouth. "That's a violation of trust."

Julian could feel any hope of discovering the slightest thing about his mother slipping away. He swallowed. "I'm sorry," he said.

Nicholas raised his hand, silencing Julian.

"Don't apologize. I want to tell you what I know. But I need to know that you really are with us."

Julian frowned as he realized what was happening—Nicholas was dangling everything he promised before Julian's eyes, and then denying it to him. A deep, itching, burning, painful anger bloomed in his chest. He looked at his hands. His nails were beginning to dig into his palms. He made a conscious effort to release them. They left little white divots in his flesh.

Julian looked up from his hands. "So, what can I do?" he asked icily.

Nicholas tried to straighten his grin into a sober expression, but he could not tame the curls of it at the edge of his lips.

He was plainly savoring this.

"Like I mentioned earlier . . . poor Clayton has gone AWOL." He made a pitiful frown and shook his head gently. "So, if you take his place tonight and burn for us, with no hesitation, no prep . . . then I will trust you. I will believe you are truly ready to dedicate yourself to us."

Julian looked at Nicholas with amazed revulsion. How did this happen? How did Nicholas maneuver him into killing himself *right now*? He was a bold-faced demon. A devilish imp parading as an angel in a crisp white jacket.

"If you do this burn for me now," Nicholas continued, "I would be able to stand up to any previous Gold Star and say, 'This kid is a Burner through and through, and he has earned the right to our trust.'"

Julian ran his hands through his hair, the anger in his chest now mixed with a ballooning sense of doom. "Is this a promise?"

Nicholas clasped his hands together in front of him like a priest. "Absolutely," he said. "I only hope the information I have is what you've been hoping for."

Julian exhaled into the sky, and his breath came out as a small puffy cloud that quickly evaporated into the freezing air.

There was no choice here. After all, he still had to burn his Two, one way or the other. . . .

He craned his head back down to Nicholas.

"Tonight?" he asked.

"Tonight," Nicholas said.

CHAPTER 21

IN HIS THREE YEARS AT LAKESHORE ACADEMY, JULIAN HAD never been to a football game. Like burning, football was something he never had the slightest interest in, even though everyone around him was obsessed with it.

And so, when he found himself that night in the stadium in the center of it all, he couldn't help but stand dumbfounded and gawking at the amount of sheer noise and nonsense that was pulled into the black hole of a Friday night.

He was with Nicholas under the scoreboard behind the Lakeshore end zone. Running back and forth in front of them was the team mascot, the Lakeshore Warrior. He wore a Trojan helmet and his face was painted a bright, almost clownish white. Completing the ensemble was a navy cape that trailed behind him like the train of a wedding dress. He carried the Lakeshore flag over his shoulder. The boy in the costume was Logan, a lanky Burner on Life Four who Julian knew as the kid who sat in the front row of Burner meetings supplying the occasional sarcastic comment.

The stands on both sides of the field were packed. The Lakeshore side was full of the school colors—navy and white—while the opposing stands were decked out in orange for the rival team . . . Poplar Heights Public High, Julian realized.

Poplar . . .

Well. At least Cody wouldn't be here to see this.

The refs whistled for halftime and the school band fired up. They pounded out a rhythm that reverberated in Julian's chest, drowning out his thoughts. As the teams left the field for the locker room, the Warrior approached Nicholas and Julian, taking off his helmet.

"Show me that Warrior spirit!" Nicholas said.

"Nope. I'm done for the night," Logan said to Nicholas, wiping the paint from his eyes with the back of his hand, the flag resting in the crook of his elbow. He blinked his eyes twice and looked at Julian, confused. "Where's Clayton?"

"He was sick today, apparently," Nicholas said. He turned to Julian with a smirk. "No cure for common cold feet."

He took the helmet from Logan. "Julian's our understudy."

"Well, I set them up for you. You just gotta knock 'em dead." Logan laughed loudly, to himself more than to anyone else, and handed the flag to Julian. He unclasped the cape from his neck and kicked off his shoes.

Nicholas picked them up and turned to Julian.

"All right, let's suit you up," he said.

They stepped into a hallway out of sight of the crowd. Julian put on the costume, then Nicholas sat him in a chair to apply the white war paint.

"So how does this burn work, exactly?" Julian said.

"Well," Nicholas replied. "It's kind of all about the surprise with this one." He bit his lip in concentration while applying the paint around Julian's eyes. His breath smelled like peppermint.

"How am I going to know what to do?" Julian asked.

"You'll know it when you see it," Nicholas said as he smoothed the paint on Julian's forehead with gentle strokes of the sponge. "Relax, please," he added. "Your brow furrowing is messing up my application."

Julian rolled his eyes and tried as hard as he could to relax his face.

"For this burn to be effective," Nicholas said, "you just need to be a good Warrior. Just keep focused on that. You saw what Logan was doing out there. Run back and forth here behind the end zone, below the scoreboard. Wave the flag. Particularly when we're trying to accomplish something, like score a touchdown. When we do, the big lights and sparklers on the scoreboard up there will fire off. That's your cue to run out into the end zone. So it's these big lights you're going to be looking for." Nicholas pointed out the large yellow orbs dangling beneath the scoreboard.

Julian swallowed.

"Close your eyes now," Nicholas said, and he gently applied the white makeup over Julian's closed eyelids. "Do you get it?"

"I get it," Julian said. "Bright lights, wave the flag."

He opened his eyes to see Nicholas's face inches away from his. "Quick study," Nicholas said.

"You know, I'm actually glad you're here," he added. "You'll do a great job. Much better than Clayton would have."

Julian glared at him from behind his face paint. "I don't like this," he said.

"I know," he said. "But that's the point."

Julian took a deep breath, and Nicholas squeezed his shoulders.

"Show us that Warrior spirit," he said. "It's banzai time."

Julian was slow to get the hang of it. The flag was heavier than it seemed, and his arms soon became sore waving it.

He hated being exposed to the gaze of so many people, but he reminded himself he was protected under the makeup and helmet. He also hoped it would shield him from the clouds of fear he felt gathering inside him. He was, after all, about to die. Right in front of everyone. In some no doubt gruesome manner.

He kept a close watch on the clock as it ticked down the third quarter, dreading every second that passed. He looked over to the stands—to where the Burners sat, two rows of white jackets behind the bench where the football team sat swilling sports drinks. Nicholas leaned back in his seat, relaxed, smiling and chatting with his disciples. His sheep, all dressed in white.

He sipped from a soda and looked over toward Julian, gesturing with his hands to say, "Keep the spirit up." Julian swallowed his rising frustration. He lifted the flag into the air and walked it one long lap of the end zone. The crowd cheered.

About halfway through the fourth quarter, Lakeshore scored a field goal and the bright lights burst above Julian. A shot of sparks exploded overhead from the scoreboard's built-in fire-works system.

Oh God, this must be it.

He hefted the flag onto his shoulder and ran out into the end zone. As he took a lap, he looked over his shoulder everywhere for death. At any moment, he thought he might step on a bomb that Nicholas had planted in the end zone. Or maybe a referee would turn around with a gun and put a bullet between his eyes. . . .

Julian completed three laps of the end zone and . . . nothing happened. He walked off the field, relieved but wary. He looked back to where Nicholas had been sitting in the stands, but his seat was now empty. Nicholas was gone.

Julian scanned the stands and the sidelines for him, but he couldn't find him. This was not good. He was out there now, doing something, making arrangements. Prepping impending doom.

Just calm down, Julian thought.

You are going to die. That's it. And you've already done that, and you came back. You know how it's going to go. So just calm down, and then you will get the information that you are looking for. That's what this is all . . .

But what if you don't come back?

Julian suddenly felt light-headed. His breathing was coming in shallow bursts, and he could hear his heart pounding in his ears. One . . . two . . . *now.*

Suddenly, the crowd rose to its feet, filling the air with thunderous screams. A Lakeshore receiver was tearing toward the end zone at full speed. The football was sailing through the air and the receiver made a lunging catch, smacking into the ground with an awful crunch. The crowd exploded into cheers, and the band pounded out a chest-rattling rhythm. Cheerleaders were tossed into the air and spun.

Julian looked up at the scoreboard. There were four minutes left in the game, and Lakeshore was down by three points. This catch put them in striking distance of a touchdown, which meant a comeback, which meant a victory. The air was dense with noise.

But Julian's attention was drawn to the ground. His feet were wet. Water was pooling under his feet, mixing with the dirt. He lifted a shoe—it was covered in brown muck. He looked closer and saw that water was spreading all across the turf behind the end zone.

Logan was standing in the entrance to the hallway where Julian had changed into the costume. He was nonchalantly holding a hose on full blast, water gushing from it into the sod. Two other hoses were turned on beside him, lying at his feet like snakes, feeding into the swampy mess.

What the hell . . .

Julian took a few tentative steps in the muck. The clouds he had been holding at bay inside him cracked open and a flood of terror entered his bloodstream.

Out on the field, Lakeshore made a play. The crowd screamed. They were now within five yards of a touchdown.

Behind the end zone, Julian spun around, searching for Nicholas.

He was about to die. He knew that, but emotionally, he

couldn't accept it. Not knowing was agony. The fear coursing through him, pounding on the walls of his veins . . . it made his body physically ache.

"Nicholas?!" Julian shouted, trying to raise his voice over the din of the crowd. He spun around again. "Nicholas!" he shouted.

He caught a glimpse out of the corner of his eye—a flash of white. He looked up to the scoreboard. Nicholas stood beside it on a service platform, placid, looking down on the game like an angel from on high. Something dangled from his hand. Something long and thick, coiled like a rope. Julian knew instantly that whatever Nicholas was holding, whatever that was, it would be the implement of his demise. He strained to see it, to understand what it was.

Behind him, out on the field, the ball was snapped, and the players crunched into one another. The crowd screamed a white noise. He watched as a receiver tore through the end zone, just feet in front of him, juking hard to the right to lose the Poplar cornerback. He made it to an open corner of the end zone, and the quarterback let loose the throw. The ball sailed through the air, and things began to slow for Julian. He saw the receiver leap into the air for the catch, and Julian turned around, back to the scoreboard. . . .

Three . . .

He saw Nicholas standing there, looking down at Julian with a devil's grin. It was some kind of cable. That was what he was holding. Nicholas stuck out his hand and dropped it. It tumbled into the swampy mess at Julian's feet.

Two . . .

In those slow moments, Julian traced the cable to its source and then he realized—the lights. The sparks. It was the electrical cable for the lights that had just smacked into a pool of water at his feet.

Now.

He heard the crash of the players behind him in the end zone and the eruption of noise from the stands. They scored.

He saw an explosion of white sparks leap from the end of the cable across the wet turf—the electricity dancing in front of him in abstract patterns, grabbing at him. He could feel it flow into him, and infiltrate his heart—a searing, white-hot pain. He fell to his knees, his head filling with heat, his vision doubling. He strained to look up at Nicholas as sparks showered down in front of him, as smoke wafted from his burning hands. Before everything disappeared into a final burst of Warrior spirit, the last thing Julian saw was Nicholas's grinning face.

CHAPTER 22

JULIAN BROKE TO THE SURFACE OF THE LAKE. HIS HANDS thrashed at the water. He sucked in breaths, but it just produced a white-hot stinging in his throat. And then, a searing pain radiated through his body.

I am freezing, he realized.

The Lake was ice-cold. Far away on the beach, he could see the guide light blinking. The signal tone sounded. Julian struggled to pull himself toward it, but he could barely keep above the water. He tried to scream, but it came out a ragged exhalation. Then a bright light lit up the water in front of him. The thrumming sound of a motor swelled up from the darkness behind him. The nurses' cold-weather boat was approaching.

It stopped just feet from him, sending up a small wake that

splashed over his face. When he blinked it away, he saw nurses moving about on the deck, shadows before the floodlights. They were reaching into the water with long poles.

A pole stabbed the water beside him. A nurse lurched it through the waves, smacking it against Julian's chest. "Grab it!" the nurse shouted over the motor. "Grab the damn pole!"

It smacked him again, but this time Julian wrapped his arms around it. The nurses pulled him to the edge of the barge and lifted him up on it.

They wrapped him in blankets and led him into the cabin, where he sat, still dripping, on a bench. He pulled the rough woolen blankets in tight around him and hung his head. He looked at his toes and counted them left to right in order to calm his breathing.

Another ten new toes.

He grappled through the fog of rebirth to recall how he got here. He remembered talking to Nicholas out on the yard. Nicholas's grin as he took Julian's demand and twisted it, transforming it into a noose he used to snare him. The bright lights of the football stadium. And then, here.

At least I made it, he thought with growing relief.

The lights inside the receiving facility were lurid, and they made his head throb. As he made his way through the line, he had to keep his head down so his eyes could adjust. But before he entered the booth to get his new number, he felt a rough hand on his shoulder. It turned him around. Julian looked up and standing there in the fluorescence was the Prelate. The black goggles bulged from the purple headdress.

"We need to see your eyes," the Prelate said, his voice stern and slightly muffled from behind the mask.

Julian blinked rapidly in the light as his eyes watered. He saw there were two male nurses standing behind the Prelate, their brows crinkled.

"Hold still," the Prelate said, gripping Julian's shoulders and looking into his face.

"Is everything okay?" Julian asked.

For a few more uncomfortable seconds, the Prelate held Julian's look with his black discs-for-eyes, and gestured to a nurse behind him.

The nurse held a device to Julian's face, like a small digital camera. It snapped with a quick burst of light.

"Am I in trouble?" Julian asked as the nurse inspected the device.

Finally, the nurse looked up and nodded to the Prelate. "Random check for retrogression," the Prelate said in his low growl of a voice. "Next time, keep your head up." He walked away without another word, the nurses following behind him.

Julian exhaled in relief and rubbed his eyes until the sting faded. Then a nurse signaled him into the booth, where Julian was marked with his Three and given a cursory inspection.

"What's the Wrinkle?" Julian asked.

"Nothing that is immediately apparent," the nurse said.

This phrase troubled Julian far more than it comforted him. There was a lot of bad shit that wasn't immediately apparent.

On the bus back to Lakeshore, he sat in the back, watching the evergreen trees roll by in the low light. He could not shake the growing sense that something was missing, that something was abnormal, though maybe not "immediately apparent." He focused on the trees. Something about them made him feel strange. But what was it?

Julian got off at the bus depot at Lakeshore. Three other rebirths got off with him, but they all had rides waiting for them. Julian was the lone walker. He thought about using the pay phone to call his father to pick him up—but no. His father would know all about it soon enough, now that he'd hit his Three, but tonight Julian just couldn't face anyone else. Even if that meant he would be walking about a mile and a half in the freezing cold.

The road home was lined with evergreens. He stopped under a branch that hung out over the road. He grabbed it by the tip and pulled it in close. He fanned the needles out on his hand. They looked . . . gray.

Not green. Not even close.

He pulled some of the needles off and stuffed them into his pocket.

At home, he stepped gently so as not to awake his father and brother. He locked the door to his room and took the handful of needles from his pocket. He turned them over in his palm. In the light, he could see them clearly. Yes . . . they were *gray*.

Julian sunk onto his bed and laid his head back on his pillow. He blinked at the ceiling.

Did he just lose the color green?

Was that even a possible Wrinkle? Losing a whole goddamn color from the spectrum?

He pulled the shoebox out from under his bed.

On his mother's Lake-issued ID card, her eyes were deep pools of green. It was *the* picture that constituted his mental image of his mother. And now . . .

Her eyes were gray.

He stared into his mother's time-frozen eyes—and her *gray*, time-frozen eyes stared back at him. It was true. Julian had lost green. He lay back down on the bed and stared at the ceiling. His eyes became hot again, and he could feel the tears rising. He closed his eyes and let them leak out the side.

The tears continued to flow, but Julian kept himself as quiet as possible. He choked down any sound of his crying so as not to wake his father or brother through the thin walls. It was as if a cork had popped somewhere in his psyche. A feeling of loss poured through him. It stretched on like an endless black pool. He focused on the image and controlled his breathing, concentrating on the vastness of the expanse that stretched before him.

Eventually, he lost himself in the enormity of it and drifted off to sleep.

In his dream, the black expanse was transformed into the Lake, and Julian was swimming through it. His limbs were pulling against the heavy water, struggling to reach the beach, where a solitary, skeletal tree stood. Underneath the tree sat a woman in a gray dress. His mother?

Once he was able to drag himself onto the beach, he saw that the woman in gray was not his mother. She was not actually a woman at all. It was a robe, like a nurse's robe, that had been caught, torn, on a tree branch. As he stepped forward to inspect it, the branch holding it lurched away from him. It rose up, and he realized that

the branch was, actually, a massive cat's claw. And this tree was a towering, monstrous black cat, a white patch over its eye.

That cat.

The cat.

It loomed over Julian, massive. Its body was a craggy gathering of bones jutting under a hide, stretched so thin it was tearing in places. The cat unwound its body with irregular jerks, and leaned down so that its head was level with Julian's. Its face was the size of a truck tire. Its two eyes were massive globes filled with a milky liquid and sliced with slits for pupils.

It opened its mouth at Julian, revealing a row of long serrated teeth, each the size of a kitchen knife. A horrific buzzing sound emanated from the creature's throat. It started softly and grew in intensity until the buzzing rattled inside Julian's head so strongly it awoke him with a start. He shot up in bed, covered in sweat.

It was morning.

Time for school.

After he had dressed and packed his backpack, Julian found his father in the workshop. He was wearing dirty overalls and sifting through a pile of tools, his back to the door.

Julian said blankly, "Hey, Dad. I'm a Three now."

His dad turned around, and upon seeing the Three on Julian's neck, a smile broke through the tight lines of his face.

"Thank you, Son," he replied. In a shaft of light coming in from the window, Julian could see that tears were rimming his father's eyes.

Julian nodded and turned away. He had to get to school. There would be news waiting for him there.

Indeed, there was news.

Nicholas had led a round of applause for Julian when he entered the orchestra room that morning. *Warrior Spirit* crushed it, apparently. Whatever it was he did, Julian could still not remember it through the fog—and that's how he was going to leave it. He was never going to look it up. Never going to watch it.

Constance led the Burners to stand on their seats, whistling and cheering. Nicholas was beaming. He explained with great pride how he was able to manage Headmaster Denton and have the cleanup look like it was an unhappy accident so that the game could continue and Lakeshore could notch a victory in the books. And a victory in the Burners' Bible, too. Nicholas made a big show about entering Julian's death into it. "But," he said, putting the pen down and looking out at his disciples from the podium. "This will be nothing compared to *The Drop Dead Drop!*"

Whatever.

Julian had no interest in the future success of the Burners. All he wanted was the information he had been promised. After the meeting, Nicholas gleefully called Julian up to the stage. He put both hands on his shoulders and eyed him levelly. "You did good," Nicholas said. "You did very good."

He produced a folder from his bag and handed it to Julian.

"As promised," he said. "Hot from the LakeNet database."

Julian opened it up. He blinked rapidly as he tried to process what he was reading. He felt his head reeling again.

"This is really as much as I could find, and I did a deep dig, let me tell you," Nicholas explained. "But like I said yesterday, I lack a context to put this information into."

Julian's eyes were racing over the text, reading it again and again.

Nicholas continued, "Nevertheless, I hope this little morsel can bring you some solace."

Julian looked up at Nicholas, his mouth open, dumb.

"Well," Nicholas said, clearly unable to deal with Julian's awkward response. "I'll leave you to it."

He tapped Julian's shoulder as if waiting for a response. But none came. So he shrugged and left.

Julian was left alone in the orchestra room, reading and reading again what Nicholas had given him.

The Attison Project.

According to the date, this was Julian's mother's last assignment at the Lakes before being dismissed.

An in-depth study on the behavior, biochemistry, and evolution of the local fauna, especially the cat population, as affected by Lake phenomena.

CHAPTER **23**

"A *THREE* NOW?"

Cody stood on the porch of Cat's Cradle, a deep, dimpled frown etched on her face. Julian wished dearly that he had a scarf or a handkerchief to tie around his neck. He shrugged his shoulders, trying in vain to obscure his number.

"Yeah, a long story—"

"Aren't they all?" Cody said, cutting him off, and went inside, obviously pissed.

Julian followed her through the living room, where two girls who looked about twelve or thirteen years old were sitting on the carpet, sorting boxes of clothing—donations maybe?—into piles by color. There was a red pile, a blue pile, and a gray pile, which, Julian realized with a sinking feeling, might actually be a green pile.

They entered Glen's computer room. Cody closed the door behind him and leaned against it, her arms crossed and her face stern. Glen swiveled in his chair and nodded to Julian by way of hello, then swiveled back to his monitor, where he brought up a screengrab labeled "Test Subject 32."

"So," Glen said. "We certainly have a Lake cat on our hands. Or in our freezer, as the case may be. Not only that, and a bonus for us, is that the chip it had was a more advanced model than the ones we've collected to date. It had a bit of firmware still on it, which looked slapped together and had plenty of little exploits left behind by sloppy coding. I used it to get deeper into the database than I've been able to before. Reverse engineering—it's your friend."

Julian blinked at him in confusion, but Glen continued, "And I found a name. Test Subject 32. Not a great name for a cat. I would've gone with Shadow or Tracer or something more interesting myself, but there you go. Check out the info on the chip." He gestured to the screen. "Age, time/date of scans . . . *Scans.* Like they do with us when we're reborn."

"That was exactly my supposition," Cody said. "Now it's finally confirmed."

Julian was floored. "So, they *are* being reborn. The cats. This is unbelievable."

"Well, believe it," Glen replied. "Because it's right here."

Cody walked over to Julian. "You said you had something to show us."

Julian fumbled in his bag for the printouts Nicholas had given him. Cody pushed Glen's keyboard out of the way and spread them on the table.

Julian explained: "It's some kind of staff list for the—"

"The Attison Project," Cody said, her eyes darting over the page.

"That mean anything to you?" Glen asked.

Cody scrunched up her face, thinking. "You see the word 'Attis' thrown around a lot by the Lentic Research Unit. Attis was a Greek god that represented decay and rebirth. The nurses liked to think of themselves as demigods. A real self-absorbed bunch." She kept reading. "This is a staff list. Lucy Dex. So, that's your mom, Julian?"

He nodded.

Glen laughed and leaned back in his chair. "Too good to be true. Son of Attis! Does that make you a demigod? A quarter-god?"

"I have no idea what this is," Julian said. "My mother never told me anything about any Attison Project, and I'm sure my dad has no clue. All we knew was that she worked in the Lentic Research Unit."

"This is the research program for these nine-lived cats," Cody said, handing the sheet to Glen, who held it close to his glasses. "This is the program all the chipped cats came from."

Glen nodded. "Yeah. Sure looks like it."

"Maybe the cat had a bond or something with my mother," Julian interjected. "Maybe that's why it came to my house when it . . . died."

Cody turned to him. "Possibly," she said. "Have you seen the cat in any other unusual circumstances?"

Julian frowned, remembering the nightmare last night. The cat on the island, with the terrible hiss and gleaming fangs—its mouth hinged open, about to swallow him whole.

"I've been having dreams about it, actually."

Glen's eyes bulged, and he turned to Cody. "Look, I get this is a good sign, but that's just creepy," he said.

Cody didn't respond. She just went back to studying the document.

Glen continued, "Maybe we should step back from this for a bit. Especially right now, with the nurses turning up pressure on the Friends, it doesn't seem wise to be getting involved with some crazy dream-cat experiment quarter-god boy."

Still, Cody didn't respond.

"Hello?" Glen said.

Finally, Cody looked up.

"Look at this," she said, stabbing the document with her finger. "Callum Collins." She snorted. "So, he *was* in the Lentic Research Unit. Why didn't he tell me?"

Glen read over her shoulder, his eyes scanning the page quickly.

"Callum? Hell no. Didn't you hear what I just said?" he said.

"I was strategically ignoring it," Cody replied.

"You guys know this Callum Collins, I take it," Julian interjected.

"He was one of the original Friends. He donated this house to us," Cody replied matter-of-factly. She stacked the papers back into a pile. "And now we're going to go see him."

Glen shook his head. "I said, *hell no.*"

"Glen, don't be a contrarian," Cody snapped. "I know Callum has his concerns, but he's involved with this. Even though he's been hiding it from me . . ." She frowned. "Why has he been hiding it? What does he know?"

Glen shook his head. "Callum was pretty clear about us

staying away from him. I believe the words he used were, 'Stay the hell away from me . . . forever.'"

Cody shrugged. "Glen, I have to."

Julian stopped their argument cold. "Can he tell me what happened to my mother?"

Cody looked at him, a curious brow raised as she evaluated his sudden gusto.

"Glen?" she asked. "You coming?"

Glen shook his head and closed his eyes. "No," he said again, under his breath. "Hell no. . . ."

Julian followed Cody to the kitchen, where she retrieved the dead cat from the freezer and wrapped it in several layers of plastic wrap. She ignored Julian's gaze and said nothing to him, as if she had also wrapped herself in several layers of protective coating.

"Hey," Julian said. But she didn't respond.

She stuffed the cat into her backpack and went to her room, the one with the red door. Julian followed her, but she turned to him abruptly outside the door.

"You wait here," she said. She slipped into the room and closed the door behind her, careful to prevent him from so much as getting a glimpse of what was inside. After a few moments, she returned, zipping up her hoodie. "Let's go," she said curtly.

They sat in silence on the drive, their vigilant scanning for pursuers keeping them occupied. Finally, when it became obvious that no one was following them, Julian turned to her. "Let's talk."

She turned to him like she was inspecting, well, a dead cat. "Okay, let's talk," she said. "I've been looking into degradations at the Lakes since well before you even *considered* burning your One," she continued. "And now, it seems like you are an important part of this. This cat that was following you and your mother's recently discovered identity are some of the biggest leads I've had yet. However . . ." She looked over at the Three on his neck. "Your continued burning is an obstacle to my trust."

Julian frowned. Not this again.

"Is it?" he asked. "Do you not *trust* me? I'm sorry, but you don't even *know* me. You don't know that my mother disappeared one day and then came back and attacked me before she went off and *permadied* right in front of the Lake. You don't know that she never wanted me to burn, and after seeing what happened to her, I didn't want to, either. You don't know that I have a father and a brother, and our family's life score is *pathetic* because of me, and the bank was about to take our house. You don't know that the Burners told me they could help me find out something about why my mother went so crazy. All you *do* know is that I'm here in this car with you and a dead cat. So excuse me if I don't feel the need to earn your trust, especially considering that we are on the way to a mysterious ex-Lake scientist who apparently doesn't want to see you, and *you*—with your off-limits room and your insane theories—could be dangerous, or deluded, or both."

Cody gave a slow-clap.

"Yeah, well," Julian said. "Trust is a two-way street. You need to tell me why the hell you care so much about any of this."

After a moment of silence, Cody nodded. "I suppose it's personal for me, too, like it is for you," she said. She stared out the window. "The Department of the Lakes took my parents from me."

"Are they permadead?"

"Yes," Cody replied immediately.

She brushed the hair from her face and tied it back into a ponytail, then continued matter-of-factly. "My dad was an engineer who worked for the army. He was part Japanese, and he could speak the language. So they wanted him in Japan during the Kyushu Crisis."

"What's that?" Julian asked.

"Big overpopulation problem. The Buddhists started revolting against the life schedule. My mother went with him. She was a chemist, and the army gave her a posting out there analyzing the Lake water. I was born there. My father helped build the famous Tori Wall around the Kyushu Lake. He was promoted up the chain after that.

"But when they transferred him to Lakeshore, he realized something was wrong. He was high enough on the food chain at that point to figure out that the nurses were covering up the fact that the Lakes were . . . changing. He quit, and he and my mother went underground. . . ."

Julian nodded.

"You know about the 6/12 incident, right?" Cody said. "When the army burned down that compound in Florida that was making the synthetic Lake?"

"Of course," he said. The 6/12 incident was a big deal. A group—a *cult*, really—was using stolen water, trying to form a Lake beyond the reaches of government control. It was a week-long standoff, and it ended in flames. That was when they started really censoring the news.

"Thirty people died, including my parents," Cody said. "They were just trying to continue their research. All they did was ask questions."

"I'm sorry," Julian said. This wasn't making him feel more comfortable. In fact, it deepened his misgivings: Cody had connections to such a high-profile incident, and she was being tagged by unknown followers, and they were on their way right now to meet someone who didn't want to receive them.

Cody looked over at him, her frown dimpling her cheeks.

"I was just a kid. I didn't want anything to do with the authorities. I went on the run. I ended up back in Lakeshore, living on Retro Row. That's when the Friends found me."

"So you do know what it's like," Julian said, "to lose a parent."

A moment passed as she studied him.

"Tell me," she said, "are you going to be a Four the next time I see you?"

"No way in hell," Julian replied.

Her dimples faded as her frown flattened out. It wasn't a smile exactly, but it was a start.

CHAPTER 24

THE DRIVE TOOK THEM OUT OF THE ELM FOREST AND DOWN
through Lakeshore to the wide, manicured fields of the West
Side Hills, to the lawns and stables and ranch houses of the upper-
crust suburbs.

When Julian was little, the family would have a Sunday picnic
out in the state park, and on the drive home through these hills,
they'd talk about what it would be like to have a ranch or a farm
of their own. Julian's father always said he could give a retired
racehorse a good home, and he could board two or three more
horses from the folks downtown—the stables would end up pay-
ing for themselves. Julian would watch these fields whip by the
window, trying to imagine himself on a horse, tackling acres of
the rolling green like one of the knights in his childhood story-
books. He watched from the back seat as his father kissed his

mother's hand. She had just gotten a new job at the Lake. This was going to be the future. These hills were where they were going to live. . . .

These now *gray* hills.

Callum Collins lived among these hills, in a white two-story house down a winding driveway. As they approached, Julian stole a glance at Cody's face. He saw her eyes were hard and determined, flickering in and out of the light as they passed through the shadows of the fence posts.

They knocked on Callum's door for what seemed like ten minutes. Finally, once Julian's knuckles were raw, it opened. Standing there was a thin man in a flannel shirt who looked about the same age as Julian's father. He had a short, closely cropped beard and thick, black-rimmed glasses.

He looked directly at Cody. "How did you find me here?"

"The Friends . . . left some of their financial records behind at Cat's Cradle," she said.

"Please leave," Callum said. "I made it clear that I have nothing to do with you people anymore."

"I'm not here asking you to come back." Cody opened the bag, revealing the dead cat. "I'm here about the Attison Project."

Callum flinched at the sight of the cat, but it wasn't disgust or shock—it was a kind of weary recognition. Callum scanned the horizon, as if making sure no one else was with them, then stepped outside onto the front step. "Don't talk and just follow me around back," he said.

Behind the house, Callum grabbed a shovel from a pot of tools and led them through the backyard to the edge of the forest. A small stream ran through the underbrush.

"The house is probably wiretapped," he said. "The stream washes out the noise, but keep it to a whisper just in case." He gestured toward his foot—there was a black ankle monitor strapped above his boot. He was clearly on some form of house arrest.

Cody took the cat out and set it on a tree stump. Callum kneeled down next to it, carefully unwrapping the plastic until the dead cat was completely exposed. Callum muttered something indistinguishable to himself as he examined the cat. He turned the cat's head around in his hands, looking it in the eyes. "Yep," he said, as if that meant anything. Julian looked to Cody, but she was just as perplexed as he was.

Callum then checked the cat's ear, pulling back the fur to reveal a small black tattoo. He sighed and stood up.

"He's a Nine," he said. "That's the end of this one. He was a real sweet boy, too. Really loved the soy cream."

"You know this cat?" Julian asked.

Cody spoke over him. "Callum, we have files on the Attison Project. We know you were on the team, and now we need to know what it was about."

Callum's eyes darted between them, and he clenched his teeth.

"I've been trying to understand what's been going on at the Lakes," Cody said. "I'm continuing my parents' work. Please, help me understand."

"No recording," he said.

Cody nodded and pulled her backpack off her shoulder. She retrieved a notebook and a pen. "Notes only," she said. "No voice or video."

Callum watched her uneasily, then picked up the shovel and spiked it into the earth.

"Attison was a project we ran out of the Lentic Research Unit. We were trying to find a cure for retrogression and rebirth Wrinkles. The cats and the cicadas were the only other animals that we knew of who were responding to the Lakes like we were. The cats, being more intelligent organisms, were the ideal test subjects."

Cody scribbled furiously in her notebook. Callum forced the shovel into the ground with his boot.

"That was the intention," Callum continued as he began excavating a small hole, the musty black earth piling up beside him. "We might've gotten somewhere, maybe, but then the new Lake director was installed. He put a new lead on Attison. We had new orders, and I didn't like the new direction, so I was bumped down the chain until I walked away."

He worked at the hole until it was a few feet deep, then he gently lowered the cat into it. "He deserves a proper burial," he said.

Julian watched as the dirt piled up around this mysterious visitor who had intruded into his life. He nodded toward it, a silent goodbye.

"What was the new direction?" Cody asked.

Callum wiped his hands on his jeans, then regripped the shovel. "You should leave here. This is liable to get you into trouble."

Julian frowned. "Wait. Did you know a Lucy Dex?"

Callum was filling in the cat's grave, but upon hearing Lucy's name, he suddenly stopped. He studied Julian's eyes.

"Thank you for bringing this old boy back to me," he said,

gesturing toward the little mound of earth. "But you need to go now."

His eyes scanned behind them and all around the edge of the woods. He tightened his grip on the shovel, as if it were some defensive weapon, as if Cody might at any moment unzip her skin and reveal some kind of monstrous form he had to defend himself from.

"Leave," Callum said firmly. "For your own good. You kids have too many lives ahead of you to get messed up in this."

But Cody pressed him.

"Something is happening at the Lake, and I need to know what it is. It's not just that the cats are behaving differently. Retrogression is even worse now, a lot worse than it was when you were studying it. But even scarier than that . . . ," she said. "People aren't getting all nine anymore."

A pall fell over Callum's face. The corners of his mouth twitched.

Cody continued, "The Lake is covering it up, labeling anyone who is defective a retro and sending them down to the Row. Right?"

"Is she right?" Julian asked. "Is it true?"

It was plain in Callum's eyes that he wanted to say *something*, but fear held him back.

At last, he spoke: "The one thing I can tell you is that you need to stop extinguishing—right now."

"Because people aren't coming back? Please, you have to tell us," Cody argued.

He looked away from her.

"There has to be something more you can do," she said.

"When you first came to Retro Row, you wanted to help us."

Callum stared at her.

"Now's your chance to really help."

Callum looked at them for a long moment. He slung the shovel over his shoulder with a sigh. "Look for the Spoofs," he said. "Now, go."

"Wait, what's a—"

"Go!" He swung the shovel menacingly toward them, then turned it to point up the hill.

Wordlessly, they walked to the front of the house. Callum disappeared inside, and the door slammed shut.

Cody and Julian got in the car and drove down the long driveway to the main drag. Julian's hands were trembling on the wheel. He felt light-headed. Cody sat beside him, the notebook open on her lap, filling out her notes more completely, trying to ensure she had captured everything Callum had said.

What was this project, and what connection did it have to his mother? His mind was buzzing, but he was cognizant enough to notice the strange tops of the fence posts as they approached the exit to Callum's driveway.

"Cody," Julian said.

"I'm concentrating," Cody said, working on her notes.

"Cody," Julian said again, more urgently. "Keep your head down."

"What?" she said, looking up, confused.

He grabbed her and pulled her down so that she was hidden in the passenger seat. He ducked down, too, peeking up over the dash just enough to see where he was driving.

Once they were out of the driveway and a little distance down the main road, he stopped the car and craned his head back to look at the fence posts. They were capped with little black monitors.

"Cameras," Julian said. "Shit."

"They filmed us coming in already, didn't they?" Cody asked.

Julian nodded.

"Double shit," Cody said.

CHAPTER 25

SCHOOL FELT LIKE A DIFFERENT UNIVERSE NOW. TRIGO-
nometry. The history of the Lake Superior rebellion. Group
discussions of the unfolding Ukraine crisis in Civics . . . It all just
bounced off Julian.

All he could think about was his mother, this Attison Project—
whatever the hell it was—and that dead cat, the dirt filling up
around it, the shovel tamping it down, sealing it into the earth.

If classes were bad, the Burners meetings were worse.

Julian had burned the two lives he needed to, and yet still he
sat in the meetings. Why did he need to be there? Nicholas went
over final preparations for *The Drop Dead Drop*—Halloween was
the following night, which was fast approaching. Apparently,
they had succeeded at getting the old roller coaster running again

at the abandoned fairgrounds (or at least the test run worked), and Nicholas was now going through a list of death totals on the screen, showing how, with the new influx of Burners members, they were on track to kill more people this year than the notorious Georgie Vander ever did.

Julian felt sick watching it.

All this death.

All this morbidity.

As if it were just a game.

Plans and schemes to kill people faster. More death. More quickly. In larger quantities.

Was his mother like this on the Attison Project? Was she some more official version of Nicholas, charting out death totals?

And—worse—what if Cody was right? What if people weren't coming back?

For what other reason would Callum tell them to stop burning now?

Julian wished he had someone to talk to. Someone who could understand. Someone who knew what it was like to live and die at Lakeshore Academy.

He wished he had Molly.

But Molly still hadn't returned his calls or messages. Her phone now went straight to voice mail every time he tried. She hadn't been in any Burners meetings either, and he never saw her in the lunchroom.

Julian scanned the auditorium just in case—but still, there was no Molly.

It was as if she'd just vanished.

After the meeting ended, Julian stayed behind at the door, watching the Burners file out past him, checking all of their faces in case he had missed her in the crowd.

She wasn't there. But Constance was. Julian stepped up next to her.

"Hey, Constance," he said.

She gave him a look of supreme annoyance. "Yes?"

"Have you seen Molly recently? I've been having trouble getting hold of her."

Constance's eyes lit up. "Molly who?"

Was Constance playing some kind of game? Of course she knew Molly.

"Ah, yes," she said, as if suddenly recalling her image. "The little pudgy dark-haired girl. Perhaps she quit. It wouldn't surprise me if she couldn't handle it." Constance studied her carefully manicured fingernails. "She always struck me as the overly delicate type."

She pushed past Julian, done with the conversation.

Delicate? Not Molly. But if she had quit, surely Julian would've found out by now. Surely Nicholas would have called out any quitter as some kind of public example. Or, at the very least, Molly would have reached out to Julian and tried to convince him to quit, too.

Wouldn't she?

Julian continued his search all day at school. He scanned the hallways, staked out her locker, and searched through the parking lot looking for her car. But there was absolutely no sign of her.

He pulled other Burners aside during lunch. Amit still hadn't seen Molly, either. He shook his head gloomily as he thought about her absence. "It was the Burners," he whispered. "The Burners took her away."

This caught Julian's breath in his throat. "What do you mean?"

Amit shrugged, looking over to the Burners' table in the back as if to say he couldn't talk about this here, and then shuffled away.

The Burners? Did they *do* something to her? Did they . . .

No. He couldn't let himself think that. Not yet.

Julian cornered Logan at lunch. He had noticed Molly's absence as well. And something else: Anastasia was also missing.

Julian immediately made the connection: Anastasia, Molly, and he were the only three kids in the academy on scholarship.

The current version of the story, according to Logan, was that Molly and Anastasia had both gone to Constance's house for some kind of initiation ritual shortly after they joined, and that's when they vanished. No one saw them after that. Logan said everyone was trying to keep it quiet. No one wanted to leap to any conclusions or make any accusations. After all, "Nicholas is a little nuts," Logan said with supreme understatement. Logan even suggested that not everyone was as eager to go through with burns at Nicholas's big Halloween party as Nicholas thought they were.

Julian was taken aback. "Constance acted like she barely knew what I was talking about when I asked her."

Logan giggled. "The Burners wouldn't be *lying to you*, would they?" He winked at Julian and got up from the table, a stupid grin still plastered to his face.

Julian's head spun. The whole world had become unhinged.

He needed to go to the source.

He found Nicholas at his locker right after the eighth-period bell. But Nicholas was as elusive and saccharine as always. He cooed in his singsong voice, "Of course, I did notice Molly had stopped attending the meetings. And Anastasia as well, for that matter. It was on my agenda to sort that out, but what with all the new pledges, and *The Drop Dead Drop* just getting more and more complicated . . ." He shook his head, exasperated. "Time is in short supply, and intelligent people who can get things done in even shorter."

"Can't you find out what happened to them?" Julian asked.

Nicholas looked at him with theatrically exaggerated pain, as if wounded by Julian's implication that there was something in this world that he couldn't figure out. "Of course, I *could*, but it doesn't seem like a mystery to me. The Burners have always had a high attrition rate."

"But would they really miss school for days to avoid the Burners?" Julian asked.

Nicholas shrugged and wedged his schoolbooks into his bag beside the big white Burners' Bible.

"The thing is," Julian said, "I heard Constance performed some kind of initiation ritual with them. Right before they stopped coming to school."

This made Nicholas stop. There was a subtle tremor in his face—a quavering in his immaculate smile—that made Julian realize he was now heading down a fruitful path. Either Nicholas knew something and was covering it up, or possibly he didn't even *realize* that something was happening right under his nose. Julian had to press this.

"Maybe Constance is doing things that you aren't aware of," he said. "Maybe she's hiding something from you?"

Nicholas darkened.

"No," he declared, spitting the word out like it was bitter fruit. "No one is doing anything behind my back. I can't believe you would even suggest it."

"I'm just telling you what I heard."

Nicholas made a tiny, condescending snort. "Look at you. You get two lives under your belt, and you think you've figured out how everything works."

"I just want to find Molly," Julian said, defensive. Weeks ago, he couldn't imagine being this aggressive with Nicholas Hawksley. But since then, the world had grown so much bigger—and more dangerous—than Nicholas and his little power plays.

"Why do you care so much about this Molly, anyway? You should be focused on the bigger picture. Tomorrow is *The Drop Dead Drop*, and you're our superstar. Don't you even care? It's going to be the biggest burn in Burner history!"

Switching gears? Nicholas was definitely rattled.

"It shouldn't matter to you what I care about," Julian said.

Nicholas's face darkened. "It damn well should," he hissed. "Considering I made you who you are." Nicholas glared at Julian now, his eyes as hard and black as little volcanic stones.

He closed his locker with a hard click, slung his backpack over his shoulder, and walked off without another word.

Julian was left standing in the hall, frustrated, worried—and alone.

He went back to his own locker, peeled off his white blazer, and flung it inside. The idea of having this damn thing draped over him now—this flag of death—made his skin crawl.

That night, Julian sneaked out after a late dinner, which this time included soy cream for dessert, thanks to his father's high spirits at Julian's delivery of the life score they desperately needed.

Now he was parked across the street from Molly's house, in the shadow of an elm tree. There was no sound except the dull scratching wash of cicadas. No lights were on in Molly's house—the windows were inky black squares.

He got out of the car, the door's loud ding intruding into the stillness of the night. He shut the door gently and made his way to Molly's front porch.

He stood in the gloom for a long moment on the front step, straining to make out any sounds, but there was nothing to be heard inside. Just a silence, deep and steady.

He knocked twice, but no one came. He knocked again, a series of knocks this time. And still no one came. Then he tried louder and louder. Almost two minutes of knocking. But still, there was no answer. He tried the handle. It was locked.

He sneaked around to Molly's window. The curtains were closed. He called her name but was met only with more of the same terrible silence. Then he remembered something: the kitchen door had a dog entrance.

Julian kneeled down in front of the dog door, sizing it up.

He had come this far. . . .

He lay flat against the ground and pushed his arms through

the flap. He pulled himself all the way inside, snaking in, and stood up.

This was Molly's kitchen, all right. He had been here countless times with Molly's family. But now everything was gone.

The big wooden table they would play board games on—gone. The refrigerator where he once spilled a two-liter jug of soy milk and then stood, petrified of his mistake as Mrs. Terra yelled at him—gone.

He tried the light switch, but there was no power. He lit the way with his phone lamp.

The living room was also empty. There were deep gouges in the floorboards leading to the front door. Someone had been dragging furniture out.

As he crept down the hallway to Molly's room, Julian felt a pang of fear. The house was eerie, like the essence of the family still hung in the air, ready to coalesce at any moment into an apparition.

Molly's room was also entirely empty, all the furniture removed. Even the carpet had been stripped. His footsteps echoed on the hardwood floor.

What the hell was going on?

People didn't just vanish. They didn't just pack up all of their stuff, say nothing to no one, and just vanish.

Julian felt a lump in his throat.

There was still that something he dared not think. . . .

But how long could he continue to avoid it?

He walked back through the house, through the empty cavern that was once a living room, to the front door. He unlocked it to let himself out, and that's when he noticed a single sheet of paper lying on the floor. It must've been slipped through the crack.

It was marked with the official government seal.

NOTICE—This residence has been seized by
Lakeshore Lentic Research Unit Holdings Ltd.,
a subsidiary of the Department of the Lakes.

For a long moment, Julian stood—alone and shattered—in the empty gloom of a world he no longer recognized.

CHAPTER 26

CODY IMMEDIATELY LINKED MOLLY'S DISAPPEARANCE TO
the Burners. She had been suspicious of them from the moment
Julian had told her about them.

"Have you ever heard of the Orphids?" Cody asked. Julian
and Cody were drinking hot chocolate soy in the café across from
Bardo Books.

Julian shook his head.

"A secret society in New York City. They host cabaret shows.
You know, with half-naked women and all that. Once the show
is over, they close the doors, and that's when the real sick stuff
begins. No one leaves alive."

Julian frowned, trying not to conjure the ghastly image.

"Then there's the Society of the Hemlock," Cody continued.
"They're foodies all about avant-garde cuisine, but every dish

contains a lethal poison. Or the Jumpers out west," she continued, gesturing theatrically. "Extreme sports, but particularly focused on cliff diving."

Julian nodded. "Okay," he said.

"Or Gabriel's Army," Cody continued. "You *must* have heard of them."

He had—they were an aggressive cult with a quasi-religious bent that would infiltrate institutions like universities or the army and urge mass suicides. At one point, they had raised the money to air a national advertising campaign promoting suicide. Julian recalled their ads—"Everyone is doing it. *Except you.*"

"Yes." Julian nodded. "Where are you going with this?"

"These clubs are basically all the same. No matter what their philosophy," Cody said, "there are always two fundamental traits: their adherents had to kill themselves frequently, and, no matter what they did, they never got in trouble with the law." She sipped from her hot soy. "The Best Practices in Extinguishment Act is supposed to have relegated all suicides to ex clinics. Any death outside one is illegal, as you know. And yet, these clubs have never had any high-profile arrests."

She put her mug down and narrowed her eyes at Julian.

"Either they are tacitly encouraged to exist, or they are outright funded and protected by the government."

Julian watched the cats across the street as he mulled this over. "I suppose it is possible that the head of the Burners could be involved in something," he said. "He's a kid called Nicholas Hawksley, and he—"

"Hawksley?!" she asked, incredulous. "Is he related to Director David Hawksley? The man who runs our Lake?"

Julian nodded. "Yes. His father is the Lake director."

"That is no coincidence," she said, as if all the connections were self-evident.

"The Department of the Lakes officially runs the life score and they run the ex clinics, and all the while claim they have the moral high ground—they're not officially *making* anyone kill themselves," she said. "It's purely voluntary. But these clubs are given free rein."

Julian frowned. "Maybe," he said. "But if retrogression is getting worse, and if people aren't returning, then what is their goal here?"

"That's what we need to find out," Cody said. "But the Department of the Lakes is like a hydra. Lots of heads popping up wherever something seems rotten. It's possible that one head isn't aware of what the other one is doing, but I'm sure everything is adding up according to a bigger plan."

But no matter how he tried to get his mind around this potential connection, Julian felt that the Burners still seemed too peculiar to the history of Lakeshore Academy. The worn leather of their Bible, the hundred-year history with the school, and Nicholas's long-simmering rivalry with the alumni, epitomized in his mad race to one-up Georgie Vander.

And yet . . .

Molly was gone.

Her house was seized by the Lake.

"Take me to this *Drop Dead Drop*," Cody said. "This Burners club is clearly taking things to another level, and I want to see it myself."

"I don't know," Julian replied. "I think it might be better if I stay away."

But then he thought about it some more.

"On the other hand, everyone in the school is going to be there," he said, as if arguing with himself. "If there's any chance Molly is still in the area, anywhere . . . she might show up."

Cody cocked her finger-gun.

"We're on, Mr. Julian," she said, firing.

The field outside the old amusement park was packed with cars.

A throng of kids dressed like fluorescent skeletons was laughing and drinking from liquor bottles as they headed to the carnival entrance. Cody snapped a picture on her phone.

"So many people," she said. "Is every party like this?" she asked.

"Everyone at the academy feels like they *have* to go to a Burners party. If you don't, you're some kind of outcast," Julian said. "This is, basically, the entire school."

He watched her documenting the party and frowned, uneasy. Things had a tendency to get out of Julian's control when either Nicholas or Cody were around. And now his two worlds were about to collide.

They followed the neon zombies to the entrance. The old carnival sign that once read "Thriller Land" still hung over the gate, but the Burners had stretched a banner over it, proclaiming *The Drop Dead Drop*. Below it, written in a spooky red scrawl, it said: "Check Your Squeamishness at the Door."

Inside, clumps of kids had gathered near kegs in abandoned snack stalls now lined with booze bottles. A massive roller coaster loomed above the grounds, craggy and derelict. Its huge loop was broken in half, hanging jagged like the broken claw of some sinister fantasy beast.

Julian pushed through the horde of kids in neon paint and glow-in-the-dark skeleton T-shirts, feeling exposed in his plain hoodie. Cody's recording didn't help his unease.

The fairgrounds were set up so that all the attention funneled toward the roller coaster. The loading platform was retrofitted into a stage, where all the Burners had gathered. Ribbons of twinkling LED lights hung in thick clumps over the platform, casting it in a yellowish glow. Music boomed from speakers mounted on the sides of the platform. A microphone stood in the center of the makeshift stage. Julian knew who would soon be standing behind it, directing his flock from on high.

He turned around to find Cody talking to two jocks in glow-in-the-dark face paint. She was shouting to them over the thumping music.

"Are you coming here to burn?"

One of the jocks downed his drink. "I'm all burned up and square on my score," he said. "So it depends on how drunk I get."

"It's a party. Free booze!" the second one said. He completely downed his cup in one gulp. "Who cares what it's for?"

"What if they ask you to burn a life ahead of schedule?"

"Lives are supposed to be used up," he said, tossing his empty cup into the dirt. "You're cute. Want a drink?"

Julian scanned the grounds for Molly or Anastasia, but he didn't see either of them. He did, however, see a group of Burners descending from the stage and fanning out through the crowd. He stepped in close to Cody. "Something's up," he said, grabbing Cody by the elbow. "Let's hang back."

But before they had a chance to say or do anything else, Franklin stepped in front of him. His face was expressionless, his mouth a thin, dry line.

"Nicholas wants to see you," he said.

Julian took a step back and swallowed. Cody looked to him, concerned.

"I'm good right here," Julian said.

Franklin took a step toward Julian, puffing out his chest. "He wasn't asking."

Cody stepped between them. "Actually, Julian was just taking me home." She grabbed him by the arm and tried to pull him away. Franklin regarded her like a naturalist might consider a curious bird, then put his hand in the middle of Julian's chest, stopping him from going anywhere.

Julian brushed off Cody's grip. "It's okay," he said. "I'll deal with him."

"You're crazy if you think I'm not coming with you," Cody said, and followed beside him as they headed for the stage.

They had to push through a mosh pit of kids. Franklin pulled a drunk kid off the steps so Julian could climb up. He turned to Cody. "Just stay here," he said. He glared at her as hard as he could. "*Please.*"

She frowned and reluctantly nodded.

Franklin led Julian across the stage. As he crossed behind the microphone, someone from the mosh pit yelled, "Warrior spirit!" The crowd cheered. Julian staggered away from the mic, startled. And that's when he saw him.

Nicholas was approaching Julian from the wings, his arms stretched out as if receiving a long-lost friend. He met Julian in the center of the stage, grabbed his hand, and thrust it into the air. The crowd cheered. Nicholas walked him to the microphone, his arm still held up triumphantly. "Julian Dex here," Nicholas shouted into the microphone. His voice echoed across the fairgrounds, drowning out the music. "The true Warrior spirit!"

The crowd exploded in cheers. Julian tried to pull away from Nicholas's hand, but his grip was tight. After the cheers died down, Nicholas led him to the wings.

"Amazing, isn't it?" Nicholas yelled back at Julian over the noise. "The whole school. Eating out of the palm of my hand!"

In the wings, Constance, in a sexy skeleton costume, was filming the scene with her phone. She turned to Julian. "We're streaming on DeadLinks," she said. "But where's your stain?" she asked, pouting. Julian looked down dumbly at his gray hoodie. Constance leaned toward Julian and kissed him on the forehead. It was long and hard. She pulled away, wiping the red lipstick that had smeared around the edges of her lips. "There you go," she said, and winked, then turned her camera back to the crowd.

Nicholas threw his arm around Julian and walked him over to a control panel off to the side. Franklin was already standing behind it, inspecting the controls.

"It would be nothing without you here," Nicholas said into Julian's ear. He reeked of alcohol and sweat. "And just in time for the main event, too." Nicholas flipped a switch at the control panel.

The floor shook as machinery beneath it came to life. The lights on the track lit up one by one, running up the broken loop-de-loop. Two trains rumbled up and stopped beside the loading platform with a shrill hiss.

"What a sight," Nicholas said, beaming, almost in a daze.

Julian wanted to get the hell off the stage. He wanted to find Cody and get out of these fairgrounds right now. "You wanted me?" Julian shouted over the noise into Nicholas's ear.

"I wanted to apologize for my aggressive nature the other day," Nicholas said, putting his hand on Julian's shoulder. "And I wanted to say that I didn't 'make you.' You made yourself." He grinned, his eyes sparkling in the lights.

Julian realized he might be looking at the real, genuine, actual Nicholas right now, standing before him, drunk on his own lunacy. There was a small, hard feeling like a rock in the bottom of Julian's stomach.

Pity.

That's what it was.

"Now watch this," Nicholas said as he strode to the center of the stage and took his spot behind the mic.

"Lakeshore senior class!" he shouted.

The crowd cheered. From the wings, Franklin turned down the music so that Nicholas's voice was all that boomed across the grounds now.

"This old, crumbling roller coaster here," Nicholas said, gesturing up at the dramatic rise and loop on the track behind him, "was once known as the Nose Dive. Long ago, it provided thrills and amusement and adventure. How quaint. But we in the Burners don't need roller coasters . . ."

He held a long pause.

"Because death has become our thrill!"

The crowd cheered.

"And so I re-dub this roller coaster the Drop Dead Drop!"

More cheers.

"The most burns ever done in a single year was conducted five years ago by the Gold Star Georgie Vander. He burned forty students. But we . . ." He gestured behind him to the loop-de-loop on the track. It was cracked at its pinnacle, about seventy yards up.

"We will burn fifty students tonight, *at once*! We will run our entire senior class up the loop, and fling you off. You will crash and you will . . . burn!" Nicholas shouted, his eyes bulging. Strands of his perfectly coiffed hair fell loose across his face, and he returned them to formation on his head. "There is no better metaphor for senior year!"

The Burners who had earlier spread out among the crowd began funneling the mosh pit toward the stairs, where Franklin was already leading kids up to the platform one by one and strapping them into the coaster.

Julian looked with concern to their faces, to their eyes behind the makeup—some of them were *scared*. These weren't all Burners who fetishized death. Many were ordinary seniors. They were Twos and Threes. They've been going to ex clinics, following the rules. They didn't need to burn for years. They just wanted a party. Free drinks. And now they were going to be flung into this godforsaken ravine . . . all for one person's amusement.

He watched as they were led, reluctantly, up to the stage.

Cody suddenly grabbed Julian. She was on the stage now, pulling at him.

"We have to stop this," she said.

But Nicholas suddenly yanked him toward the mic.

"We all know Julian Dex here was a One—a goddamned

ONE—until just a few weeks ago," Nicholas shouted into the mic. "Until he saw the light! So, why don't you strap in first, and lead us off for the evening?"

"What?" Julian said, shocked. "No! We never discussed this."

"Julian, don't be shy," Nicholas whispered, his hand over the mic. "You're our star, after all!"

But Julian yanked his arm free from Nicholas's grasp. "I said *no.*"

The microphone squealed. Nicholas stepped back, confusion bleeding through his mask of enthusiasm. "But Julian—"

Cody intervened. "We're not participating in your psychopathic suicide cult," she shouted. The mic picked it up and broadcast it out to the crowd. There was a murmur of confusion as people tried to understand what was happening onstage. Nicholas stood still behind the mic, his mouth half-open.

"And who are you?" he asked. His confusion, and the sting of Julian's rejection, seemed genuine.

Julian pushed Cody away from the mic. "Don't get involved in this," he said.

But Nicholas brought the mic to them. Julian realized what was happening—they had defiled Nicholas's sacred stage. The mount from which he preached to his flock. But you don't just run an angel off his pedestal and walk away.

No.

Nicholas was going to take his stage back.

"Now, now," Nicholas said into the microphone, an icy-cool confidence eerily restored to his voice. He looked out at his crowd. They were rapt now. Whatever other antics were going on, things were far more interesting up on the stage.

"Suicide cult? I find that description totally wrong, little . . ." He peered at her beaten-up old hoodie. "Homeschooled girl?"

Cody snorted. "You kill yourselves over and over ahead of schedule. You get nothing out of it except for laughs," she said, grabbing the mic from his hand. "But someone gets something out of all of your deaths. Who wins? You? The Department of the Lakes? The academy?"

Nicholas's eyes practically bulged out of his head. He released a tiny disbelieving laugh. His nose twitched, like an animal detecting the scent of a predator on the wind.

There were audible gasps from the crowd now. Some of them—probably most of them—were drunk and spoiling to watch a fight. But there were other faces in the crowd that looked disturbed—kids who, like Julian or Molly, had been coerced into the Burners and felt Cody's words resonate. The mood shifted from something jovial into something . . . unpredictable, dangerous.

Which meant it was time to go.

He tried to back Cody away from the mic, but she was fired up. She wasn't budging. She pushed away from him, clutching the mic to her. "It seems like some kind of sick scam to me! You are taking all these people for a ride, all right. Just not the one they think."

Nicholas snatched the mic with a fierce swipe that knocked Cody back. He forced his face into a grin. He paced the stage, a thick strand of his usually impeccably coiffed hair stuck to the sweat on his forehead, spoiling his perfect image.

"The world demands we die. It demands we extinguish our lives to get into colleges, extinguish our lives to get jobs, extinguish our lives to get promoted, get married! The government plans our lives out for us. They tell us when to extinguish down to the *day*. They tell us where to do it, too—in their antiseptic, white-walled clinics with the nurses and the elevator music and all that boring garbage."

He shook his head dramatically, like a television evangelist.

"But the Burners . . . ," he said. "We do not *extinguish*. We *burn*! *When* we want and *where* we want. These are our lives, and we burn them bright."

He turned to the crowd. "Am I right?"

There were some cheers, but the response was muted. It was not the reaction Nicholas was hoping for. He yelled again, this time his voice cracking. "Am I right?!"

"Wrong!" Cody shouted, loud enough to broadcast it to the crowd. "The Lakes are changing, and some people are not coming back! You all need to know this!"

There was a grim murmur of shock from the crowd.

Julian saw movement from his peripheral vision—Franklin was coming toward them from the roller coaster.

Nicholas was breathing hard now, fuming, stalking toward Cody like a panther.

Julian looked to the crowd. To the individual faces. To all the pending waste. To all the pending death.

Cody was right: *No.*

Julian stepped in front of her, shielding her from Nicholas. He wrestled the mic from Nicholas's hands. Nicholas pulled back and after a brief tugging match, Nicholas stumbled, crashing to the floor of the stage. Julian whipped the mic up to his mouth.

He took a ragged breath, and the sound of it squealed over the

PA, silencing the crowd for a moment.

"Where's Molly?" he asked simply.

Nicholas shook his head in disbelief, pulling himself to his feet.

"Where's Anastasia?" Julian asked.

"Julian!" Nicholas shouted. "You don't know what you're talking about!"

"Where *is* Molly?" a voice shouted from behind them. Julian turned—it was Amit, strapped into the roller coaster.

"Where did she go?!" he shouted, his face red. Tears were streaking his now hollow cheeks.

"I have no *fucking* idea!" Nicholas shouted. He was totally unhinged now.

Julian looked out into the crowd. Everyone was watching him.

"Molly and Anastasia joined the Burners. They went to Constance's house," he said, looking over to the wings. Constance was glaring daggers at him.

"And then they were gone."

Julian moved toward the steps leading off the stage, ushering Cody behind him with his arm.

He had to think the unthinkable now.

There was no other way.

"Retrograde?" he yelled. "Or . . . *permadead*?!"

Muted gasps rose up from the crowd.

Franklin charged at them from across the stage. Julian slammed the mic down, producing an earsplitting squeal. He grabbed Cody by the hand and they leaped from the stage into the crowd. All at once, the crowd melted away from the stage, away from the Burners. The kids already in the coaster unstrapped themselves and joined them, pushing past Franklin. The entire student body poured through the white jackets, who tried vainly to keep them funneled toward the death coaster. As they left, some flipped over tables, grabbed kegs, and tore down lights and decorations.

Among the chaos, Julian saw Nicholas in the center of the stage, standing alone and still, clutching the microphone to his chest as the senior class streamed away from him. His eyes tunneled into the core of Julian's being.

Julian turned his back and sped up. He gripped Cody's hand tighter as they charged away toward the exit.

PART TWO

CHAPTER 27

WELL...

This was a disaster.

Franklin looked out at the orchestra room. It was a hell of a lot emptier. Just last week, white jackets would fill out the whole wing. Forty members in regular attendance. Now, there were ... twelve, by Franklin's count.

Twelve.

Tragic.

In the center of the stage, Nicholas stood behind the conductor's podium, hunched over the mic, intoning in a dull voice about meeting minutes as if everything were normal. Franklin pushed the red wristband he wore as the stain of blood aside to check his watch: it was ten to eight. Surely Nicholas would wrap this up now, if he had any dignity left.

After that whole . . . incident, when everyone trashed the carnival while Nicholas paced the stage with his head hung low, mumbling into the mic like an idiot—rumors started flying.

The fact was, Molly actually *was* gone. There was no denying it. Amit had checked with Headmaster Denton, and he confirmed as much. After much coercion, Denton made an announcement that he had received a notice that Molly's father had been reassigned by the Department of the Lakes, and they'd had to move. But not everyone was buying it. Some said Molly simply ran away, and then her family, devastated, moved out of state.

Anastasia was gone, too. Another undeniable fact.

Gloria Merriweather's father, who worked at the police station, told her that Anastasia's single mother made a missing persons' report, and the police started an investigation, but kept it all very quiet. They could've been protecting leads. Or covering something up.

And then, when Anastasia's mother also disappeared . . . Well, maybe she was involved in her daughter's disappearance and fled. They were one of those scholarship families, after all. Who knew what went on in those parts of town?

At the edge of all these rumors was one other rumor that few dared to mention. . . .

Maybe, as Julian had so unhelpfully suggested during the incident, Molly and Anastasia were actually permadead.

That seemed pretty ridiculous to Franklin. They were both only Threes.

Constance suspected they were secretly dating. She told Franklin that the two girls simply couldn't handle the Burner's life and were spooked by her little secret lesson, and ran away together to wherever it was that Molly's father was transferred.

That sounded far more plausible.

Franklin knew that there had been rumors and conspiracy theories about the Lakes for as long as there had been Lakes. You would have to be some kind of a weak-ass motherfucker to let them get to you now.

Speaking of weak-ass motherfuckers . . .

Franklin narrowed his gaze at Nicholas. He was still dully reading from the Burners' Bible, recounting past glories in a sad attempt to inspire the twelve—*twelve*—people still here.

It was pathetic how rattled and flustered Nicholas had become since these rumors started spreading, and the Burners stopped showing up.

Finally, Nicholas snapped the book shut. He looked down at the mostly empty room and released a sigh into the microphone, a feeble scratch of anguish that ricocheted off the room's expensive acoustic soundscape.

"Dismissed," he said.

The twelve remaining diehards—or braindeads, Franklin suspected—shuffled their way to the exit. Nicholas stuffed the Bible into his bag and looked over at Franklin.

"They'll come back," he said. All of Nicholas's usual verve and energy—not to mention, bullshit—had escaped him like a ghost from a corpse.

Franklin had nothing to say in response. He just watched as Nicholas trudged down the aisle to the exit.

"Hey." A girls voice.

Franklin turned.

Constance was standing in the stage left wings.

"Let's talk," she said.

She led Franklin, curiously, to Headmaster Denton's office.

They took a seat opposite Denton's thick Lakespawn red oak desk. Denton sat behind it, snaking his fat tongue over his lips in that way he did when he reveled in his authority. Behind him, a man in purple robes stood tall and stoic. His purple mask and cowl were gathered around his neck, a pair of black goggles nested inside them. The man, who looked to be in his mid-twenties, had tidily cropped hair parted on the side, a clean-shaven face, and a vacant, unnerving stare.

"This is the Prelate of the Lake," Denton said.

"He's an alumnus, actually. George Vander."

Holy hell.

Georgie Vander became the Prelate? At such a young age?

That was seriously impressive.

"The Honorable Prelate Vander is here today to talk about this little organization of yours," Denton said.

Georgie—the Prelate—stepped forward.

"The Burners," the Prelate began.

Denton squirmed in his seat at the word. He still obviously hated outright condoning the club, and this must've been an arrangement it had pained him to make.

"You know they are the most prestigious, if unofficial, club in your school. But they also play an important role in the wider world." The Prelate's voice was surprisingly deep and gravelly.

What number was he on? Franklin couldn't see behind the folds of his robe.

"The Burners are one of the key ways we find our next leaders."

He nodded to Constance.

"I have been watching your club, just as the previous prelates had been watching me when I was the Gold Star. I like the looks of you, Franklin. And Constance here had very good things to say about your leadership potential."

Franklin looked at Constance, arching his eyebrows in confusion. She grinned.

"Truth be told," the Prelate said, "I had approached her first, through your headmaster's recommendation. We did a little a test run, actually, with two of your scholarship students. But then, after what happened at the abandoned fairgrounds . . . with those *wild* accusations." He shook his head solemnly.

"I don't need to tell you that having thinner ranks in the Burners lowers your school's overall life score, which was something I personally worked very hard to elevate when I was here."

Denton frowned at this as well and shook his head. "Not good," he muttered. "Not good."

The Prelate continued, "Constance proved her worth, but we both agreed that if there was going to be a new face in charge of the Burners, it should be someone untainted by *the incident* at the abandoned fairgrounds. Someone who can inspire faith in the student body. Unlike your current . . . *leader*," he said, spitting that last word out of his mouth like curdled soy.

Franklin had to suppress a grin—the Prelate wanted *him*. The

Prelate of the damn Lake was making *him* head of the Burners.

"Because you're so far behind on the score target now, I've arranged for some rewards to get things back on track," the Prelate explained, looking to Constance. "Early acceptance to Azura University, for example."

As if this could get any more interesting.

Denton leaned forward. "I don't have to tell you that an opportunity like this for Azura is a rare and highly—"

"Just raise the score by any means possible," the Prelate interrupted.

Denton shut his mouth and leaned back.

The Prelate opened a briefcase that had been sitting on the table. He took out two official-looking pieces of paper and handed one to Franklin and one to Constance.

Marked with the official DoL seal, they were exemption letters authorizing one Franklin Overton and one Constance Zandt, acting as agents of the nurses, "to administer and hasten compliance extinguishments."

Franklin looked up at the Prelate. In the light coming through Denton's window, the Prelate's robes had an iridescent shimmer, like a rare bird basking in a halo of morning glow. Beautiful. Just beautiful, Franklin thought.

"The time for subtlety is over," the Prelate said, clicking shut the briefcase.

Denton nodded to them both. "Dismissed."

Franklin and Constance left together, each with a letter in their pocket permitting them to get away with murder.

CHAPTER 28

WITH MOLLY GONE, JULIAN BEGAN SPENDING MORE AND
more time with Cody. Her presence, and her determination
to unravel the secrets of the world, to find some kind of truth
behind the chaos of their nine lives, made Julian feel more at
ease. She was not afraid to grab Nicholas's stage and upend it.
Julian couldn't help but admire that.

For a simple, undramatic week after *The Drop Dead Drop*, he
had been meeting up with Cody after family dinner. Almost
always, it was at a different location in downtown Lakeshore or
Poplar Heights in the hopes, as Cody put it, of "throwing a curve
ball" to any prying eyes who might be following.

It was much colder out now. The winters around Lakeshore
and Poplar were infamous for the sudden onset of plunging fri-
gidity. On a few particularly windy evenings, Julian and Cody

got hot chocolate soys and visited the alley behind the bookstore to feed the cats—they still shrank away from his presence.

Cody had taken to checking them behind the ears for life numbers. She filled out a grid in her notebook with the numbers. Her notebook was also filled with pages about *superpalingenesis*, the scientific description of the rebirth process, which, she was quick to explain, was still poorly understood. In her opinion, the field needed to be integrated with quantum physics if anyone wanted to find a unifying explanation for the phenomenon.

On one night so cold it felt like Julian's breath froze before it could escape his throat, he met Cody at the harvest market in Perennial Park.

She slipped ahead of him through the crowd, like she always did, a girl on a mission, even though the mission now was simply to find the synthetic cider booth. Julian jostled among the puffy winter coats, following her rusty tangle of curls through the crowd, trying to keep up. The colors and the scents were overwhelming, and chasing Cody through a throng of anonymous people, Julian felt alive and grateful for it. For a moment at least, his worries about Molly and his mother and the Attison Project had receded. . . .

This is what life should be like, he thought. Your heart beating, your skin tingling, your mind bright and alive as you run headlong toward a future. Toward answers. Not death, after death, after death . . .

Once, they met at Lover's Leap—the jagged rock overhang that looked into a deep, limestone gorge. The trees were evergreen there, not that Julian could see their color anymore, and the air was rife with the scent of needles and musty leaves. Standing at the precipice of the rock, Cody had grabbed Julian's hand all of a sudden and mock-jumped, terrifying him. She laughed at how easy it was to scare him, and then she pecked him on the cheek. It was, technically, Julian's first kiss. It made him dizzy with excitement and confusion.

Cody was strange. There was no denying it. While most girls Cody's age were thinking about college applications, Cody was continually shaping and abandoning theories about the Lentic Research Unit and the Attison Project. She was going to prove to the world that the rebirth system was failing—she had become more determined than ever after witnessing that spectacle with the Burners at the abandoned amusement park.

More than once, she told Julian a variation of "they got my parents, but they didn't think about me." Or "they'll never see someone like me coming."

She had convinced Glen to focus his efforts on reverse engineering the OS they found on the cat's microchip to find a way into the LakeNet servers, in hopes of uncovering anything they could about the "Spoof" Callum had told them about, whatever that was.

It was promising, but it took time, and Julian could tell patience wasn't Cody's strong suit. In fact, it drove her to do things like take him to the harvest market, or kiss him on the cheek.

On the final day of that week, Julian met Cody at Cat's Cradle. Glen had a breakthrough. They crowded around his monitor as he explained what he had found, in between sips from a chocolate soy jug.

"I can tunnel in through a server connected to the cat ID database. It's all supertechnical, and I'll spare you the details, but the point is, I found a way in with administrator privileges. I got to the root of the admin server and . . ."

He took a huge glug of soy.

"I found the index table with a list of files with 'Spoof' in the title. But . . ."

He exhaled heavily.

"I got locked out. I tripped something up. I'm not sure what, but the system sealed it all up once I was booted."

Cody crossed her arms, her brow furrowed. "Wait. So, we don't have anything?"

Glen smiled broadly. "Who said that?"

He brought up a spreadsheet containing a long list of names. "I did manage to download this database file before it froze up. It's a Spoof-marked file. I've been trying to figure out what it is exactly. I have a theory."

They studied the spreadsheet. Beside each name were two numbers and a date for each.

Glen continued: "My guess is it's—"

"Two sets of books," Cody interjected. "Like an accounting fraud."

Glen nodded. "Right. This is exactly how the Lake formats their tables to input into the life score database, but this extra column here . . ."

"They're giving people fake life scores," Cody said, her voice focused and sharp. "Those assholes."

Julian leaned in closer to the screen.

There were a couple of hundred names total. Glen scrolled through them.

"Wait," Julian said. Something had caught his eye. "Just stop

222

for a second." He gripped Glen by the shoulder and leaned in close.

A name.

He turned to Cody. She snorted.

"Nicholas Hawksley," she read.

According to this, he wasn't a Five. He was . . . a One.

Julian had lost a color, Amit had lost his sense of taste, and Molly had vanished, had maybe permadied, all because of Nicholas.

And yet, Nicholas never once took a risk. He threw them all under the bus, while he sat safely in the driver's seat.

It was all a lie. All of it.

Cody stepped away from the monitor, her brow furrowed. She put her hands on her neck as she paced in tiny circles, thinking.

"Think about this. Nicholas Hawksley has a fake number. Who is Nicholas Hawksley? He's the son of the director of the Lake, David Hawksley. Why has Nicholas been prevented from burning? Maybe because he, or more likely, his father knows the Lakes are changing."

Julian nodded. That was feasible.

"And you," Cody said. "And Molly and Anastasia . . . You're all the scholarship kids, right? The poor kids. This is not a coincidence," she said. "Maybe the rich are hiding their numbers while the poor are burning faster."

This made sense to Julian. It was how the world seemed to work, after all. The haves straddling the dead bodies of the have-nots.

Julian asked Glen for control of the screen. Glen conceded, scooching his chair out of the way. Julian scanned the sheet up and down—and noticed something else.

Something that made his blood run cold.

At the top of this spreadsheet, there was a small printed legend under the SPOOF stamp. It was in small type, like part of an automated filing system.

It read, "Issued by Attison Project Director Lucy Dex."

"Guys," Julian said. He pointed to the screen. "My mother didn't just work there. She was *in charge* of Attison."

Cody leaned over him to inspect the monitor. "Holy moly, Mr. Julian. Director."

Julian's heart sank.

He closed his eyes and grasped at the strands floating in the murk of his mind: Nicholas, faking his number while running a suicide club, the obsession with topping Georgie Vander's score, the dead cat, and now his mother, involved in this, whatever it was, hiding Nicholas's number—but no, not just *involved* but *directing*. . . . There was a kind of grim logic lurking in this, a puzzle falling into place. But the key missing piece was the truth of what the Attison Project was actually doing.

"Callum," Cody said. "He told us about the Spoof files, but that's not enough. Not anymore. We have to make him talk to us."

Glen shook his head. "You said there was surveillance. You were recorded on the premises. What if there are guards now, or they have the place on lockdown?"

Cody shrugged. "We won't be so stupid as to just drive up this time."

She insisted that they move on this tomorrow night. Glen gave up the fight quickly and volunteered to stay back at the house with the kids. "The only risks I'm comfortable with are the ones I can take from this chair," he said.

Cody looked to Julian. "You in?" He had vowed weeks ago that he would find out the truth of his mother. So, of course, there was no backing down now.

"I'm in," he said.

Then there was a knock on the door.

A little girl with a pink scarf, who looked about eight or nine years old, entered.

"Cody, the Friends are here to see you," she said.

"Thanks, Carly," Cody replied, rubbing the girl's hair. She walked with Carly to the door, but before she left, she turned to Julian and Glen—"Tomorrow night."

After Cody left, Julian stood and straightened his jeans. He needed to walk, to move and clear his mind. . . .

He followed Cody into the hall and leaned against the handrail to the stairs at the edge of the living room. He watched as Cody received a woman—the woman who ran Bardo Books with the rectangle glasses; they called her Johanna—and led her into the kitchen. They were carrying bags of groceries.

He thought of his mother's eyes. The deep green pools that were gray now. He recalled his last memory of her alive— crashing through their living room, calling out to him: *What the hell are you doing here?* His father dragging her away, the sound of blows out on the porch . . .

The recollections made his head spin. Julian squeezed his eyes shut to chase them away, to give himself a moment's peace, but when he opened them again, he noticed something.

The red door to Cody's room was open. A lamp was on inside,

casting the room in a yellow glow.

He realized that he was, once again, standing on the precipice of something. He was now involved with Cody, with Glen, with Cat's Cradle, and Callum, and the Attison Project, and the secret cameras, and the cars following them down the streets of Poplar Heights. . . .

Soon there would be no going back.

So, if he was going to step across that line, then he needed to know what this was. He needed to look.

Julian knocked softly on the door, then stepped into the room after no one answered. There was a bed in the corner. Clothes piled on the floor. An ordinary-enough-looking room. He saw a brush on the dresser, a tangle of red hair trapped inside it.

There was a small black box beside the comb. It was open, and a photograph inside caught Julian's eye. A pale-skinned kid with white hair and a white splotch on the side of his face.

He recognized the face instantly: Robbie. The retro who stalked the halls of Lakeshore for him.

Stay away stay away stay away . . .

There were more. Photos of Robbie and Cody embracing in the park. Robbie and Cody reclining in a chair, Cody in his lap, a group of cats all around them.

Robbie and Cody kissing at Lover's Leap.

All those strands he had been pulling together . . .

He felt them all slip from his grasp at once, whipping backward into the unknown.

CHAPTER **29**

THE NEXT DAY AFTER SCHOOL, JULIAN BEELINED ACROSS
the yard to the parking lot, his head buzzing with anxiety.
Tonight they were going back to Callum's.

Julian threw his bag into the back beside his crumpled-up
blazer and then hopped into the driver's seat.

He turned his car on and looked up, only to discover Nicholas
Hawksley standing casually in front of it, one hand tucked into
his white blazer pocket, the other holding a paper cup of steaming coffee. Nicholas nodded toward Julian's front passenger seat
as if to say "May I?"

Julian thought about putting his foot on the gas—the tires
squealing, Nicholas dodging out of the way. Just driving out of
here and not looking back. But . . .

This was clearly a different Nicholas Hawksley standing

before him now. His shoulders were sunken and his face, usually bright with the glow of his perfect white teeth, was glum.

He had been the angel of death. But now he was just another awkward twelfth grader. A lanky poser in a tacky white jacket, pretending he had all the answers. And now Julian held something dangerous over him: the truth of his number.

Whatever Nicholas wanted, Julian could handle him.

He unlocked the door.

Nicholas sat down gingerly in the passenger seat. "Good afternoon, Julian," he said. He surveyed Julian's car, and his eyes landed on Julian's white blazer lying in the back. His left eye twitched slightly at the sight.

He brought the paper cup of coffee to his lips.

"Black, bitter, and full of dregs," he said. "Sometimes what you really need in life is vile, imitation insta-coffee. It wakes you up to the world."

Nicholas set the cup down, then removed a napkin from his pocket. He used it to wipe a film of dust off Julian's dashboard. He inspected the napkin, frowned, then folded it up.

"So, what is it?" Julian asked.

"Listen," Nicholas said, taking another sip of his vile coffee. "I have no idea what happened to Molly or Anastasia. I swear. If I did, I would share it with you."

Julian looked at him stonily.

Nicholas continued, "The Burners are more than just some club. We have a purpose. I don't think I need to tell you again about our philosophy that, when—"

Enough of this.

"Why me, Nicholas?" Julian asked, cutting him off. "There's

plenty of other Burners who quit besides me."

"It's just, I thought we were becoming friends," he said.

Julian sighed. "Cut the shit, okay? You want me to burn again, don't you? I was the one who told everyone that some people disappeared on your watch, and ruined your party, so if I burn again, then everything looks like it's fine, right? Or, at least, it looks like you're still in control?"

Nicholas stared him down. "See? You're clever. That's why we were becoming friends."

"I'm not burning ever again," Julian said flatly. "So, don't waste your time."

Nicholas sighed and reached for something inside his jacket.

"Well, the thing about that is . . ."

He took out a piece of paper.

"I've done my research on you, Julian, and I'm sorry to tell you that, in fact, you do need to burn one more life."

Julian screwed up his face in puzzlement.

"I recall quite vividly you telling me that you were burning just to raise your family's life score. Well, this is the long-form life score report for your family right here," he said, tapping the paper.

"I looked it up, and even with your two burns, it's still not enough." He leaned over with the paper, pointing to a specific line. "You see, there is still the lien on your house right here." Nicholas looked up at Julian.

Julian could smell the bitter coffee on his breath.

This was beyond pathetic.

"This paper is a lie," Julian said, pushing the report away. "My father is taking care of everything right now."

Nicholas scrunched up his face as if he were genuinely baffled.

"But Julian, this is the genuine article, right here."

"You're *lying*," Julian insisted.

Nicholas's face flushed, animating his sickly pallor with blood and spirit like a real human being. Who knew you could turn the beast back into a boy just by calling him out on his deceptions?

"It's *not*," Nicholas replied. "It came straight from the LakeNet server. The same place I got the information on your mother. And . . ." He looked away. "Frankly, I'm offended.

"I admit that I may have crossed the line sometimes. I may have twisted things or manipulated situations. But I have never, ever, outright deceived anybody."

Julian looked to Nicholas's number. A perfectly articulated Five, bright in its blackness on his ghostly white skin.

A fraud. A total fraud.

That was the secret truth of the angel on high.

Julian had to suppress a laugh. He had to resist, also, letting Nicholas know what he held on him. Because if Julian had learned anything from his time in the Burners, it's that when you have a card to play, you hold it until the time is right.

But that time wasn't now, because there was a simple response to this sad, defanged version of Nicholas Hawksley sitting beside him: "Get out," Julian said.

Nicholas sighed. He put the paper back into his jacket pocket, he picked up his paper cup, and he opened the door. Slowly, he stepped out.

"I'm trying to help," Nicholas said.

But Julian did not reply.

Nicholas closed the door, and Julian pumped the gas and sped off to meet Cody.

CHAPTER 30

A COLD MIST SNAKED THROUGH THE WOODS, LIKE THE TEN-tacles of a ghostly sea creature. Julian and Cody, dressed in dark sweats and hoodies, crept through the elm forest to the back of Callum's ranch house.

There was a low-register buzzing that permeated the air, and the ground seemed to almost quiver beneath his feet. At first, he thought he was just crunching through wet leaves. But then he looked closer and saw what he was crunching through was not leaves. They were, in fact, cicadas. Or, pupae, actually. Young cicadas that spent their lives hibernating underground, coming up for their first taste of the waking world, only to be crushed under his foot. Hundreds of them.

Cody, noticing his disgust, put her hand on Julian's shoulder. "Don't think about it. Just keep moving," she said.

There was a lot Julian had to keep from thinking about right now.

Like, who was this girl with the notebook full of quantum physics that she may or may not really understand? The daughter of the renegades of the 6/12 incident. The girl who would expose the deadly secrets at the Lake. The girl with the psychopathic retrograde boyfriend who warned Julian to *stay away stay away stay away* . . .

And what about his mother? She had been a director of this strange project at the Lake, and then she was found dead there. Why?

He had to push these worries from his mind. He needed to stay here, in the present. Vigilant. They couldn't be sure how closely Callum was being monitored. They couldn't set off any alarms.

Cody crept up past him, taking the lead. Julian kept focused on following her through the forest, trying not to look down, trying not to register what he was mulching up underfoot.

Finally, they were at the stream, the wash of the water bleeding into the buzz of the cicadas. They found a narrow edge and hopped across it, emerging near the workshop where they'd spoken to Callum the first time. Julian looked at the small mound of dirt where the cat was buried. He suddenly remembered finding it under the living-room window, a dead ball of fur. It had tried to claw its way inside. . . . To find him, maybe . . .

No. Focus.

"Lights are on," Cody said, gesturing to Callum's house.

"But who's in there?" Julian said.

A dark silhouette stood behind the curtain of an upstairs

window—it was hunched over something and tossing dark shadows of objects over its shoulder, as if it was rifling through a desk or a drawer. A second silhouette appeared downstairs. Cody pulled Julian into the shadow of an elm tree at the edge of the yard. They lay down in the brush to hide themselves and watched the windows.

The figure walked into the kitchen, where the curtain was pulled back.

A bearded man wearing a powder-blue robe. A nurse.

"Nurses. They must have got him," Cody whispered. She punched the ground in frustration.

The nurse in the kitchen flung open the cabinet doors and yanked out the plates and cans in huge armfuls, searching for something.

"We have to leave," Julian said, pulling back toward the forest. "We're too late."

But Cody wasn't moving.

"Cody," Julian said, more urgently. "We should go."

But she just lay there on her arms, her eyes flicking back and forth, studying the movement in the house. She pulled her hood over her head. "Callum quit the Lake for a reason," she said, whispering.

"We can talk about it later," Julian said.

Cody shook her head. "He took us out of the Row. He worked with the Friends. He knew the risks of what he was doing. He wanted to help us."

Julian grabbed her by the sleeve. "Let's get out of here."

She pulled out of his grip and then stood in a crouch. She slunk to the outdoor work table and ducked behind it. She palmed around on top of it, feeling for something. She found a gardener's spade.

She looked back at Julian. "You stay there."

He watched in agony as two more nurses appeared in the kitchen. These were carrying flashlights. They were ransacking Callum's place, bagging whatever objects they found of interest.

Cody dashed across the yard to the spot where the cat was buried and dropped to her knees. She started digging furiously.

A swish of light flashed down from the top of the hill. A group of nurses had entered the backyard, carrying flashlights. Julian's breath caught in his throat. The nurses were searching through containers leaning against Callum's house. They were carrying bags emblazoned in a white text that read "Evidence."

Julian looked to Cody. She was digging furiously at the spot where the cat was buried. Did she see them up on the hill?

He needed to warn her, but that would only draw more attention. He was going to have to run out there and grab her. There was no other option.

Shit, shit, shit.

Another swish of light, now coming down the hill. It landed on the workbench and scanned the area. Julian flattened himself on the ground, pine needles stabbing into the palms of his hands. He noticed another movement: a white cicada head, about the size of a quarter, pushing up from the soil, inches from his face.

And still, Cody was out there, digging.

Another light joined the first and now they were jostling, shaking up and down. The nurses were coming down the hill. In a split second, Julian made the calculation, and before he could process what he'd decided, he was up, running across the backyard, the flashlights bright in his peripheral vision. Muffled shouts floated down to them from up on the hill, voices shaking as they ran for him. But Julian's focus was solely on Cody, who was furiously digging at the hole. He ran up behind her and scooped his arm under her chest.

She grunted, her hands pulling out of the soil where the cat was buried, the dirt falling away in clumps. Something flashed in her hands, something shiny and plastic. But there was no time to look closer. He pulled Cody to the tree line.

She started running as well, and the two of them were soon crashing through the forest like frightened deer. The lights searching behind them swished through the fog. Julian ran ahead of Cody, leading her on a series of turns, disappearing farther and farther into the mist. The beams behind them grew fat in the diffusion of the fog. They were putting distance between them and the nurses.

They kept running at full speed for some time, the sound of their breathing a ragged rhythm over the horrible crunch under their feet. They finally made it to the edge of the forest, where it met a back road. Julian recognized where they were—his car was parked in a turnoff a few bends up. He pulled them down behind a large stone in the gutter to catch their breath.

"What the hell were you doing?" Julian said, his breath coming in gasps, his heart skipping every other beat.

"I was right," Cody said, sucking in huge gasps. "Callum did want to help. He left this for us." She was holding a plastic bag covered in dirt. She tore it open. Inside was a note.

C—

I half hope you get this letter, and I half hope you don't.
Because I know it will lead you to trouble.

I'm sorry.

I'm sorry for not being able to do more. But I have to leave, just like I left the Friends. The nurses have been following me ever since I left the Lentic Research Unit. Plainclothes faces in the crowd. Nondescript cars parked across the street, the windows tinted. They were never going to let me out of their sight. For years, I wondered why they didn't just put me down and permakill me, but then I realized, they probably wanted me as a lure. They want to shut down the Friends. They want to tie up loose ends. They're worried about things getting out.

Things about the Attison Project.

As long as I hold this information, they will never let me go.

But someone has to know.

As one of the founding members of the Attison Project, I can tell you that we began with the best intentions. Retrogression and Wrinkles can be a crippling part of the rebirth process, and they were getting worse. We were trying to find a way to eliminate the Wrinkles, reverse them. Imagine a world with guarantees that we wouldn't come back warped or missing memories or senses?

This is where we started. With the cats.

Then things started to change.

The director installed a new project lead. Her name was Lucy Dex. Under her, we switched from cats to human test subjects. We found that repeatedly extinguishing a fresh rebirth created a sustained window of rebirth sickness. Subjects literally could not remember anything that had happened to them during the course of this process. Subjects who were re-extinguished repeatedly had no concept that this was happening to them. This meant their numbers could easily be manipulated.

A subject who woke up on Life Three could be immediately killed again. He'd wake up in the Lake and be brought back into the receiving center, where he should be on Life Four. But then, before the fog of his mind would abate, he would be killed once more. He would wake up, again, in the Lake and by now be on Life Five. He would then be brought back into the receiving center with no memory of the previous two deaths. This process could repeat. Again. And again. Until the subject would awaken in the Lake on what should be Life Nine. Then, once again, he would be brought into the receiving center. But instead of a Nine tattoo, they could give him what he expected to receive. A Three. He'd be on his very last life, but have no knowledge of that fact.

Suddenly, the Department of the Lakes had a way they could directly control the ballooning population numbers without having to resort to martial law.

You're a smart girl, Cody. You know why this was vital to the Lake's interests.

This is a tragedy on multiple levels. Our work for a cure turned out to become a cancer. But the biggest tragedy is that because of this misuse of the Lake, it has started changing, possibly degrading. No one cared to listen. All anyone cared about was maintaining control.

The Attison Project was carried out at the Lakeshore receiving center on a floor that was not marked on the elevator.

It could only be accessed with an authorized keycard. We called it the Spoof floor.

If you access the floor, you may find what you need to get the truth out there.

Again, I'm sorry.

$$-CC$$

Cody put the note down. Julian leaned against the boulder, his hands cradling his head.

He had burned two lives.

There was a Three on his neck, but maybe—he just found out—this Three could be a lie.

And his mother engineered all of this?

She had warned his father to prevent them from burning. Why would she, unless she knew the truth?

His chest started heaving.

He could do nothing to stop the tears from flowing.

CHAPTER 31

GLEN POURED HOT CHOCOLATE SOY FROM A POT INTO three mugs.

Julian and Cody sat at the kitchen table. The light was bright and harsh. Cody's fingers were still grimy with dirt. Julian looked down at his own hands. He pulled a pine needle out from under a nail. His thumbs—too small. Always too small, in every body he'd ever had.

Glen set the steaming mugs in front of them. Julian looked at his dumbly. The smell of the synthetic chocolate stirred something in his gut. He suppressed a hiccup, his insides still raw from crying.

Glen sat down at the opposite end of the table and pulled Callum's letter toward himself.

"So, a handwritten confession isn't really a smoking gun," he said.

"I know," Cody said. Her voice had a flat, hard edge to it. Now that she had finally got hold of the thing she had been searching for, it seemed, the "gee-shucks, Mr. Julian" affectation had vanished.

"Who's to say Callum really wrote this? I could have written it for all you know," Glen argued.

"I realize that," Cody said.

"Who are we, anyway? Just a bunch of orphans living in an abandoned house in the woods? We go to the media, they'd dismiss us as retrogrades."

"I know," Cody said.

"This is . . ." Glen touched the page again, as if to confirm it was real. "This is worse than I ever thought it would be. But what can we do about it?"

Cody looked at him for a long, silent moment.

"We're going to break into the Lake. We're going to get that smoking gun."

Glen sighed. He hung his head low, his fingers idly rubbing Callum's confession.

"Cody," he said. "Not again . . ."

"We have to," she said.

Not again?

"Cody," Glen said. "The last time we did this, it was a total—"

"We didn't know what we were doing," Cody said, cutting him off. "Now I know exactly what I'm looking for. The Spoof floor."

Julian tried to pay attention to them, but it was difficult. He kept retreating into himself, pulling back the curtain in his mind and peeking at the revelation that his mother ran this project, a truth that loomed over everything else like a roiling storm cloud. Bit by bit, he would take in a portion of it but then freeze up, close the curtain, and return to the world. Return to the table, and his hands spread out on it, and Cody talking about breaking into the Lake, and running right into the center of everything they were trying to escape from. . . .

And then, finally, Julian spoke.

"Who is Robbie the retrograde?" he asked. "Who is he really?"

Glen froze, his mouth hanging open. He looked to Cody, who was staring at Julian with hot coals for eyes.

"You didn't tell him?" Glen asked.

Cody didn't react. She just stared at Julian, the silence heavy between them.

"He calls himself Robbie now, but his name is Jake. We used to be . . . friends."

Glen shifted his weight in his chair, and Cody blinked.

"More than friends," she continued. "He was my boyfriend. We met after moving to Cat's Cradle. And . . ." She frowned, dimpling her cheeks.

"We broke into the Lake receiving center once, trying to steal a numbering gun. The nurses caught us, and we ran. I got away, but Jake was caught. And . . ."

She looked down at the dirt covering her hands.

"Well, now . . . After what we found tonight, I can only assume they kept him as a test subject. The next time we saw him, he was retrograde. He didn't remember anything about who he was. It was . . ."

She had to turn away. Her eyes were hard and dark, almost shiny in the fluorescent light.

"It was shitty," she said, her voice growing smaller. "Pretty shitty for everyone."

She let out a long exhale, then snapped her look back over Julian.

"I understand that might change your thoughts about breaking into the Lake," Cody said, her voice once again studded with firm assurance. "But I know what we're looking for now, and I can avoid the mistakes we made before."

That was all he could bear.

Julian stood up from the table.

He had to go home. He had to go home and check on his brother. He should be asleep now, since it was late on a Thursday night, but he had to make sure he was actually there, in his bed.

And he had to make lunch for his family tomorrow—it was his turn.

And he had to tell his father what he had discovered about Mom, if he could summon the courage, if he could hold the curtain back long enough to observe the knowledge as it laid waste to everything.

And finally, he had to tell his family never to burn again.

"Julian, your mother set all this in motion. You have to undo it. You know this," Cody said, serious and unblinking.

Without another word, Julian left, his mug of hot chocolate soy still steaming on the table.

CHAPTER 32

"MEETING ADJOURNED," NICHOLAS SAID AS THE LAST remaining Burners trickled out of the orchestra room.

Logan was last at the door.

That good old boy, Nicholas thought. Bless him.

"Logan," Nicholas called.

Logan stopped at the door.

Nicholas lifted up his cup of coffee.

"Thanks for your dedication," he said. "You're the real Warrior spirit."

"Don't mention it!" Logan shouted, a slanted grin plastered to his face, giggling to himself.

Hmm, Nicholas thought. Never mind that he might be brain-damaged by retro. Loyalty still counts for something.

He sipped from his cup and held the hot liquid in his mouth, turning it around until it filled him with its bitterness.

Vile coffee.

At least he would always have that.

Nicholas looked over to stage left. Constance was approaching from the wings.

He turned to stage right. Franklin was approaching from that side.

Nicholas set his coffee down and closed the Bible sitting on the podium. So this was it.

Franklin spoke first.

"It's not personal," he said. "We need to put the club first."

Nicholas ran his hand across the white leather of the Bible. He snorted. "Franklin, if I may, while I'm still in charge for a few more seconds—shut your ugly mouth. Speeches aren't your forte."

Franklin glared at Nicholas, balling his fists. All bluster with that one, Nicholas thought. Good luck trying to put the club back together with that kind of attitude.

"I don't suppose you'll give me another week?" he asked. "If I can just convince Julian to renounce what he said and return to us, I—"

"The Bible, please, Nicholas," Constance said, interrupting. The grin that Nicholas was attempting vanished.

He picked up the Bible—for the last time, he supposed—and he appreciated the weight of it in his hand. This old tome was passed down through one hundred years of Burner Gold Stars, a grim log of thousands and thousands of student deaths. It was never his—it was always meant to be passed down to the next

Gold Star. Now it was just a matter of accepting that it had all ended much sooner than he had hoped.

"Tell me, my dear Constance," Nicholas said. "Do you know what actually happened to Molly and Anastasia?"

She shrugged. "I asked them to burn, is all," she said nonchalantly.

"Behind my back," he said.

She shared a look with Franklin and turned back to Nicholas.

"I was just . . . stretching my wings, you know," she said.

Something happened to Molly and Anastasia, that was for sure. Something involving Constance. Something that had unfolded under his very nose, and he was in the dark the whole time.

Maybe he didn't deserve the Burners, in the end. Maybe this was meant to happen. He sighed and handed her the Bible. She struggled a little with the unexpected weight of it but kept a straight face.

"Didn't even come close to beating Georgie Vander, did I?" Nicholas asked.

"Not even close," Constance said, her pretty red lips forming a sinister grin.

Nicholas picked up his cup of coffee and held it out over the orchestra pit, as if in a toast to an imaginary class of Burners who were still sitting before him, hanging on his every word.

He turned the cup over and watched as the thin brown coffee pooled, steaming, onto the orchestra pit carpet.

Banzai, then.

CHAPTER **33**

JULIAN WOKE UP LATE.

The exhaustion of the previous evening had taken its toll on his psyche. After he got home from Cat's Cradle, he lay in bed for hours, pushing away the thoughts of his mother on a secret floor in the Lake center, orchestrating rekillings on unsuspecting people.

Eventually, he had managed to empty his mind by concentrating on the steady rhythm of his skipping heartbeat and soon, a black nothingness had taken over, blotting out his consciousness.

It was as if no time had passed at all, but it was almost noon already.

He looked out the window as he poured himself a glass of water from the kitchen sink. Gray clouds hung low over the horizon. A swarm of black cicadas arced across the scrapyard down below before dissipating into the forest, like a blob of ink bleeding down a drain.

He checked his phone. There was a series of text messages from his father:

Where are you?

Where were you last night?

Thank you for burning your two lives to raise our score. I needed to burn one more myself. I know how you feel. I couldn't ask you to do any more than two. So I am doing the last one.

My appointment is at 10 a.m. Please meet me at the bus stop at 6 p.m. I should be there not long after that.

No.

Julian reread the messages again and again. Nicholas had tried to warn him—they *did* need to burn one more.

Nicholas was right—but Julian couldn't imagine that it meant his father's life, not his.

He tried to call his father's phone—but he could hear it ringing in his bedroom. Of course, you don't bring your phone with you to the ex clinic.

Julian checked the time: it was almost 12:30.

He was far too late to stop him.

No!

He pounded his fist on the countertop, knocking his glass into the sink with a clang.

He looked out over the gray banks of clouds hanging over the world, like they were about to crash into it.

"What's going on?"

Rocky was at the door to the kitchen, still in his pajamas. His little brother's presence calmed Julian for a moment.

Everything might be fine. Yes, his father had gone to extinguish, but people extinguish every day. Yes, Lakes might be changing, but what are the odds that, out of the thousands of rebirths in the Lake that happened that day, something would happen to his father? He had to believe this now, for Rocky's sake.

"Hey kid, you're just in time to help me make lunch," he said.

"Ugh," Rocky replied.

Julian pushed his fears away and roped Rocky into lunch prep. He concentrated on the process, on the motions, pushing away the dread threatening him, like the clouds that threatened to tear open outside.

Together, they made soy-cheese macaroni, but they only had enough for one serving. They also had one tofu brick left in the fridge. Rocky, of course, hated tofu, but Julian had a trick to make it palatable—he fried it in corn syrup oil and added chocolate soy milk to it, making a slimy sweet dessert.

As they ate lunch, Julian reminisced about all the harvest meals they had eaten before—it was a good way to keep his mind occupied. Coconut curry chicken was Julian's favorite. Rocky loved apples—he said he still sometimes had dreams of the candied apples and pie they had at the harvest fair two years ago.

Julian pushed through the rest of the day, anxiously counting down the time to 6:00 p.m. Everything might be just fine. His father would show up on a new life and their house would be saved.

And here was Rocky, still on his One. He had no idea of the meat grinder of a world that was waiting for him. A world that would begin for him in just a few short hours if their father didn't return . . .

The rest of the afternoon, they played video games together until it was time to drive out to the bus stop to pick up Dad.

At 6:00 p.m., they sat in the car at the bus stop. Rocky was lost in a game on Julian's phone. Julian watched as rebirths in their paper gowns got off the buses. Most had family or friends there to greet them, but some didn't—confused strangers in paper gowns, shuffling through the cold into the heated bus terminal. Was someone coming for them? *Who* were they, anyway?

Who were any of these people?

Fours. Fives. Sixes. Sevens. Even an elderly Eight.

What had they lost in all of their lives? What colors were they missing? What flavors?

The buses cycled through the lot, a new one arriving every fifteen minutes. For the bus drivers, this was their life. They checked in every day at work and carried rebirths back from the Lake. The rebirths were just following the life score, devised by actuaries in Lake Tower, who were also just doing their jobs. Julian suddenly remembered the little fat man with the bald head at the Tasty's. It was a job for him, dishing out the flavored protein bricks that kept everyone's new bodies fed. All these people, with their multiple lives, and their appetites and hungers and desires, spreading out among Lakeshore valley, across these lands, stretching on to cover America and beyond, out to every unclaimed scrap of land available. Each was a tooth in a giant gear that kept grinding and grinding for the benefit of a select few.

This was the world that Julian was born into: a kaleidoscopic tapestry of lives—nine per person, or maybe less now?—raying out across the world until it consumed everything. Not so long ago, he had dreamed of living alone in a shack on a Lake-less island in the Indian Ocean. Now, he realized what a naive dream that had been. Even there, the machinery of the human race would surely come for him.

He saw glimpses and fragments of these apocalyptic visions in all the faces climbing off the buses. But none of those faces belonged to his father.

He allowed himself to sink into a powerful, deep pool of envy for Nicholas Hawksley. A boy outside the system who never needed to burn. He could hoard his lives until he needed them in an emergency, or to prolong his old age to the absolute limits of the human life span. Julian had a vision of an elderly Nicholas Hawksley sitting in a room at the top of Lake Tower, looking out giant windows, crunching into a bright green sour apple—eight more lives left to live.

Julian looked over at his brother. He had fallen asleep, his head propped against the window, Julian's phone limp in his hands.

Exhausted from the worry, Julian laid his head back as well, and he drifted in and out of a fitful sleep. In his spectral half dreams, he saw that cat again, with the white eye patch. It was sitting on the hood of Julian's car, staring into the window, watching him, its tail flicking like it was about to ambush its prey.

His eyes shot open, and the cat was gone. A dream, it must've been.

He looked around. It was dark out now, the loud thrum of the cicadas drowning out the occasional hiss of the air brakes from the buses, which by now had slowed to a trickle. One every half hour maybe.

One or two rebirths milled around in the bus stop.

It was almost midnight.

Their father wasn't coming home.

CHAPTER 34

THERE WAS A BANGING ON THE DOOR.

The sunrise was a faint orange glow quietly smoldering from behind the clouds. It was barely morning.

That's when the nurses arrived.

Two nurses and a doctor stood at the door. Two of them were middle-aged men with dead eyes, in powder-blue robes. Behind them stood an older doctor holding a clipboard—a woman with frizzy hair and a Seven on her neck.

This woman introduced herself as Dr. Tazia, and she led her two colleagues inside, uninvited. Julian and Rocky were standing in the living room, still in their pajamas and underwear.

"What is this?" Julian asked. He flushed in a hot feeling of panic as it dawned on him that what he was seeing was actually happening—the nurses walking through his house like they had through Callum's, taking notes and bagging evidence.

"I'm sorry to have to tell you that your father reported for an appointment at the extinguishment clinic, but he failed to register with us after his rebirth." Dr. Tazia's voice dripped with the condescending authority of all the worst teachers at the academy.

Julian was cognizant enough to put those words into some kind of order and ask her back in bold-faced terms what she was trying to sugarcoat: "Is he . . . permadead?"

Her lips made a grim line, and she looked over to Rocky, who was clutching Julian's arm.

"Unfortunately, we have to assume so," she said.

It felt like the roof tore off the house, like the sky had cracked open, and a terrible black doom was descending upon all and everything.

The two male nurses were now going through the drawers in their father's desk, in the corner of the living room.

"Because you are both under eighteen, we have to take you to the group home. Now, I know this might seem scary to you, but the home is a safe place."

Julian grabbed Rocky close to his chest.

"Get out of here! All of you!" he shouted.

Dr. Tazia tried to soothe him: "I know this is hard to understand."

"This is our house," Julian said, his voice hard and angry, almost in a growl.

Dr. Tazia became sterner. "Now, about that, I'm sorry that I have to inform you that, actually, this house belongs to the

Adirondack Bank. Mortgage payments are long overdue, and we have no choice but to repossess the house."

The lien. That was what all this burning was about in the first place—but maybe there was some loophole he could find. Some way to buy some time.

"If that's true, then where is the bank person?"

"The Adirondack Bank is a wholly owned subsidiary of the Department of the Lakes. I'm here on their authority to seize this house."

Julian grabbed Rocky and ran for the hallway, but the two male nurses stepped in front of them. The fatter one with the thick beard grabbed Julian by the arm. Julian tried to yank out of his grip, but the nurse pulled him so hard he felt his shoulder burn.

"Be gentle, Raymond," Dr. Tazia said. "They're just boys."

"They should wait in the van," the nurse said, a weary kind of authority in his voice, like he had done this many times before, and they had forgotten the simple fact that you put the kids in the van before anything else.

Dr. Tazia nodded, and the nurse gripped harder on Julian's arm, twisting it. The nurse practically dragged Julian out to the van, the other nurse escorting Rocky. Rocky's face was red, his eyes puffy, tears welling up in them.

They sat in the back of a van, and the nurse locked the door. Julian wanted to climb into the front, steal the keys, just start driving and never look back, but a metal grate separated the cabin. The grate extended over the back windows too. It was like they were arrested, like they were common criminals.

All Julian could do was watch as the nurses carried out their possessions and tossed them into a crate they had set up outside the door. They even took the shoebox out from under his bed—the one stuffed with all of Julian's memories—and tossed it into gray plastic bins labeled "Property of the Department of the Lakes."

He wanted to pull the grates off. He wanted to run and scream and fight those nurses and grab his things and set fire to the house they thought was theirs now.

But Rocky was crying, his face bright red, the tears flowing down his cheeks.

Julian pressed Rocky's face to his chest.

"We'll get through this," he said. "I promise you, we will get through this."

The group home was a long gray building in Retro Row, reminiscent of an army barracks. It was ringed by a brown yard of dead scrub that extended to the river, bordered by a fence at least twenty feet tall.

Dr. Tazia led Julian and Rocky to a concrete room containing two beds divided by a small table. She made it sound like she was doing them a favor by arranging a double room for them.

Julian sat with Rocky under his arm, looking at the floor, as Dr. Tazia explained what was going to happen next: since their home was owned by the bank, which was owned by the Lake, and since they were both under eighteen and both of their parents were assumed permadeceased, they would become the legal wards of the Lake. They could live here in this home until Julian turned eighteen, at which time he could apply for custody of Rocky if—and she arched her eyebrows to emphasize the hypothetical nature of this *if*—he could prove financial security, and, *of course*, an exemplary life score went a long way when figuring such things. She gave them a menacing smile and added, "I'm sure you can work it out if you set your mind to it.

"Regarding your vehicle and your personal effects," she added. "They're being held at our evidence collection center. Once our censors have cleared them, they will be returned to you. School will resume for you once we have checked your life score records and paperwork. We have buses that will take you there."

She stood.

"Do you have any questions?"

"Leave us alone," Julian said.

Dr. Tazia released a condescending puff of air from her nose. "I'm sorry about all this, but we're not your enemy."

"Yes, you are," Julian growled. "You work for the Lake."

The doctor frowned, as if she had bitten into something bitter. "The Department of the Lake ensures the smooth operation of the rebirth process. We serve the entire community."

Julian didn't answer this, wary that perhaps she was baiting him into saying something that would come back to haunt him.

The rest of the day was a blur.

The doctor had them taken to an examination, which checked their numbers and their chips. She also gave them a tour of the facilities: the cafeteria, a study hall, a library, and the yard pockmarked with steel picnic tables and playground equipment that stood, stoic and untouched, like dead vegetation on a dying tundra. They were fed three meals—a soy porridge at midmorning, fried tofu squares for lunch, and some kind of stew at dinner. The other kids in the home looked like they ranged in age from younger than Rocky to Julian's age; in terms of numbers, they ran from Ones to Fours. But there were also a Five and a Six. They all watched Julian and Rocky with wary, judging eyes—sizing up the new kids. Julian refused to engage with any of them. He refused to engage with the nurses, either. He only talked to Rocky. He was not going to see these people for long, he had decided. He was getting out of here with Rocky one way or the other.

Lights were out at 10:00 p.m. Rocky, exhausted from the stress of the day, fell into a deep sleep under Julian's arm. But Julian couldn't sleep—his mind was racing. How could he get them out of this?

He got up, being careful not to disturb Rocky, and sneaked into the hall—he didn't care if it was allowed or not. He walked outside into the cold night air, past the steel picnic tables and the brutal-looking playground. He walked to the edge of the fence and looked out to the river beyond it. The buzz of cicadas was thick in the air.

Something had drawn him from his bed. Drawn him out here.

And, on the other side of the fence, there it sat.

The cat with the white eye patch.

The dead cat.

Its ninth body buried on Callum's ranch, now in possession of the Lakes.

And yet, here it was, alive.

The cat stared at Julian, the tip of its tail ticking in the wind like a wicked metronome.

"What are you?" Julian asked.

The cat, of course, said nothing.

"What are you?!" Julian shouted.

The cat's mouth opened. It let out a horrible screeching cry.

The cicada drone seemed to swell in response, to rise in a horrific cacophony of buzzing that rattled his head and forced him to cover his ears. From the horizon, over the river, a massive swarm of cicadas filled the night sky, barreling toward him with terrifying force.

Julian ran as the cicadas began to crash around him, exploding into the picnic tables, into the slides. The swing set seats were blown back, as if in a hurricane-force gale, but actually, it was a dire wind of pestilence.

Julian ran back inside as the horrific *plinkplinkplink* of cicadas exploding against concrete echoed down the hall. The lights were flicking on. Dr. Tazia was shouting commands. Security guards were rushing to secure the windows.

Plink, plink, plink, plink!

The awful explosions of cicadas smacking into the building rang out like the ricochet of gunfire.

Julian burst into their room. Rocky was sitting up in bed, and Julian gathered him in his arms. That awful buzzing, the horrible scraping of wings echoed throughout the home, pinging off the concrete walls.

"What's going on?" Rocky asked, terrified.

"It'll pass," Julian said, holding Rocky close as the bugs exploded against their window.

CHAPTER **35**

THE SUNLIGHT STUNG. IT ALWAYS STUNG THE FIRST THING IN the morning.

Molly rubbed her eyes and crawled out of her sleeping bag.

Her eyes would get used to the light, and the vague headache that was scratching around in her skull would fade.

Robbie was already getting dressed, pulling on a flannel shirt, a vague form in the shafts of light bleeding in through the smudged-up windows of the old gas station. He reached into the crate beside the counter and pulled out a yellow propane tank—last night's score—and hooked it up to the two-burner stove. He grinned at Molly, his face briefly lit in the glow of the flame as it flared up.

"Morning, Cass," he said, and winked. "Ready for some *huevos Robbieneros?*"

He pulled a carton of real, honest-to-god chicken eggs from the minifridge. It was a good score last night.

Molly couldn't remember her real name. Nor could she remember where she came from. In fact, she couldn't remember much of anything from earlier than four or five weeks ago. But she did remember that real eggs were few and far between.

Robbie fried them up and served two plates on the old Formica table in the corner. Cass, as she allowed herself to be called even though it didn't exactly feel right, sat across from Robbie. They drank mugs of insta-coffee and, for today at least, they ate like kings.

Four or five weeks ago—the exact date was still hazy in her mind—Molly got off a bus down by the river. "Got off" isn't exactly the right term—she was dragged off by nurses. They wore dark black coats over their blue robes. They pulled her out, along with four other rebirths. The fifth one—a young kid about her age with dark bangs that obscured his eyes—refused to budge. So the biggest nurse whipped a baton out of his bag. Bangs ended up getting off the bus just like the rest of them, but with a stream of blood trickling down from the top of his head and spreading across his chest like the mouth of a river opening to the sea.

The bus rumbled away and the six rebirths were left shivering in the cold. The nurses called them retros. Molly knew what retrogression was. She knew that sometimes minds wasted away with rebirth, and retros were often afflicted not just with amnesia, but with other mental defects and syndromes as well.

But she felt perfectly fine. She felt like who she was. The only weird thing was that when she tried to think back and remember where she came from, there was nothing there. It was just a blank sense of time and place that made her think of the billions of years that passed well before she was born—a whole lot of time and space that had nothing to do with her.

Three women retros—one of them probably in her thirties, and the other two looking like they were early twenties—stuck with Molly for the rest of the day. They found a place under a bridge where two men already had a fire going and huddled around it for warmth. The men offered them blankets and jackets, which they gladly accepted. Molly kept looking down to the riverbank, where the bangs kid just sat on his knees, in the freezing cold, the stream of blood hardening on his neck.

They ate scavenged algae bars with the men and kept warm, trying to figure out who they were, where they came from. But, unlike the other two women, Molly had no nostalgia for what she was missing. All she was focused on was the moment, and then the moment after that one.

The next morning, the three other women woke her up. They had gotten up early and pieced together that they were both from Lakeshore, and were going to go back to the town. Molly wasn't interested. The women tried to take her, but she pulled out of their grip. The women left without her.

Later that morning, she saw Bangs was still down by the river. She went down to him. His body was cold. Dead. She checked his number: a Five. That's when she remembered to look for her number, too. She stood over the edge of the river, in the flea-infested jacket given to her by the strangers at the campfire, and looked at her reflection. She pulled her hair back—she was a Three.

A few days passed, and the two men from the campfire

became possessive of her. One by one, they tried to coerce her to sleep with them in their bag, but she always refused. Eventually, a fight broke out between them over who she belonged to, and that's when Molly grabbed the hot metal rod they were using to stoke the fire and turned it on both of them. The men stopped fighting among themselves long enough to grab weapons of their own—shovels with the spade-ends filed into sharp edges. Maybe they could share her, they joked.

That's when Robbie arrived. He came up from the river, and he kicked over their pot of water into the fire. As the cloud of steam hissed into the air, scalding the men, who scrambled away from it, he turned to Molly and said, "Follow me."

She did.

Robbie never forced her to do anything.

For a week or so, they roamed the Row in search of somewhere to squat. Eventually, they found the abandoned gas station, which was tucked far enough off the Row and had a small hot plate. They shooed away the big, mangy cats that had made a home there and cleaned it up.

Robbie was strange—he talked all the time, mostly about his theories on the world and philosophy of life (he was a big believer in living only in the present moment), and sometimes he would ramble at length about somewhere he used to live once, a house up on a hill in the elm forest where no one had life numbers, but he had lost the way to get there—it had vanished from his memory except for the vaguest of images. As with most things Robbie said, Molly didn't know whether to believe him or not.

Every day with him was a unique kind of struggle—looking for food or clothes or propane—but they were always stocked at least one day ahead and Molly soon discovered an odd kind of serenity she could appreciate in the duller moments. She would find herself idly watching the swirls of the river where it pooled and eddied around the rocks of the shore. Once, she spent maybe an hour watching a cicada warm itself on a stone, its body remarkably iridescent—a shiny rainbow in its wings, in the right light.

One day, on one of their longer journeys that took them down the river to where it met the Lake fence, she noticed the big houses far in the distance up on the hillside. Something lurched inside her—a faint outline of a memory. She knew those houses had far more resources than they would ever need, and she knew that you could get to them from the woods and probably only have to scale a single fence. She knew too that they would probably be lightly populated, and so they would have a good chance of getting what they wanted and getting out unnoticed.

That's when things really clicked with Robbie.

They worked together well as a team, hitting the rich, lightly guarded estates on the hillside for food from the guest houses and propane tanks left out at barbecues. Soon, they had stuffed their gas station with all kinds of staples. Stuff she knew, instinctively, that she had lacked in her previous life. Whatever that life was, she knew that it did not contain eggs or honey or bananas.

Once, when they were breaking into an exceptionally large home with a breathtaking view of the Lake, she saw something on a chair that caught her eye—a white blazer, a crest emblazoned on the shoulder: Lakeshore Academy.

It stirred something inside her, but she couldn't place it.

There was a name, though, that the sight of that crest brought back to her: Julian.

But that's all it was—a name. She thought long and hard about it that night, trying to see if that name could stir other memories back up.

The only thing it brought to mind was burning and life numbers . . .

Which led to thoughts of the nurses, and the nurses gave her nightmares.

They gave everyone on the Row nightmares.

One thing she learned quickly among the retros was that everyone—*everyone*—feared and hated the nurses with all the energy they could summon. The sight of a Lake bus was a reason to flee as far and as fast as you could.

Sometimes, the nurses picked people from the Row and put them *back* on the buses. No one knew where they went because anyone who returned after this was far too jacked-up to say anything coherent.

The prospect of being spotted by the nurses was the reason she and Robbie had to be careful to kill all lights and fires after dark, so that they wouldn't be rooted out. There was a jump-bag always ready by the door.

But *Julian* . . .

The name didn't have a direct attachment to the nurses.

Instead, the more she pondered it, the more it brought back a different kind of feeling: a sense that the name might, somehow, lead her away from the nurses, if they ever came for her. It might, in some weird unexplainable way, be a kind of protective talisman for her. At least, that's how she accepted it eventually.

Julian, the name, a talisman.

But then there was also Robbie. He would disappear,

sometimes for days, leaving her alone to hunt for food and to hide from the nurses.

Julian, her talisman, never did that to her.

It was morning. The sunlight, grainy through the smeared gas station windows, was the start of another day. Robbie zipped up a heavy winter coat he had pinched last night and tossed her one.

Another day was about to begin out on the Row, keeping to the shadows, and doing whatever it took to stay the hell away from the nurses.

CHAPTER **36**

BREAKFAST HAD ENDED, AND THE SERVICE STAFF WERE
gathered in the kitchen on a morning break, chatting. Gossiping,
probably, about the poor state of the Hawksley family.

David Hawksley—the esteemed director of the Lake of
Lakeshore—had been away for most of the year on an administrative tour of the Lake facilities of America. The mother, too,
was barely home—there was always a charitable function downtown that needed her, or a dinner party in the Federal District
that required the urgent presence of the softer side of the intimidating director. And, if she was home, she was more often than
not tied up in the parlor room, where she was hosting the wives
of the Councilmen of the Awakened who were in town. As for
their only son, Nicholas—no need to worry about him. Lakeshore Academy was keeping him plenty busy, no doubt.

As Nicholas walked through the kitchen, he gave the staff a curt nod by way of acknowledgment and then proceeded into the dark, cavernous hallway that led to his father's study. The director was home for only a few days before taking off to visit the Lakes of the West Coast—and Nicholas had been summoned.

Nicholas had always hated the tile in this hall, polished every weekend with large machines that scared him when he was a little child. He remembered being that child now, sneaking down the hallway, his bare feet stepping gingerly on the cold marble like he was walking on ice. He recalled the thick wooden door, and the awful, scratching creak it made, like in the horrordocs he obsessively watched despite his parents' proclamations that it wasn't a proper thing to do and didn't behoove someone of Nicholas's standing. Too bad there were lots of rooms—and lots of televisions.

He remembered crawling up onto his father's leather chair, cold in the morning stillness, and going through his father's drawers, pretending to be him, to wield these implements of power—pens, documents, disk drives—pretending they were his and that he, too, was very important. And then the harsh reprimand he received afterward: five days and nights locked in his room upstairs.

"Control," his father had said. "You need to learn to control yourself. Otherwise, you'll never learn to become a leader."

Control.

Boy, he thought. Really cocked that one up, didn't you?

Director David Hawksley—or "Dad"—nodded to Nicholas as he entered. He was standing by the table in the back of the room, near the big windows that framed the Lake down below.

"I'm back home for only a few precious days, and this is not how I want to spend it, on the phone with your headmaster."

Nicholas cringed, his teeth grinding—here we go.

"Your test results are flat-out terrible, Nicholas," his father said. "I'm not sure there are favors I can pull to get you into Azura with results like that. There is a bare minimum standard."

Nicholas turned away. "I've been really occupied," he said, sheepish.

"It would be one thing," his father continued, "for you to say that you've been so busy with that ritualistic club, but look where that got you."

He shook his head gloomily. "I heard from the headmaster how you are no longer part of the Burners Society. On bad terms, no less."

Nicholas frowned and turned away from his father. He looked over at his desk: a giant mahogany–colored slab of authority hewn from the rare Lakespawn red oak. Just looking at it now, and the empty, impossible promise it represented, made Nicholas's stomach turn.

"That was your best chance," his father continued, "given where you stand academically. They are an odd club, with their pranks and rituals, but they were prestigious, with important connections."

"I know that, Father," Nicholas said, quietly.

"You know, George Vander was a member," the elder Hawksley said. "And look how far it has gotten him."

Growing up, Nicholas hated how his father had taken such a shine to Georgie Vander. He was the phenom from the academy, son of the esteemed Councilman Vander, the only person in the

Lakeshore area to have ever been elevated. Georgie's record test scores were written up in the newspaper. He was the valedictorian. He took over the Burners and impressed all the alumni who worked at the Department of the Lakes. He even interned there when he was back on summer breaks from Azura. He was hired straight out of his senior year as a supervisor trainee under Director Hawksley. He was given control of the Lake floor in his first year—a Prelate in his first year!—an unheard-of feat. Georgie fucking Vander.

"I can't believe you had that chance right in front of you, and you blew it," Dad said, shaking his head. "It's supposed to be you taking the reins of the department once I'm nominated for elevation. But it looks like George Vander is the only suitable candidate now. There's so much about the job I wanted you to know, Nicholas. I had big plans for you. But now I'm afraid you won't be part of this. Not if you couldn't even handle a little school club."

Nicholas refused to look over at his father. His shame was hot, burning in his cheeks.

"Do you think it's easy for me to arrange to get your number updated regularly like I do?"

Updated, Nicholas thought.

Faked, he meant.

"Not everyone is as lucky as you are," he continued. "The Lake is becoming far more unstable these days, and I gave you a free pass, thanks to a lot of work and string-pulling. I gave you every advantage I could find, but it seems you failed to realize you were meant for bigger things. You really should've taken the time to speak to George Vander about this. Perhaps he could've given you some advice."

"Excuse me," Nicholas said, the bile rising in his throat. "Why are you talking about Georgie Vander?"

His father blinked at him in a curious way. "You don't know?"

Nicholas turned to look at his father, an awful dread bubbling inside him.

"George had to bail out the Burners Society. He heard about what a disaster it was. Some god-awful thing in the Row you set up, at some crumbling amusement park?"

He shook his head.

"George stepped in and made some recommendations to turn things around."

Wait.

What?

Georgie Vander stepped in and had Nicholas ousted from the Burners? And his father is celebrating this?

"Why?" Nicholas asked.

"I suppose . . ." His father turned back to the window. "He didn't care to see his legacy spoiled like it was."

His father was holding out on him—there was clearly something more to the story of the Prelate deigning to step in to the affairs of a secret society at the academy, but it was also clear that Nicholas was no longer worthy of this knowledge.

"If there's anything I can do to salvage this situation, I'll do it," his father said. "But for now, I'm afraid you had better set your sights on something other than Azura University."

Nicholas flexed his jaw, grinding his teeth together.

"I wish that I could have done better," he said, "but—"

"There's no 'but,' Nicholas. There's no excuse. You know who wouldn't make up an excuse for himself? George Vander."

"Well," Nicholas replied. "We both know I'm not him, am I?"

"You are certainly not. Dismissed."

Nicholas's father waved his hand.

Nicholas's shoes clicked down the hallway tile. Georgie Vander. Georgie Vander. Georgie Vander. Nicholas repeated his name with the martial rhythm of his steps.

His jaw was grinding now so much it hurt. His entire face ached. It burned, and not just with pain, but with a white-hot anger that he could see in incandescent blobs floating across his vision.

Control, Nicholas thought.

Control yourself.

Because your time will come.

Yes.

It will.

CHAPTER 37

THE GROUP HOME RAN A BUS TO ALL THE SCHOOLS IN THE district. Julian discovered this upon awakening to the loud rapping of a baton on the door in the morning.

Dr. Tazia and an angry-looking lump of a nurse opened the door and explained that school would continue as usual. She dropped a bag of their clothes that had finished inspection on the floor beside the door and looked at him and Rocky before moving on to the next room.

Julian made sure Rocky got off the bus at the middle school. He leaned in to whisper to him so that none of the security stationed on the bus, or any of the other students, could hear: "I'm going to look for Dad. I'll meet you back at the home tonight, and we'll go from there. You just keep your head down and don't talk about what I'm doing. We're going to get out of this," Julian said.

"I hope so," Rocky said. Julian watched from the bus as Rocky went into the middle school and was received by a teacher.

Julian was the only kid getting off at Lakeshore Academy. There was little chance that anyone else at the academy would ever end up on a group home bus.

He dodged the crowd thronging to beat the 7:30 a.m. bell and made his way to the parking lot, making sure to stay out of sight of any of the teachers or guards. He took a shortcut through a copse of trees and walked about a mile down Academy Drive to the nearest public bus stop. By the time he got there, his cheeks were bright red and his fingers felt cold and dead. He tried to warm himself in the bus shelter, pulling his collar tight to his neck. Finally, a bus arrived that took him rattling down Lake Road and out to Retro Row. He paid with the few coins he had in the bottom of his pocket—the sum total of everything he had left to his name.

Julian's best-case theory was that his father had merely gone retrograde. Maybe it was a long shot, but there was a chance.

He got off near the Tasty's just north of the Row and followed the river down into the thick of it. He spent the morning searching the encampments near the shore. He talked to several retros—the lucid ones at least—mostly older men about his father's age, but his father was not among them. He walked another mile up the river, asking everyone he saw if they had seen anyone who fit his father's description. None had.

He saw some nurses midmorning unloading a bus full of retros near the pier. He hung back away from them and observed. When they left, he checked the new arrivals—a group of confused and lost people, some of them quite young looking, maybe only a little older than Julian. But again, his father was not among them.

Soon enough, the sun was starting to fade into the steel-gray sky. He was ready to give up, to return to the home and huddle with Rocky and figure out a backup plan. Cat's Cradle—surely, Cody could take them in. The home had confiscated his phone, so he couldn't call her—but he was pretty certain he could recall the route by heart now. Maybe he and Rocky could sneak out tonight, climb the fence near the river, then find a car somehow and make their way toward the winding road to Cat's Cradle. Or maybe it was faster and safer to go to that bookstore first. Maybe Cody was there, visiting her cats, and she would know what to do.

That's when Julian noticed lights go off in an old gas station.

Julian approached a girl lurking around in front of it.

"Hello?" he said.

She spun around, holding a knife. He recognized her instantly.

"Molly?" Julian exclaimed.

She held the knife up in a defensive posture, but something flickered in her face—some kind of dim recognition.

"It's me. It's Julian," he said.

At the sound of his name, some deep, animal instinct lit up in her face. She lowered the knife.

He approached her, his hands up. "I'm so glad you're alive!" he exclaimed.

She backed away from him. "Just chill, okay? Stay in your space."

Julian looked at her neck—a Three. The last time he saw her, at the fire ring during Amit's dead man's party, she was also a Three. This confused him.

"Did you burn?" he asked. "Did Constance make you burn?"

"I don't know what you're talking about," she said. He stepped closer to her, and she jerked away. But he moved slowly, reassuring her of how glad he was to see her, that she wasn't permadead or gone, and eventually she allowed him to come closer. He reached for her shoulders. She flinched as he touched her, but then she accepted it and let him put his arms around her. He squeezed her to his chest.

"How did you get here?"

She pulled out abruptly. "The nurses dropped us off on a bus," she said simply.

Julian was horrified, but he tried to stifle it. He tried to look at this girl and find the old Molly he knew.

He was flooded with a crash of memories: Molly and Julian climbing a tree when they were six, finding the best place to build a fort. Molly and Julian in the back seat of the bus on the way to the middle school with a pack of playing cards, dealing out a game of Born Again Bones. Molly and Julian on the first day of freshman year, the only Ones in the school, watching with condescending disgust as the white jackets walked through the cafeteria. Molly at the fire ring with her new friends, all of them in white jackets now. Julian turning and walking away from her. . . .

And now here she was, wielding a knife and fending for herself in an abandoned gas station on the Row. These memories were now his alone—they might as well be his own private hallucinations.

"Molly," Julian said. "Something really messed up is happening at the Lake, and I think you got sucked into it."

"Cassie," she corrected him. "I'm Cassie."

Julian frowned—the name didn't suit her, but that was hardly the strangest thing about the situation he was now in.

Especially now that he caught sight of someone emerging from the gas station down below. That white-blond hair, the pale face, the bright white patch stretching down his neck . . .

Robbie the retrograde.

"You," Robbie asked, a vicious edge in his voice. He was holding a pipe in his hand, defensive.

"Let's just be calm," Julian said. "I was looking for my father. This has nothing to do with you."

"I told you to stay away," he said. "To stay away!" He came toward Julian with the pipe held back, ready to swing.

Julian stumbled back, putting his hands up—"I don't want to fight!"

"It's okay, Robbie," Molly intervened, stepping in front of Robbie. "He doesn't mean anything bad."

But Robbie pushed past her. "I told you," Robbie said, pointing the pipe at Julian. Julian grabbed the pipe and tried to wrestle it from Robbie's hands. Robbie pulled against it. As they tussled, Robbie kicked Julian in the leg. Julian let go and stumbled backward.

"Stay away from her," Robbie said. "She's mine."

Julian gathered himself. "I can't stay away! She helped me. Cody, she took me to Cat's Cradle."

The phrase "Cat's Cradle" seemed to shake something in Robbie's mind.

"The house on the hill?" Robbie asked, the gears turning in his head. "Cat's Cradle," he said, declaring it as if he had just discovered it. "Do you know where Cat's Cradle is?" His ferocity seemed to have melted away all at once.

"I'm going there tonight," Julian said.

Molly helped Robbie up. Julian couldn't let her stay here—he couldn't let her rot away in the Row.

"Come with me," he said to Molly. "Cat's Cradle is a safe place, away from the nurses."

"You're taking both of us," Robbie interjected.

Julian looked warily at Robbie.

"I trust him," Molly said. "He saved me."

The sun was gone by now, just a dimming filament behind a bank of clouds. Julian tried to calculate the risk he was about to take, bringing Robbie to Cat's Cradle, back to Cody, without her permission. But he soon realized calculations were useless, really—he was not leaving Molly here. There was no way. Even if he had to bring this Robbie kid along.

He nodded to the two of them.

"Fine. But I have to get my brother first," he said.

But something was deeply wrong when they arrived at the group home.

The front gate was choked with vehicles from the Department of Lakes, the light on an emergency van rotating in the night. Nurses were hustling in and out, some of them reading off a clipboard, others prepping a row of vans.

Julian held Molly and Robbie back across the road. They hid behind two Lake-issued sedans.

"Is this some kind of setup?" Molly asked, looking at the nurses.

"Kid, I'm going to smash your face in," Robbie growled.

"I have no idea what's going on," Julian protested, his voice laced in panic. A nurse emerged from the entrance to the group home, leading a line of young children behind him. At the end of the line, Julian saw Rocky. Behind him walked a man in purple robes—the Prelate of the Lake—along with Dr. Tazia.

Suddenly, something broke inside Julian.

Some tiny wire that had been holding him together.

It snapped, and unwound, and fell tumbling into the void.

"They're not taking my brother," Julian said.

He burst out from behind the car. He charged up past the nurses, rushing in so quickly they didn't know how to react. Dr. Tazia looked over, her mouth gaping open.

Rocky saw Julian and broke free from the startled nurse restraining him. He ran for Julian, his face wet and puffy from tears. "Julian!" he shouted. Rocky grabbed his brother by the waist and Julian scooped him up in his arms and turned to leave.

But two thick arms wrapped around his neck—a nurse from behind. Another nurse, his face a strobing shadow in the flashing light of the van, grabbed Rocky and pried him out of Julian's arms. He could feel his brother's fingers, clutching at his jacket, being peeled off.

Julian's arms were twisted behind his back and he was thrust toward a bright bulb of light. It was a flashlight, glaring into his face, stinging his eyes.

A hooded figure stepped into the light and leaned in close to Julian, a silhouette behind the brightness.

"Child." The Prelate spoke, his voice a deep scratching of stone on stone. "You need to stop this and calm yourself down."

"That's my brother. Where are you taking him?" Julian demanded.

"He's a One," the Prelate said. "All the Ones are being enrolled in the Attison Camp, a special educational program at the Lake."

It felt as if the ground crumbled beneath his feet and Julian had entered free fall.

"Don't worry," Dr. Tazia added, stepping beside the Prelate. "He will get full school credit."

No!

Julian pushed against his restraint, and the nurse responded by wrenching his arms so hard it felt like they were tearing from the sockets. He looked over to Rocky, who was crying now, wailing, as a nurse hoisted him up into the van. All Julian could do was watch as Rocky slipped away from him . . . like Molly, like his father, like his mother.

"Let him go! Let us go! We didn't do anything!"

"Child," the Prelate said, "this isn't a punishment." He shook his head. "This is just how things work."

The Prelate stepped back and signaled to the nurse behind Julian.

"We'd better put him in detention," he said. But then he stopped still, noticing something. He grabbed Julian's chin. He leaned in close to Julian's face, so close Julian could smell the clinical, antiseptic stink coming off his robes.

"I've seen you before," he said. "You were with the Friends. Visiting dear Dr. Collins." The tapes.

Damn it, the tapes.

The fabric of the Prelate's mask shifted. He was probably

contorting his face into a grin. "What good fortune to have you here tonight," he said. "Makes my life much easier."

The nurse yanked Julian onto his feet and turned him to the van.

Just then, a bright flash lit up beside them. A violent crashing sound tore through the air. Julian felt the nurse's grip slacken in the sudden rush of noise: a car had crashed into the fence, flames tumbling out of the open windows.

The nurses were shouting. The Prelate was barking indistinguishable, gravelly commands to his scrambling nurses.

Julian seized the opening: he elbowed the nurse holding him in the ribs and slithered out of his grasp. He fell in the dirt and scrambled to his feet before the nurse could grab him again. He rushed toward the van containing Rocky, but the Prelate signaled to it and it sped away, the tires throwing up a cloud of dust.

There was a powerful gust of heat on Julian's back, and he turned to see that the fire in the car had grabbed hold of the back seat and ignited it. The flames were towering several feet in the air. Two nurses sprayed it with feeble-looking fire extinguishers, but the flames just ate the spray up. In all the chaos, Julian had a single moment of clarity—enough to realize that the flames would soon grab the gas tank, and it would explode.

And so he ran as fast as he could back the way he came, his legs thundering, his heartbeat throbbing in his head. He jumped off the road and tumbled into the ditch where he had been hiding earlier. Molly was suddenly there, grabbing him by the collar, pulling him up.

"This way," she said, breathless. She pulled him to one of the other cars they had been hiding behind.

Molly tumbled in on top of him and slammed the door shut. Robbie looked up from under the steering wheel, a mad grin plastered on his face.

"You just cross wire A with wire B," he said as he cranked the engine on. "And voilà."

Robbie gunned the car and they sped out onto the road with a sharp squeal. Robbie was hunched over the steering wheel, his movements animated with a jittery but reassuring sense of control.

Another blinding flash of light filled the sky behind them, and then a millisecond later, the booming sound of an explosion cracked so loud it rattled the car. Julian cupped his hands over his ears and ducked down. Molly was crouched beside him, covering her ears, too. He looked at her, and she looked at him. They both seemed to be saying the same thing with their eyes: This was happening. This was real.

Robbie, up front, didn't look back.

He just gunned the car, the engine growling, and they disappeared into the night.

CHAPTER 38

CONSTANCE, BITING DOWN ON HER LIP IN THAT POUTY WAY of hers, was tying a cute little bow.

The bow was on a rope cinched around Amit's gut.

He was tied up nice and tight now, the All-State Football Champions trophy strapped to his chest. The big brass cup was about three feet tall and must've weighed 120 pounds. The team carried it off the football field together last year after winning States. It was a group effort, so Franklin didn't get a sense then of how truly heavy it was. But lugging it around today, Franklin came to understand that yes, sometimes you had to measure your prestige in weight. And damn if this thing wasn't a lot of prestige.

Amit's eyes were squeezed shut, little twitches jumping at the edges. But at least they were closed. They'd been shot through with blood this morning. He'd clearly been up all night worrying about this. Amit absolutely didn't want to do another burn, and his eyes had started tearing up that morning, and then he started begging, literally *begging*, there in the orchestra room. . . .

Franklin coughed to clear his throat.

He thought again about football. He had that championship on his résumé. His All-State recommendation, too. Even better, he also had *summa cum laude* right up there on the top—a little laurel leaf next to his name: Franklin Overton, *summa cum laude*, laurel leaf.

Now he could add another distinction. A little Gold Star in the extracurriculars. Of course, the Burners weren't an *official* club, but that's what the star was for. It's a dog whistle. Any Burner alumnus out there reading his curriculum vitae would recognize it instantly. The *Gold Star*. Leader of the Burners. Pleased to meet you, young man. Very pleased.

All that, plus Georgie Vander's recommendation.

Welcome to Azura University.

The most prestigious university in America.

Franklin's grandfather burned his lives in the shipyards back in Boston, making enough to start a construction business that turned into a mini-empire. That empire was passed on to his son, Franklin's father. Franklin's father used that to get him into the academy.

His father played the game, and his grandfather played the game.

Looking at Amit, his eyes squeezed tight, the edges of them trembling, Franklin suddenly recalled the moment when he wheeled his elderly grandfather into the ex clinic to take his Eight. Right on schedule, as always.

But there was something off with the old man that day—he didn't speak, he just kept his eyes glued shut, like Amit's, squeezed tight as if trying desperately to keep something locked into his head. Franklin remembered watching his grandfather wheeled away down the hall. And then, when the old man came back on his Nine, he was changed: bored, uninterested, exhausted. He seemed to not even recognize who Franklin was. Whatever his grandfather was trying to hold in that day had clearly been robbed from him then in that ex clinic. . . .

But that's the game.

And now it was Franklin's turn. The path from here was clear—do your homework, study hard, and go after the opportunities in front of you.

You may not like the game, but you had to play it. Sort of like football. Learn the rules, and win.

Poor Amit here, though . . .

Tears leaked out of the edges of his eyes. He was mouthing something too, mumbling indistinctly.

Constance cinched the last few ropes up tight against him and took out her phone. There was a damn cold wind up here.

Constance started filming. She had a knack for filming burns. She had a great sense of composition. She was also adept at finding a way to include herself in most videos.

She filmed a panorama of the bridge they were standing on, then craned the camera over the edge—it was a thirty-foot drop into ice-cold water.

She then squeezed in close to Amit, holding the camera in front of them as if taking a selfie.

"Let us hear it," she said. "Banzai?"

She's cute, but she's stone cold, Franklin thought. He wondered if they might still be hanging out together next year, at Azura.

She winked to the camera and then flipped it over to film Amit directly. She looked over to Franklin and gave him a nod. Franklin snaked his foot in under the frame, so it wouldn't be caught on the video, and gave Amit one solid nudge with his toe.

Amit tumbled over the edge, emitting a pathetic, muffled yelp.

Constance rushed to the ledge to film his descent. There was just a ripple in the water down below now, and a stream of gurgling bubbles that soon enough stopped.

Did it worry Franklin that students were dying faster, and more often, now that he was in charge of the Burners? Did it bother him that in many cases, he was the one directing the killing?

No. The world was full of dying.

Murder was punishable by two lives or two years in the Pit. But Franklin had that letter exempting him from any prosecution. Indeed, it was something else that troubled him about this—something more than the unlikely prospect of a two-or-two . . .

It was those missing kids, Molly and Anastasia. What had happened to them? And Clayton had recently stopped coming to school too. Where were they all? The question scratched at him, a burning under his skin.

But . . .

You play the game.

You may not like the game, but you have to play the game.

After school, they were called to Denton's office. Denton was there with Georgie, dressed up in his full Prelate outfit, except his mask was off. The goggles were resting around his neck, but he might as well have been wearing them—his eyes were like two hard orbs of obsidian. Second time this week he had met with them.

Georgie gave them no greeting—he just asked them for an update on the life score.

"We're at thirty-four total for the year," Constance said.

"Thirty-five," Franklin corrected. "After this afternoon."

Denton grinned, pleased with the progress.

But Georgie was not moved.

"With Amit Sandoval this afternoon," Franklin said. "We've also hit almost everyone on your list, Mr. Vander."

"What about this Julian Dex?" Georgie asked.

Julian.

Franklin sighed.

He was going to be a problem.

"Not yet," Franklin responded. "But we can—"

Georgie raised his hand, silencing Franklin.

"Actually," he said. "That's fine. I need something else from you, regarding Mr. Dex."

Franklin cocked an eyebrow in curiosity.

You gotta play by the rules, even though you don't get to make them.

But someone gets to make them.

And someday, we might all become someone.

CHAPTER 39

ROBBIE PULLED THE CAR UP TO A STOP UNDER AN ELM OUT-side Cat's Cradle.

Glen and Cody stood on the porch, worry bordering on panic written on their faces.

As the car rattled to silence, Robbie sat, his left eye twitching as he stared up at the house, lit in the headlights.

Julian hopped out of the car and ran up to the porch. "It's me!"

"Julian?" Glen asked. "What are you doing in a Lake car?"

But Cody barely acknowledged his presence. Her eyes were locked on Robbie, who was climbing out from the car. Cody's eyes were boring into Robbie, who moved swiftly toward the porch. Glen tried to step in front of him, but Robbie pushed him aside and charged for Cody. He grabbed her and threw her up against the door.

"I'm home!" he shouted. He was up in her face. "You told me to keep away, but here I am!"

Glen wrapped his arm around Robbie's neck and Julian grabbed him by the waist, trying to pry him off Cody. Robbie strained against them, his eyes bulging and his face reddening under Glen's thick arm.

"You need to calm down!" Cody shouted. "There are kids in here!"

Robbie gurgled a spittle-laced hiss from under Glen's choke hold. Glen and Julian managed to wrestle him to the ground, then Glen sat on his stomach.

"Trust me, no one wants this," Glen said as Robbie moaned.

Now Cody grabbed Julian and pushed him toward the front steps.

"What the hell are you doing bringing him here?!"

She looked over to Molly, who was now on the porch, struggling to pull Glen off Robbie, while he swatted her away. "And who is that?" Cody demanded.

"Everyone stop!" Julian shouted.

Julian pulled Molly back and helped Glen hoist up Robbie and push him over to one side of the porch. Like a referee at an out-of-control football game, Julian shouted for Glen and Cody to stay on one side and Molly and Robbie on the other. Once everyone was calm and in separate corners of the porch, Julian explained what had brought them there: his father's likely retrogression or, more likely than that, his permadeath, the group home, Molly and Robbie on the Row, his brother being taken, the explosion, the stolen car . . .

Glen became distraught. "They were taking kids from the group home. . . . I knew it. . . . I knew it. . . ." He kept shaking his head darkly. "Cody, did they see you at Callum's? Are they coming for us next?"

Cody stopped Glen's questioning with a hand and turned to Julian. "Were you followed?"

"No," Julian said. "I made sure we took the back roads. But the Prelate of the Lake recognized me. He knew we were at Callum's."

"Even worse than being followed by the nurses, I'm here now," Robbie said from the other side of the porch, rubbing his neck.

Cody turned to him. "You were violent. You *are* violent. That's why you got kicked out."

Robbie leaned over the railing and spat. "You did this to me," he said. "I loved you!" he shouted. "And you did this to me!"

Everything seemed to stop out there on the porch—Molly, Glen, and Julian sizing up the situation as Cody stepped closer to Robbie.

Even as she glared at Robbie, Julian could see Cody's eyes trembling, her expression taut and on the verge of cracking.

"You don't understand," she said quietly.

Glen stepped between them, trying his hand at peacemaking. "Guys, look, we're already here, and the nurses are riled up. They're going to be looking for a stolen car. So how about we all go inside and figure things out without tearing each other up?"

Cody stared at Robbie for a long, hard moment, then turned to Glen.

"Fine," she said, and headed for the door.

Molly grabbed Robbie and watched icily as Cody slammed the door behind her. She led Robbie to the other side of the porch.

After a few minutes of relative calm, Glen and Julian checked the Lake car for any trackers or bugs—none found—and then drove it to the garage around back.

Glen was troubled. "We've stirred up too much. They're going to find us." Julian wanted to calm him, but he couldn't even calm himself—he kept seeing Rocky slip away from him into the back of the van, feeling angrier and more helpless as the memory looped.

At the kitchen table, Julian sat with his head in his hands, his mind racing through plans to find his brother and free him before . . . before . . .

He couldn't finish the thought.

"Julian," Molly said.

Julian looked up at her, snapping out of it.

"So, you're saying my name is Molly, and we used to be friends?"

Julian nodded.

"Weird," she said, rubbing her chin in that familiar way of hers. "A Molly just seems like a dumpier kind of girl than me, don't you think?"

Julian laughed, the mixture of exhaustion and fear that had coursed through him held at bay for a moment.

"That sounds exactly like something Molly would say," he told her.

She nodded, a tiny glimmer of a smile. "I'm sorry your brother was taken," she said. "Did I have a brother?"

Julian frowned. "No. But you had a mom and dad. They're gone now. The Lake took your house."

She frowned. "Why would they do that?"

Glen sat down beside them, placing mugs on the table.

"Hush money. It happens a lot with retro families. They sign nondisclosure agreements saying there's nothing wrong with the Lake, they take the money and they take the new house and they're gone."

Molly frowned. "Sounds like they don't really care about what happened to me, then."

Julian looked up. "They were probably heartbroken," he said. "They were told you didn't know who they were anymore. That you ran away. You can't blame them."

Molly shook her head. "Well, I *don't* know them."

Julian sighed. He'd been told that in this world, death was rare. It was . . . managed. But really, death was there all around them: in every moment that had vanished. In every face and interaction that had been forgotten.

Robbie—standing in the corner darkly, his arms crossed—turned down Glen's offer of chocolate soy. He watched and stewed as they chatted.

After a few minutes, Cody emerged from her room holding a box of stuff. She tossed it on the floor in front of Robbie. Their photos spilled out.

"This was Jake," she said, pointing at the photos. "Not you."

Robbie glared at her. Glen rose from the table, ready to intervene.

"Jake built this house with me and Glen and Callum. But you are not Jake."

Robbie tensed his jaw. "You made me into this," he said.

"Jake knew what he was getting into."

"You left me behind at the Lake."

"No," Cody said. "Jake . . ." Her voice cracked, then she swallowed it and composed herself.

"Jake went off script. He led the nurses away from me. He sacrificed himself so I could escape. I spent weeks searching for him on the Row. I found you, and I wanted to believe he was still inside you. I brought you here, and I thought maybe I could undo what had happened to you. But it was impossible. You got worse and worse. Then you stole our car. You ran off with our kids, taking them down to the Row to teach them to steal. You almost brought the nurses right to us. I had no choice but to kick you out."

Robbie glared.

"I loved Jake," Cody said. "But you're not Jake anymore. And the truth is," she said, looking down, "I was relieved when you forgot about us."

She stormed out, tears welling in her eyes.

A distant, lonely glaze fell over Robbie's face, and he gathered up the pictures scattered on the floor. He peered closely at one of them and then chuckled softly. "I thought maybe this white spot was some retrograde thing," he said, touching his neck. "But I guess I've always had it." He released a sad little laugh and walked outside to the porch.

Molly followed after him, leaving Glen and Julian alone at the table.

"She's never lost her edge," Glen said after a moment of uncomfortable silence. "In all those years I've known her."

"Did you know her in Florida?" Julian asked.

Glen blinked. "Florida?"

Julian explained what Cody had told him about the 6/12 incident, and her parents, the Lake scientists, and the artificial Lake they were building somewhere west of St. Augustine.

Glen laughed. "Sometimes I forget you were a One until just a few months ago," he said.

"What do you mean?" Julian asked, puzzled.

"Cody's lived in Lakeshore her whole life. God knows who her parents were. They might've worked at the Lake. Or maybe they worked for the army. That's another story she used to tell. For a while there, they worked in the president's military council." He shook his head.

Julian was flummoxed. "She's . . . making it up?"

Glen shrugged. "She's from the Row. Like the rest of us. Her parents maybe went retrograde. Or maybe they just dumped her there. It's a convenient place to dump kids."

He ran his finger around the inside of his mug, getting as much of the leftover sugary dregs as he could. "But having parents who were the renegades in the 6/12 incident sure sounds a lot better, don't it?"

So, Cody was just another kid from the Row, trying to make sense of what had happened to her, trying to gain some control over this world.

Julian shook his head, feeling even more deflated. Did she really know about any of the things she seemed expert at? But just as soon as he had the worry, he realized that it didn't matter—because right now, he needed to get Rocky out of the Lake facility, and Cody was pretty much his only hope of doing that.

Just then, Cody emerged from her room, her face bright and recomposed from a fresh wash, and her hair tied back. She went to the porch and knocked on the door. Robbie and Molly walked over and stood in the doorway.

"You guys can stay," Cody said. "If you promise to play nice."

"Thank you," Molly said. But Robbie was stone-faced.

"Well?" Cody said.

Robbie nodded.

"The moment something sketchy happens, you are out of here," she said.

She turned to Glen.

"Can you show them the extra room in the basement, please?"

Glen nodded.

"And you're telling me to do this because—"

"Because, if I'm not mistaken, *we* have a break-in to plan."

She looked at Julian.

He nodded.

Damn right.

"For what it's worth," Cody said, waking Glen's computer from sleep mode, "I'm glad you're here to do this with me."

Julian nodded, and Cody pulled a blueprint of the Lake facilities up on the screen.

"We've been busy since Callum's. Glen wrote a script that can broadcast a cease order from the Lake, which will tell everyone to stop all extinguishments. He's also designed a program to sniff the database for the Spoof folders, which should contain all the

Attison Project files, and download them to a data stick."

"I'm going to find my brother," Julian said. "And get him the hell out of there."

"Right." Cody nodded. "We'll do that, too."

She zoomed in on the map of the facilities.

"Do you see an Attison Camp on here?" he asked.

Cody frowned.

"No. We need a more current layout. Also, we've been trying to find any hidden traces of the Spoof floor, like venting or a strangely placed stairwell, or an unmarked elevator, but it's not on these old blueprints."

"Cody," Julian said. "We can make this work, right? This is not impossible?"

Cody nodded firmly. "We can do this. I learned some things last time. The direct approach is not wise. We cut a hole in the fence and came in from the beach. I know now that is what they're expecting. So, I figure the best way to approach it this time is to go exactly against what they're expecting."

"You mean, come in through the Lake?" Julian said.

"Exactly," Cody said. "We burn to get in."

"But," Julian said. "We could get caught by the nurses and go retrograde like Molly or Robbie."

"Not if we sneak in from the beach, disguised as nurses."

Julian continued to frown.

"What if we don't wake up? We might permadie."

"I know," Cody said. "But neither of our names were in the spreadsheet we found, so our numbers are most likely genuine. However, we can't eliminate the risk entirely. We'll just have to take it."

Julian frowned. Did they *both* really need to take it?

"Cody," he said. "I'm getting my brother back. I have no choice. But you don't need to do this."

"I was born to do this," Cody said firmly.

Julian frowned, thinking about what Glen had told him about her parents, who she maybe never knew, who maybe were just regular old retrogrades like so many others, folks who lost their memories and lost their kid.

"You have these kids here to take care of," Julian said.

"I'm doing this," Cody said, her voice hard and cold. "I'm going to honor my parents' memory."

Julian nodded—he got it. It was just like his fantasy of living on Mauritius, hidden away from the world. Cody wanted a reality she could deal with, that she could live through. If her parents had to be heroes for Cody to keep putting one foot in front of the other, then so be it.

"Okay," Julian said.

She sucked in a hard, sharp breath through her nose, then untensed her face.

"However. None of this is going to work unless we get an inside man. Someone who could get into the Lake facility and be willing to steal us robes, smuggle in the data stick with Glen's programs, and sneak us into the building. This is really the complication for us right now."

Julian's face lit up.

He had a card to play.

And now he had a time to play it.

"I know just the right person," he said.

CHAPTER 40

IT WAS HARD TO ESCAPE THE FACT THAT NICHOLAS Hawksley—the Burners' Gold Star, the angel of death on high, the hunter with a list of meticulously researched targets—was no longer wearing the white blazer.

Nor was he the first one in the Lakeshore halls in the morning anymore. He used to be the sole student walking the main hall to the orchestra room at 6:30 a.m., a full thermos of coffee steaming in his hand, drawing disapproving looks from the teachers exiting their own morning meetings, who thought it was unhealthy for a kid to drink so much coffee—even though, probably, they were secretly envious that their rations for genuine coffee beans were so small.

No.

These days, Nicholas was just another kid in a navy blazer,

thronging into the lobby as close to the 7:30 a.m. deadline as possible.

These days, it was Franklin who hosted the Burners meetings, and was held in a fearsome regard, especially as more students began disappearing.

Just like Molly and Anastasia, so went Clayton, and just yesterday, Amit Sandoval . . .

Julian stood at Nicholas's locker, watching the lost little angel approach.

"I need to talk to you," Julian said.

"That's nice." Nicholas opened his locker, sullen. "But frankly, I don't want to speak to you ever again."

Julian put his hand on Nicholas's chest and stepped in front of him.

"Here's the thing about people like you," he said. "You're always talking. Everyone is just an audience waiting for your orders, for your directions. You think you have this natural-born right to speak. Some *right* to have everyone follow your words. It's the same with the life score—we *have* to follow it. Not anymore." Julian shook his head. "Today, you're listening to me."

Nicholas sighed. His eyes were baggy, and he looked exhausted. "Out with it," he said.

Julian took a single piece of folded paper out of his jacket and handed it to Nicholas, who studied it. His face turned pale and ashen.

"You're a liar," Julian said. "A fraud. A *One*."

"Where did you get this?" Nicholas hissed.

"I've been looking in all the right places," Julian said.

Nicholas glared at him, a pathetic little gulp worming its way down his throat.

"The Attison Project," Julian said. "What do you know?"

Nicholas shook his head feebly. "I don't know what you're talking about."

"Why'd you fake your number, then?"

"You think it was my choice?" Nicholas said, swallowing whatever putrid thing was in his throat. "You think I *liked* it? Everyone I knew was burning . . . except for me."

"Then, why?" Julian insisted.

Nicholas blinked rapidly, clearing his eyes, and looked around as if to ensure no one was looking.

"My father started taking me to the Lake once every other year or so since I was about eight. We'd go into a room, and someone would erase my old tattoo and give me a new one. It hurt, and I hated it. But I was told to never ask questions. Of course, I wondered why . . . but my father said I'd find out only when I started working for him. Until then, I was told to never talk about it."

He shook his head. "Now, well, maybe I'll never know."

"I'll tell you my guess," Julian said. "It seems like plenty of other people are getting fake numbers too, but they're going in the other direction. They have fewer lives than they think they do."

Nicholas blinked dumbly—the kid with all the answers was genuinely dumbfounded.

"The Attison Project," Julian said. "The Lake is using it to move people to permadeath much faster than they realize."

Nicholas blinked. "That sounds like some nutso conspiracy."

"Says the person with a fake number," Julian replied.

Nicholas shook his head, disbelieving.

Julian explained the evidence he'd collected from Callum. How it all started with the file Nicholas gave him on his mother. "In fact, you can check all this out yourself if you don't believe me."

Nicholas was stunned stupid like he had been stricken with retrograde. "I am talking to you honestly right now, Julian. I know you may not believe me, but I truly have no idea what you are talking about. All I know is my father gave me my numbers, and I wasn't allowed to question it. You don't know my father. There is no second-guessing him."

"Fine," Julian said, realizing he was at a dead end. "It actually doesn't matter what you know. All that matters right now is *that I have this on you.*"

Nicholas glared. "So," he said, "I assume you want something. That's the point of all this, right?"

"I need you to help us break into the Lake."

"Julian," Nicholas said with a thin crackle of a laugh, "you're supposed to be clever, remember? Why are you talking about something so stupid?"

"My father is gone. Permadead or retrograde, I don't know."

Nicholas frowned. "He must've been chasing that score. I told you, Julian. I told you, but you didn't listen."

Julian silenced him with a vicious look.

"I was taken to a group home with my little brother, and then they took *him* to Attison Camp at the Lake because he was a One. They didn't realize I knew what the project was."

Nicholas's jaw tightened—was this finally adding up for him?

Was the sick web of the world finally making itself clear to him?

"I'm getting my brother out," Julian said. "And you're going to help, or everyone is going to find out you're a One. Then what? You going to burn five in a row to catch up? Good luck not going retro."

Nicholas eyed him severely.

"Look," Nicholas said, trying to grab hold of the tables and spin them back around in his favor. "This whole Machiavellian thing you're doing"—he gestured theatrically—"it doesn't exactly suit you."

Julian glared. "So that's a no?"

Nicholas looked up at the ceiling, thinking. The moment was long and uncomfortable. Finally, he looked down at Julian—a flash of the old Nicholas briefly glimmered across his face.

"I'll do it," he said.

"Good choice," Julian replied.

Time was of the essence, and he needed Nicholas to retrieve keycards and secret LakeNet files right the hell now.

But Nicholas slowed him down—he would need to break into his dad's office, and the time for that would be when his house staff went on lunch break. He would download whatever updated maps he could find of the facility. They would reconvene after school and drive up together to Cat's Cradle. In the meantime, Julian would prepare a DeadLinks post with evidence of Nicholas's fake number, ready to publish in case something fell through.

"Ah," Nicholas said softly when Julian explained his fail-safe. "I knew you didn't lose your little spark of wit."

Finally, as they agreed on the plan and were about to head

off on their own ways for the morning, Franklin and Constance emerged from the orchestra room and strode toward them—the gold star on Franklin's lapel and the silver star on Constance's were glinting in the light.

"It's so nice to see you two are still connecting," Constance cooed as they approached.

Nicholas gave her an ugly frown. "Shouldn't the school's most popular Goth cheerleader be down at the cemetery smoking or whatever grim nihilist thing you do?" he said and then turned to Franklin. "And take your mascot with you."

Franklin stepped closer to Nicholas, shifting his weight to make sure his gold star was prominent on his lapel. "I'm brushing off your little insults, Nick. I know you're upset," Franklin said. "But no one asked you to totally quit the club. You could have stayed."

"What, and listen to you garble your way through some speech up there every morning? With all those inarticulate *ums* and *uhs*? You know, I hear good things about the public speaking class here."

Franklin frowned and stepped close to Nicholas's face, peering at him angrily.

"Besides, no one has stayed," Nicholas said, standing his ground. "I even saw Logan without the white blazer yesterday. *Logan*. That kid is plain sick in the head, and even he quit. Rebuilding the Burners wasn't as easy as you thought it might be, was it? You have to force people."

Franklin glared. "We're restoring honor bit by bit."

"Boys," Constance said, intervening. "Let's not fight now, okay? What's done is done."

"Why are you here right now?" Nicholas asked, entirely out of patience.

Constance smiled and suddenly grabbed Julian. She put her arms around him and kissed him, pressing her lips hard against his cheek. It happened so quickly that Julian was momentarily stunned, but then he regained his senses, and he pushed her off. She stumbled back.

"What is wrong with you?" Julian said, wiping his cheek, smearing the back of his hand with red lipstick.

"A goodbye peck," she said.

Nicholas grabbed Julian's arm. "Let's go," he said, pulling him away. "There's some kind of clumsy, desperate game here."

Constance and Franklin stood there, grinning, as Julian and Nicholas headed away from them down the hall.

"They make a real cute couple, don't they?" Nicholas said darkly.

"This is what it's like," Julian said, wiping the last bits of lipstick from his cheek. "Being a target for the Burners."

A strange kind of somber pall fell over Nicholas. "Listen, Julian . . . ," he began. Julian waited for him to continue, but he never did. He just shook his head, clucking his tongue quietly.

They made their way down the hall, and when they reached an intersection, it was time for Nicholas to head to his homeroom, and Julian to his. Julian turned to him. "The coffee machine after lunch, right before the start of fifth period. Don't be late."

Nicholas nodded, and then continued to his homeroom, not looking back. For once, Nicholas Hawksley seemed to have nothing to say.

CHAPTER **41**

THE BELL RANG, USHERING THE LUNCH CROWD INTO THE halls for fifth period.

But Julian remained behind at the imitation coffee machine, nervously fidgeting with his phone. He hoped dearly that he wouldn't have to push Publish on that DeadLinks story because that was his one card. Once used, he would be out of leverage, and they would lose their inside man, and then what—what could they do then to get Rocky back?

But just as the last few kids trickled out of the cafeteria, Nicholas came in from the parking lot, expressionless and waving a data stick in front of him.

They sneaked out the back door, avoiding the guards. They sat in silence as Nicholas drove them to Cat's Cradle in his car, a luxury sedan, since the Burners' van was under new management.

Cody received them on the porch and ushered them into the computer room, keeping a wary eye on Nicholas as they walked through the house.

Glen plugged in Nicholas's data stick, and brought up the updated blueprints. Julian studied them over his shoulder. "There," he said. "Attison Camp." It was a fenced-off area to the side of the facility, right off the beach, containing a half dozen smaller buildings.

"It looks like we have a bingo, Mr. Julian," Cody said. "And looky here. A locked, restricted access elevator. Is that our Spoof level?"

"Probably," Nicholas said, speaking up for the first time since they settled in for the briefing. "I've seen my father use that elevator before. Only nurses with a very high clearance level were allowed in."

Cody turned to Nicholas. He was sitting on a sofa in the back, a judgmental frown plastered on his face. His hair was perfectly styled, not a strand out of place. He had a pristine Five on his white neck and wore a crisply pressed navy Lakeshore blazer. This was decidedly not his scene.

"You have the Spoof access card?" she asked.

Nicholas retrieved a card from his breast pocket and waved it in front of him like a winning ace. "Director-level access. If this doesn't get us in, then nothing does."

She gave him a firm nod. "Impressive. I wasn't sure what to expect after seeing your proclivities at that roller-coaster thing . . . what was it again?"

"It was called *The Drop Dead Drop*," Nicholas said flatly. "And it would have been spectacular."

"Glen here is ready if you don't deliver, Nicholas," Julian reminded him. "If we fail, or if he doesn't hear from us, the post gets published."

"Dang right," Glen said without turning around from the screen.

"And Cody, let's just stick to planning, all right?"

Cody frowned. "Fair enough."

"But will you apologize, please?" Nicholas asked, a smarmy grin on his face. "I mean, I am helping you now."

Cody snorted again and looked at Julian. He rolled his eyes and nodded to her.

"I'm so sorry, my little boy prince," she said, letting the words ooze out of her mouth like some foul slime.

"Good enough," Julian said.

Nicholas made a small sound like a laugh that was being strangled, and looked down at the sofa. He ran his finger along the arm. It came up smeared with grime. He frowned, then took a tissue from his pocket to wipe it clean.

Glen ejected the data stick from his computer and swiveled to them. "It's loaded up and ready to execute," he said. Julian took the stick and tossed it to Nicholas.

"Once we're out of the Lake, you give this to us along with the nurses' robes."

Nicholas slipped it into his pocket. "I think it's a fair courtesy to tell me what you just put on this thing."

It was the sniffer program that was going to find and download all the Spoof files Glen had discovered on the LakeNet server before he was locked out. Among them, hopefully, would be the Attison Project files, which they would reveal to the world.

This, they told Nicholas about.

What they didn't tell him about was the virus, which, if run from an administration terminal, would broadcast an official cease extinguishment order across the county. The order was rarely used, but everyone knew what it meant—the Department of the Lakes tested it frequently on the radio station and drilled it into every schoolkid. The calm and reassuring female voice looping on the radio meant there was an emergency situation at the Lake, and everyone must immediately stop dying if it could be helped, even if you had just strapped into a snuff chair at an ex clinic.

This was Cody's big move. The order would stop everyone from burning, and the Attison Project leak that came right after would ensure that no one ever started again.

Or this was her hope, at least.

"All right," Nicholas said, pocketing the data stick. "I bring the robes and slip you the stick. Then we're off to the Spoof elevator. But that's the end of my involvement. I'm walking away after that. And Julian," he turned to him, glaring up from a low angle, "you're deleting the evidence of my number."

"That's right," Julian said.

Nicholas studied him for a long moment, probably trying to imagine a world where Julian didn't keep his word. Finally, he released a theatrical sigh and said, "You remember when I first asked you to join the Burners? I told you I believed in you."

Julian nodded.

"I'm going to choose to keep believing in you right now," Nicholas said.

The door to the computer room flew open, and a little girl

rushed in—Carly, Julian remembered. Her face was red, and she struggled to get words out among gasping breaths.

"They're coming!" she managed to spit out. "Archie saw them! From the hill! Cars and vans full. They're coming up the road!" She was frantically shifting back and forth on her feet in worry.

Cody grabbed Carly and held her still. "Who's coming?"

"The nurses," Carly said.

Cody turned to Julian and Nicholas, her face contorted with fury. "You brought them here!"

Nicholas looked around the room in alarm. "I don't know what you are—"

"It doesn't matter," she said, cutting him off. She rushed to the table and pulled a small safe out from under it. She spun in the code as she shouted over her shoulder to Glen, "Just like we drilled. Take them down the hill and follow the marks to the rendezvous spot."

Glen scrambled behind the table, unplugging his computers.

"But my rig. I need to—"

"Now!"

Cody grabbed the little girl. "Listen carefully: just like we practiced, you get everyone out of the house and onto the back porch. Then you're all following Glen. You do whatever he says. Can you do this?"

The girl nodded.

"Go!"

She took off the way she came. Cody turned to Julian and Nicholas.

"You two get out here and help round the kids up onto the

porch." Cody grabbed something from the safe and rushed them all out of the room. Glen ran out past them, stuffing a computer tower into a backpack.

The house was a crash of children. Cody was barking to them to get to the porch and wait for Glen's orders. She had transformed: she was mission-driven, an army commander every bit the one that her imaginary father was.

She grabbed Molly and Robbie, who emerged from their rooms confused and worried, and pressed them into service getting the children out of there. Julian helped funnel them all out the door, Nicholas trailing behind him. Through it all, Julian kept an eye on Nicholas, making sure he didn't disappear in the fracas.

Outside on the porch, Glen was taking a head count of the children. All sixteen of them were there. Cody ran up to him. "Tell me you have the route to the rendezvous memorized," she said.

Glen nodded. "Cody, I've got this."

"Let's go!" Glen called out as the kids fell in line behind him. They ran down the hill behind Glen, disappearing into the forest. "Stay close and stay quiet!" he said. "From here, no more talking."

Robbie and Molly stood bewildered on the porch. Cody turned Robbie toward her. "I'm sorry," she said. "I'm sorry for everything that happened."

Robbie glared at her, but then his eyes softened.

"Glen's going to need some help from someone who knows how to survive out there."

Robbie grabbed her. Julian instinctively moved toward them, to break things up—but Robbie only pulled her in for an embrace, and, surprisingly, Cody returned it.

She touched his face. "Thank you," she said. "Keep the kids safe."

Robbie grabbed Molly. "Let's go."

As she was taken away, Molly looked over at Julian, her face grim and ashen. Julian realized with a sense of finality that, though this girl looked like Molly, really, the Molly he'd known and loved died that night at the *Terrible Twos*.

"Julian," she said. She clearly wanted to say something more—but she couldn't articulate it, or even fully grasp what it was, a feeling lost forever in the mud beneath the Lake. She just said his name again: "Julian."

He nodded to her. She blinked back at him—then she was gone, pushed away by Cody, together with Robbie, corralled down the hill, toward where Glen and the kids had disappeared into the tree line.

Cody ran over to Nicholas next. "You," she said, gesturing toward the opposite direction in the forest. "Head down this way. It leads south and eventually connects to Lake Road. As long as you're going downhill, you're heading in the right direction. The plan is still on. We're still breaking into the Lake, and you're still meeting us there."

She urged him on. "Go!"

Warily, Nicholas made his way toward the forest, away from Glen and the kids.

Cody then grabbed Julian and pulled him toward the house. "You come with me," she said.

"But we can't get caught," Julian said. "They'd take us to Attison."

"We won't. But right now, we need to keep them distracted so the kids get some time to run."

Cody grabbed a can of gasoline from the side of the porch and the two of them ran into the house and up the stairs to the top floor. They rushed down the hall, banging on all the doors, calling out to make sure no stragglers were left behind, while Cody doused every room, every hall, every step with gasoline.

They had moved down to the bottom floor, pouring out the last drops of the gasoline, when the caravan of nurses rumbled up. Outside the window, Julian saw the Prelate emerge from the lead truck. Beside him were . . . Franklin and Constance? They were checking something on their phones, pointing out directions.

Julian grabbed Cody and pulled her down beneath the window level.

"They'll see us," he said.

The Prelate's gravelly voice was a clarion call over the din of the vehicles. "Round them all up!"

Cody tossed a lighter from her pocket to Julian.

"Burn it down."

They kept down below the window line, lighting up all the rooms they'd doused until the flames had taken hold, chewing through the wood, linking together in the hallway behind them and blazing a route up the stairs.

When they emerged from the hall, nurses wielding batons were already in the kitchen. Constance and Franklin were there, too, and they were inspecting something: Julian's jacket.

Constance's phone was dinging. She had tracked him. That's what the hell that kiss was about this morning.

"I'm sorry," Julian said to Cody. "They tracked me."

"Just be quiet," she replied.

But it was too late. The nurses were rushing toward them now, batons at the ready. Cody and Julian took off into the thick smoke in the hall. Julian buried his face in the crook of his arm as they ran, pushing through the edges of the flames. Cody led them to the back door, and out to the greenhouse.

The fire had reached up to the top floors now, flames pouring out the windows. Pieces of flaming wood broke off, falling onto the greenhouse roof. Cody and Julian rushed inside the greenhouse, the nurses dashing through the flames behind them in pursuit.

Once inside, Cody started rustling the plants, and directed Julian to do the same. "Make it look like everyone is hiding in here."

They hustled up and down the aisles, shaking the vegetation. Julian grabbed a broom and ran it through the foliage. They could hear the nurses congregating outside, and above all the noise, the gravelly commands of the Prelate: "Surround the greenhouse!"

There was an awful crunch as a portion of the flaming roof collapsed, raining glass and flaming bits of wood down into the greenhouse, setting the plants alight. A pungent organic stink quickly filled the air.

Cody grabbed Julian and pulled him down to the floor.

"Glen," she said to herself, "that's as much time as we can buy you, buddy."

She then pulled a pistol from her back pocket. She must've gotten it from the safe. She slipped a clip in and cocked it.

"I'm sorry," Julian said again. "I'm sorry I brought this here."

Three nurses burst into the greenhouse. They spotted them and charged, whipping aside the flaming vegetation with batons.

"We weren't going to be here forever," Cody said.

She pointed the gun to Julian's head.

"I'll see you on the beach, Mr. Julian."

The nurses were almost upon them.

Julian closed his eyes.

CHAPTER 42

JULIAN BURST TO THE SURFACE OF THE LAKE. THE WATER was so cold it felt like thousands of needles pricking at his skin. He tried hard to suck in air, but it was as if his lungs could not expand. They were tight and hard in his chest.

The nurses' boat was slow to reach him. Julian thought for a moment that the lights chugging toward him might be mirages, dimming and fading, and would soon blink away. He would be left there, in the freezing Lake, dying over and over in a loop.

But no.

Not today.

Rocky.

He and Cody were going to find him.

He kept above water, kept treading, kept sucking in ragged

breaths until the boat reached him.

The nurses hoisted him aboard and wrapped him in a woolen blanket. He looked out at the Lake through his dripping hair. The sun was almost below the horizon, and the cold Lakeshore night was descending. The nurses' boats were searching the black stillness of the water with lamps now, trying to locate rebirths as quickly as they surfaced. He watched the flickering lights of other boats on the horizon, hoping Cody was on one of them. There was a troubling gap in his memory, but he recalled the plan.

Clad in a paper gown and wrapped in a towel, Julian made his way from the dock to the receiving hall. He walked slowly, watching over his shoulder as the crew took the boat back out on the Lake for another round of pickups. A few scattered rebirths were making their way across the beach to the entrance. Julian held back, lingering, until he was able to slip into the shadow of the building, keeping lookout for Cody. If this somehow didn't work—if they already had her, or if . . .

Seemingly out of nowhere, Nicholas was at his side. Without a single word, he looped his arm through Julian's and led him to the side of the building.

Cody was already standing there, her arms wrapped around herself, shivering in the night air. Nicholas slung a bag off his shoulder and started rooting through it.

"What the hell happened?" Nicholas said. "The Prelate came back here a few minutes ago, reeking of smoke and looking rather pissed off."

Cody blinked, wincing, struggling to fight through the fog of rebirth.

"The last thing I remember is we were talking about the plan with Glen," she said.

Julian nodded. "A little girl ran into the room and said they were coming."

Cody shook her head and turned to Nicholas. "The Prelate didn't have the kids with him, did he?"

"Not that I saw," Nicholas replied. "Just a bunch of nurses complaining that they weren't getting hazard pay. My, you must have really touched a nerve with the Department of the Lakes."

Julian could tell that Nicholas was still skeptical, even now, about what Julian had tried to explain to him about the Attison Project.

But that didn't matter right now.

All that mattered was that they stick to the plan.

"Let's get on with it," Julian insisted.

Nicholas nodded and rooted through his bag, removing three powder-blue nurse's robes and three sets of the dark blue jumpsuits that were worn under them. Cody turned her back to them and untied her paper gown. She pulled the jumpsuit on, followed by the robe, and turned to them. It hung loosely from her small frame, like she was a little girl, play-acting.

"Will it pass?"

"Put the hood down," Nicholas said.

She flipped it over, and it swallowed her head.

"Close enough," Julian said.

"My apologies," Nicholas replied. "There was no time to get a menu of size options." He was pulling his robe on over his jacket, not bothering with the jumpsuit underneath.

Julian pulled on his jumpsuit and cinched his own robe close to his chest, and then took a few cautious practice steps. It had big sleeves that flared open at the wrist, kimono-like. It felt heavy to walk around in, but he was going to have to act natural. Keep his head down, too.

Once they had all robed up, Cody said, "Let's do it."

Nicholas stuffed the crumpled paper gowns into his bag to hide the evidence, and led them a short distance in the shadow of the building to a side door. He reached into his robe and pulled the keycard from his jacket. He scanned them in.

The hallway was awash in glaring fluorescence. Julian's head reeled from the brightness, and he suddenly felt weak. He grabbed the door frame, steadying himself. His eyes stung, like on his last rebirth, when he lost the color green. It struck Julian that he probably had a new Wrinkle in his system with this rebirth, and he didn't know what it was. He tried to blink the thought away and focus.

Cody touched his shoulder.

"I'm good," Julian said, pulling himself up.

"Just act like you know what you're doing, and people will think you know what you're doing," she said.

"Couldn't agree with that more," Nicholas added, and strode off down the hall.

Julian and Cody fell in line behind them.

Julian could feel the eyes of the nurses watching as they headed down the hall, but he just let them look. He didn't turn to see them. He kept his head straight and low, focused on Nicholas's back in front of him.

Soon, they were at a service elevator, and Nicholas jammed the keycard into it. A red light blinked on the access pad. The elevator didn't open. Nicholas tried again, but again was met with a red blinking light. Julian felt his heart drop.

At the end of the hall, a double door swung open and the Prelate emerged together with a retinue of nurses. They were charging through the hall—they clearly had somewhere to get to in a hurry.

"They're coming," Cody whispered.

"We're just nurses with genuine access to the Spoof floor," Nicholas said. "No cause for any alarm. As long as this card works." He tried it again, but again it was a red light.

"It's probably smudged or something," Nicholas muttered, rubbing the card between his hands.

The stink of smoke preceded the Prelate as he approached. Julian looked down and saw his hand was shaking. Was this it? Was this his new Wrinkle? His heart surged in his chest, a rush of panic flooding into his head. He felt dizzy again, and he started to sway.

Cody grabbed his trembling hand and held it still as the Prelate came closer.

"You know exactly what you are doing," she whispered.

Julian closed his eyes. He concentrated on the darkness. He tried to empty his mind completely, all his panic, thoughts, and worries drifting away into inky oblivion one by one, like dead leaves from a tree. He felt only his heart thudding in his chest. And then, from the darkness, two glints of light emerged.

The cat.

The white patch on its face.

It stepped forward from the darkness of his mind. It sat down and stared at him, its alien eyes unblinking.

Beep.

Julian blinked. The elevator doors opened with a sigh, a little light finally flashing on the access pad. They stepped inside as if they knew exactly what they were doing. As the doors closed, the Prelate and his entourage charged by without so much as a second glance.

The floor shifted, and the elevator started to move. Julian released a pent-up breath.

We're doing this. We're actually doing this.

The Spoof floor had been closed down for the night. The tables were lined with blank, dead screens. Workstations were scattered with the detritus of an active office: mugs, documents. . . . Cody walked through the floor, a look of stunned disbelief on her face, as if she couldn't fathom that she had actually, finally, made it to this forbidden place.

Julian looked out the window. Outside was the beach. It sloped down on the right toward the dock. Down in the other direction was a large fenced-off area with modular housing units. He spotted kids milling about in the yard, and entering one of the buildings was the sharp-edged form of Dr. Tazia.

Attison Camp.

"Guys," Cody said. "Look at this."

In the center of the room was some kind of large cube, probably about seven feet tall and just as wide. There was a dark sheet hung over it, but something was glowing underneath, a muted blue light emanating from behind the cover. She tore the sheet off.

It was a kid.

No older than ten or eleven years old.

He was suspended in a tank of water, his skin a dead bluish-gray. Wires snaked from his body, out of the tank, and connected to a terminal beside it, where a little green light blinked idly.

Julian rushed to the tank and circled it, trying to make out the kid's face.

It wasn't Rocky.

He felt an enormous sense of relief, but also shame for his relief—this was still some kid right here. God knows what the nurses did to him.

"What the hell is happening in here?" Nicholas asked.

Julian and Cody didn't consider the question. They had business to take care of. Cody found an admin terminal in the back of the room and switched it on.

"Give me the stick," she demanded.

But Nicholas just stood in front of the tank, gawking.

Julian grabbed him by the robe. "The stick," he demanded.

Nicholas snapped out of it and fished the stick from his pocket, and Julian tore it out of his hands. He hustled to Cody. Nicholas staggered up behind them, still gawking over his shoulder at the dead kid in the tank.

Cody plugged the stick into the terminal. A screen popped up with Glen's program. It started combing through the archive, hunting down anything marked with the Spoof classification, or tagged as part of the Attison Project.

File after file popped up on the screen: folders, spreadsheets, photos of dead cats, dead kids, "dump" lists of subjects that went retro and were loaded on buses destined for the Row, video files . . .

"Wait," Julian said. He recognized something. "Play this video."

"We should just download these and go," Cody said.

"Do it," Julian insisted.

Cody enlarged the video. It was grainy footage from a poorly focused handheld camera. There was a subtitle on the screen:

INTERVIEW NUMBER 2

DEPOSER: DIR. DAVID HAWKSLEY

SUBJECT: ATTISON PROJECT LEAD LUCY DEX

Julian's heart sank. His head spun. His breath gave out.

"That's my mom," he said, his voice small and deflated.

"And that's my father," Nicholas said, now looking over Julian's shoulder. "What the actual hell is going on here?"

Cody turned to Julian, still ignoring Nicholas. "Are you sure you want to watch this?"

Julian had to look.

He always had to look.

He grabbed the mouse out from under her hand and clicked play. The date-stamp on the footage indicated it was filmed nine years ago. In the video, Julian's mother looked up. Director Hawksley studied a piece of paper in front of him.

Dir. Hawksley: Why did you apply for the lead position at the Attison Project in the first place?

Lucy Dex: Attison was about fixing retrogression and finding a cure for retrograde and the Wrinkles. I'm a biologist and I wanted to help. And we *were* helping until you changed the remit.

Dir. Hawksley: Mrs. Dex, with all due respect, the Attison Project was about fixing rebirth as a whole. It wasn't just about fixing defects. I would say that the possibility that people may stop coming back to life was a far more pressing issue than dealing with Wrinkles or retrogression. Wouldn't you agree?

Lucy Dex: Of course. But this direction you sent us off on . . . Running these experiments on retrogrades? That doesn't help anything. It's . . . unethical, to say the least. It's actually . . . it's monstrous. I couldn't in good conscience—

Dir. Hawksley: There are far too many people using the Lake now, Mrs. Dex. Too many people, too often. This is causing the effects to degrade.

Lucy Dex: But, Mr. Director, that is just a theory. If we can be free to determine exactly what's going on here, before we start jumping to predecided conclusions, we could—

Dir. Hawksley: Mrs. Dex, at the end of the day, you have orders to follow. I expect you to follow them.

Lucy Dex: I'm sorry, but I draw the line at faking numbers. I saw the reports you issued. You can't taint my reputation like that. I had nothing to do with that arm of the project. I'm going to tell people the truth.

Hawksley reached for the camera and the video abruptly ended.

Julian sat for a mute moment in the blue glow of the screen. Nicholas stood beside him, looking to Julian, his mouth half hanging open in shock.

Julian opened the next video.

This one was soundless security footage from a Lake boat. A woman with dark hair was swimming toward it. The Prelate himself was on the boat, and instead of using a pole to pull the woman to safety, he was using it to push her under the waves. When a wave broke, Julian could see the woman's face.

It was his mother.

"He's killing her," Julian whispered.

"Look at the time-stamp," Cody said. "It's about thirty minutes after that interview we just saw."

Julian hardened his jaw, the realization of what he was witnessing at the edge of his consciousness. It threatened to take hold and terrorize him. But he went on, stoically, to the next video.

He had to keep looking.

Julian's mother was at the table again. Her head was slumped more this time, her gaze cast downward. She was no longer a Six. She was a Seven now. And sitting beside Director Hawksley was Dr. Tazia.

Dir. Hawksley: Let's try this again. Why did you apply for the lead position at the Attison Project in the first place?

Lucy Dex: If rebirth is failing . . . we need to warn everyone. To tell them to stop extinguishing.

Dir. Hawksley: That's not my question.

Lucy Dex: I have kids. My son is almost of age now. His first extinguishment is supposed to be scheduled soon. I have to warn him. You should understand. You have a son, too. You have one, too!

Dir. Hawksley: It's not that simple, Mrs. Dex. If we want a future for our children, one where the Lakes continue to work, then we must follow the schedule and maintain the life score. In fact, we have to speed it up. Dr. Tazia will be taking over your position on the Attison Project, effective immediately.

"This is the smoking gun," Cody said, her voice a live wire. She turned to Julian. "Copy everything to the stick and let's get the hell out of here."

But Julian was transfixed by the screen. He opened the next video.

It was the boat camera again. Julian's mother was being stabbed at with the Prelate's pole again. Pushed down under the waves again.

Julian went to the next clip. More security footage, but this was months later. His mother was running down the hallway of the facility now. Nurses were running after her. She was screaming. Ranting. Julian could not make out anything she was saying, but he saw her neck clearly in one frame—she was on Life Nine.

He recognized, also, the gown she was wearing. It was the gown she had on when she came home that terrible night, the last night he ever saw her.

In the video, she burst out the front door and ran into the bus terminal, the guards trailing after her.

She was coming for him, he realized.

She was trying to warn him.

The video cut to a blue screen, like the others.

She was trying to stop him from burning before he started.

She was trying to save him.

Julian's throat was frozen. Tears welled in his eyes. A cloud of sorrow burst inside his chest. But from inside this storm, a new feeling was born: relief. Blessed relief. It fueled him. It filled him with strength.

She had been coming to save him . . .

And he would save Rocky now.

Julian closed the videos and clicked Export on Glen's program. All the files were copied to a stick, and then a new prompt appeared on screen. "Execute 'Cease Order'?"

He clicked yes, and the program closed. From outside, a siren rang out. Then another, this one much louder, from somewhere closer. Little white emergency lights flickered on overhead, then settled into a flashing rhythm.

Nicholas looked around. "Okay, you definitely need to tell me what this is."

The cease order message came on—"The Lake is closed. Stop all extinguishments immediately, and await further instructions. Repeat. The Lake is closed. Stop all extinguishments immediately."

"That's sent out across all Lakeshore," Cody said, as the voice looped. "We're pulling the plug on all this."

"And we're getting my brother. Now," Julian said, rushing to the window.

"What's the fastest way down there, Nicholas?"

But there was no answer.

Nicholas was still standing dumbfounded halfway between the terminal and the dead kid in the tank.

"Nicholas!" Julian shouted. "You need to lead us there."

He shook his head, bringing himself out of some strange reverie.

"Right," he said. "We were going to take the elevator back, but then you did this, whatever the hell this is, and . . . I don't know." A strand of hair fell loose over his forehead. "I don't know!" he said again, this time shouting.

The elevator doors dinged. They opened, and two nurses emerged.

"Stop right there!" one of them shouted.

The nurses ran for them, and Julian picked up a chair and smashed it into the window, shattering it.

"It's only two stories into the sand," Julian said. "We'll jump."

Julian climbed up onto the window frame.

"Come on!" he shouted.

But Nicholas just stood there, shell-shocked, as the nurses came for him. Cody grabbed a chair and flung it at them, smacking one of them in the chest. She ran over to the smashed window and crawled to the edge.

Finally, Nicholas snapped out of it. "I'm coming," he said, hustling to the window.

One by one, they jumped out.

Nicholas was the last of them, a pale-blue ghost tumbling through the air, crashing into the sand.

CHAPTER 43

THEY WERE SUPPOSED TO HAVE WALKED RIGHT INTO ATTI-son Camp. With the cease order looping, Cody thought they could take advantage of the confusion—keep their heads down, their hoods on, stroll in, grab Rocky, and walk him out, acting like they knew exactly what they were doing.

But now that they were discovered, they were going to have to improvise.

Julian pushed himself up out of the sand. There was a sharp pain in his side, and it hurt with every breath he sucked in. Cody was already standing, making her way on shaky feet to Attison Camp up ahead.

"If you can move, let's move," she said over her shoulder.

Behind them, Nicholas was trying to pull himself up, moaning. Whenever he tried to put pressure on his left leg, he collapsed onto his knee. His ankle was twisted or broken. His head was hung low, and he was gasping out a long thin whine.

For a moment, Julian thought he could leave Nicholas behind. Just let him sit there, choking, in the sand. It might even throw the nurses off his tail—they'd come for Nicholas first, while he and Cody made a break for the camp.

But Nicholas was wailing like a wounded animal.

And . . .

They might still need him to find a way out.

"I have to get him," Julian said to Cody as he went back for Nicholas.

Cody held a position in the shadow of the building as Julian hoisted Nicholas up and slung his arm over his shoulder. Together, they hobbled up to where Cody was and down the side of the receiving center to the camp, the cease order still looping on the loudspeaker at an earsplitting volume, a woman's eerily calm voice requesting everyone to please stop dying.

"Why don't they turn it off?" Nicholas asked between gasps.

"I'm sure they're trying, but they can't. It's a virus," Cody said.

On their right, there was a vast, dark, and shimmering presence. The Lake. The boats were coming back to dock, probably triggered by the cease order, little flashing lights streaming steadily toward the shore.

The camp was just ahead, a large fenced-in field containing about a half dozen buildings. It was alive with activity, with nurses running in and out, rounding the children up to the fence near the front entrance. They were in some kind of lockdown protocol.

There was a gate on the beach end of the camp that had been

left abandoned when the nurses were summoned to the front entrance. Cody ran for it and yanked it open. Julian, with Nicholas's arm draped over his shoulder, limped them both in. Once they were inside, Nicholas pushed himself off Julian and stood on his own weight.

"I can manage," he said, his voice small and cracking. "I can walk. Go get your damn brother. I'll find some way out." He leaned against the building, reached into his robe, and pulled out a printout of the blueprint.

The children had all been grouped up near the front entrance. Cody and Julian kept low, slinking toward them, keeping hidden behind picnic tables where possible. The pain in Julian's chest stabbed at him with every breath. His head still throbbed. He felt like his body was bursting at the seams, ready to fall apart—but he was also alive with energy. With determination and focus.

"There!" Julian said in a whispered shout.

He spotted Rocky at the edge of the crowd. There must have been thirty kids in the group, total. The nurses were keeping them in line with swipes of their batons. Dr. Tazia was shouting some kind of command over the noise.

"They've taken all these kids," Cody said, distraught. "We can't let them do this."

"You stay back," Julian said. "Let me get this."

He straightened himself up, sucked in a painful breath, and puffed out his chest with an air of assumed confidence. Even as his body screamed in pain, he strode right up to Rocky, acting like he was one of the nurses assisting with lockdown.

"It's me, Rock. Just be quiet and come with me," he whispered.

Rocky's eyes lit up, and a huge smile broke on his face.

"Don't smile. You're following my orders."

Rocky tried in vain to tamp down his joy, and Julian peeled him off the group and started off back the way they came. He could feel excitement rising in his chest, drowning out the pain—this might actually work.

"New orders!" a voice shouted. "Take them out to the beach while we wait for the all clear!"

It was Cody.

Shit.

Shit shit shit shit shit.

What was she thinking?

Dr. Tazia turned to her. "And who are you?" she demanded. "I didn't receive those orders."

But Cody kept waving the group over.

"Don't know why you didn't get them," she shouted, her voice dropping into a deeper register, trying to make herself sound older. The nurses looked at her, confused, and then back to Dr. Tazia, who was just as puzzled. "Ah . . . ," she said, reaching for a walkie-talkie. "Let me check that."

Just then, the Prelate and his group of nurses emerged from the main building behind Dr. Tazia. "Get them!" he commanded in a gravelly shout.

Julian grabbed Rocky and started to run for the beach.

But then something struck him in the back. A hard, sharp pain brought him to his knees and knocked his hood off. A hand grabbed him by the hair and yanked him back. A nurse put him in a headlock, the last bits of air that were trapped in his lungs wheezing out of him. He saw Rocky running for him, kicking at the nurse. He wanted to yell "Go!" but he couldn't say anything. Dr. Tazia was there now, too, grabbing Rocky, pulling him away.

No!

Another nurse tackled Cody to the ground and rolled her over, pushing her face into the sand, twisting her arm behind her back.

The Prelate strode up behind her.

"I should have just waited for you both to come here," he said. "Saved myself the trouble."

Julian struggled to speak, but the nurse's arm was twisting tighter and tighter against his throat, a thick cord of muscle like a python. Little blooms of light dotted Julian's vision. The world seemed to shrink and collapse around him. The looping cease order and the Prelate's awful croak shrank and shrank in volume until all he heard was the pounding of the blood in his head.

Then everything seemed to slow: Dr. Tazia pulling on Rocky's arm, his mouth twisting open in pain. Cody pushing against the nurse to lift her head, spitting sand out of her mouth, each little grain drifting into the air. The Prelate looming behind her, reaching into his robes, pulling out a gun.

And then there was the cat.

That black cat with the white patch. Calmly, eerily, sitting among it all.

It was unbothered by the activity.

It was looking at Julian, the tip of its tail flicking in the sudden stillness.

Then there was a voice.

A low, deep, thunderous growl of a voice.

call them

Was it the cat, speaking to him?
Then louder:

CALL THEM

Julian twisted his head to find Rocky. At the sight of his brother wailing, Julian felt something dislodge inside him. Something knock loose and fall free. Some awful little black ball of hatred. Hatred for the Lake, for burning, for the world. He felt it spill out from the core of his being and flood into his bloodstream, fill up every extremity with darkness.

He grabbed the arm choking him, clawing at it with all his strength, and he screamed. He screamed into the night. A horrible, shrill sound from a place in him he didn't know existed. And yet the sound was somehow familiar. The cat screamed along with him, its fangs glinting in the night.

That's when the buzzing began.

The cicadas emerged from the trees.

Just a few at first, ricocheting through the Attison Camp, bouncing off the doors, smacking into the nurses. Their number grew and grew until they were a terrible black cloud that whipped through the air, crashing into the nurses, exploding onto Dr. Tazia's face, and bursting like mortar upon the nurse holding Julian. He tumbled free.

As the cicadas whipped past them, Julian scrambled for Rocky, pulling him away from Tazia, who was screaming as the insects pummeled her head. He went to Cody next, pulling her up. Julian looked into the heart of the storm. The children cowered in fear, screaming and hiding behind turned-over tables. But they were safe—the cicadas were arcing around them even in their frenzy, leaving them untouched.

"Cody, get the kids!" he shouted. She took off into the storm, pulled the kids together into a group, and led them like a pied piper through the mess to Julian and Rocky.

Julian led all of them to cover behind the nearest building as the swarm hammered the camp. He held Rocky to his chest and peeked around the edge.

There was an awful screech and a massive explosion of white sparks as the cicada swarm exploded into an electrical pole. The blast cracked the pole. It tumbled to the ground, landing with a crash of electricity. Live wires tumbled across the sand, flipping like a sea monster dragged out from the depths.

All the lights in the camp went off at once. The cease order squealed off midsentence. The lights in the receiving facility went dark, too. The only lights now were the bright blue-white electrical fingers of the downed cables.

"Run!" Julian shouted.

And they ran, with Julian, Rocky, and Cody at the head of the group, leading them back out to the gate where they came in, when—

Blam!

A gunshot exploded in the sand beside Julian. He turned.

A figure emerged from the swarm of cicadas behind them, holding a gun.

The Prelate, his robes smeared with insect guts.

"I'll sort you all out on your next lives!" he shouted.

He steadied his aim square at Julian.

"Hey, Georgie," a voice said.

The Prelate turned. Someone hobbled over to him from behind a building.

Nicholas.

He was holding a live wire with both hands. It was writhing like a frenzied snake.

"Banzai," he said, and tossed the wire at the Prelate. It hit him smack in the chest, and bright tendrils of blue electricity danced over him, like spider's legs cocooning a trapped fly. The Prelate fell face-first into the sand, smoke drifting off his headdress.

He writhed in the sand for a few moments that soon enough settled into stillness. Once he had stopped moving, Nicholas delicately plucked the Prelate's gun from the sand, using only his thumb and forefinger.

"I'll take this," he said. He wiped it on his robe, and then gripped it more fully in his hand.

A mad grin smeared across his face, he turned to Julian and Cody and their gathered group of lost children.

"I've found a way out," he said.

CHAPTER 44

NICHOLAS DIRECTED THEM DOWN THE BEACH TOWARD THE docks. With all the lights out and the nurses scrambling to secure Attison Camp and the receiving center, the group was able to make it to the shoreline without being followed.

"What the hell was that with those bugs?" Nicholas asked.

"I-I don't know," Julian rasped. He could barely understand it either. Did he . . . did he really call them? Was that a Wrinkle? How? But there was no time to dwell on this.

Nicholas had found a back entrance to the overnight bus parking lot. He could use his access card to break into the bus office, grab the keys, and drive out of there. A bus could fit everyone. But they needed to move now, while the confusion was at its highest point.

Cody led the kids from the front of the group, while Julian

brought up the rear, assisting Nicholas, who still walked with a limp. Rocky was not going to leave Julian's side, holding on to his arm like a vise. As they passed the dock, Julian saw all the boats were moored. Nicholas, even as he limped along, kept craning his neck to study something out at the Lake.

"What is it?" Julian said.

"Look," Nicholas said, and pointed.

In the moonlit shimmer of the Lake, Julian could see a little white crest break in the darkness, splash around for some time, then go still. Minutes later, after they had made it past the docks to the edge of the beach, the little crest surfaced once more, breaking on the opposite side of the Lake now. It thrashed again and then went still again.

"That's gotta be Georgie," Nicholas said, a wicked smile hanging lopsided on his face. "He must be a quick rebirth. Oops, too bad there's no one out there to pluck him from the icy waters."

Julian looked at Nicholas. His eyes were wild. He clutched the Prelate's gun against his stomach, dragging his left leg behind him.

At the edge of the beach, Cody, at the top of the group, came up on a row of a dozen parked buses. There was a small office structure beside them, on the edge of the parking lot.

"This is it," Nicholas said, pulling the keycard out of his robes.

They swiped in and grabbed a set of keys for the number 6 bus, then found it parked a short distance away. They unlocked the door and Cody led the kids into it, Julian, Rocky, and Nicholas rounding up the group from the rear.

Cody hopped into the driver's seat and cranked the key. The bus roared to life.

"Get on now." She beckoned to Julian, Nicholas, and Rocky.

But as Julian stepped forward, Nicholas grabbed his shoulder, holding him back.

"Wait," he said. "We still have some business to settle, you and me."

Julian's blood froze.

"Nicholas, please. Not now. We're so close."

"That's why we must," he said. "This is the only time left."

Rocky grabbed Julian's arm, his face twisted into a mask of worry.

Cody looked at them with horror. "Let's go. What are you waiting for?"

Nicholas whipped the gun up at Cody.

"This doesn't concern you," he said, his voice suddenly hard and cold and flat.

Cody raised her hands defensively, leaning back in the seat. "Whoa, whoa. Let's be calm, all right? I just want to get these kids out of here."

Nicholas nodded and then flicked the gun at her.

"I want the same, because this has nothing to do with you. So yes. Go. Now. And be thankful I even led you out of here."

"What about Rocky?" she asked.

"I'll need him, too. Now go," he said again, loud and firm.

"Julian, give me the data stick," she said.

Nicholas thrust the gun toward her. "I said, go now!"

Julian looked at Cody. He tried to tell her with his eyes—he had this. That data stick was everything they needed, and he would hold on to it.

Cody nodded back at him dismally and yanked the bus door closed.

She gunned the engine, and the bus growled as it lurched out of the lot and onto Lake Road.

All Julian could do was watch, Rocky clinging to his arm, as the bus disappeared around the bend. It felt like long moments passed in total quiet as the situation sank in.

Nicholas snorted a half laugh, shattering the silence, and Julian turned to face him.

"Here I am, looking all like the bad guy here," he said, chuckling.

"What is it, Nicholas?" Julian said, his voice suddenly small and dead, as if all of that fiery rage that had been coursing through him just minutes earlier had been compressed into a tiny, useless pebble that plinked to the ground at Nicholas's feet.

There was a catch.

Of course, there was.

He could scream until pestilential swarms filled the Lakes and gobbled up all the nurses, and still, there would be a catch.

"You remember when I first asked you to join the Burners?" Nicholas asked, with strange, out-of-place nonchalance. "I said you could be bigger than me."

He grinned. "And well, here we are. Not even I dreamed that you could do something *this* big. Breaking into the Lake, uncovering this sick little science experiment, freeing these kids." He clucked his tongue. "So impressive."

"What do you *want*?" Julian asked.

"I want that data stick," Nicholas said. "I want all those Attison Project files."

"Why? The world deserves to know this," Julian said.

Nicholas nodded. "I don't disagree with that. The world must know. But who is going to tell them? You? That *girl* Cody? And what then? What if they get you, like your mother? Look what happened to her when she tried to blow the whistle." Nicholas frowned and shook his head in pity. "Besides, do you think people will listen to a bunch of retrogrades and orphans?" he asked. "You'll be discredited in a second."

"So, what? *You're* going to tell them?" Julian asked, stunned.

Nicholas grinned. "I have certain plans," he said. "Best kept to myself for the time being. But, yes, they involve giving the press all the information right there on that stick."

Julian shook his head. "I can't do it, Nicholas."

"What? You don't trust me?"

Julian glared at him. "Don't make me answer that."

Nicholas laughed. "All right, look. You coerced me into coming tonight. But still, I helped you out. I went above and beyond, you have to admit that."

Julian nodded.

Nicholas removed something else from his pocket. A little black device about the size of his palm.

"So, in the spirit of going above and beyond, I'm going to offer you a fair trade for that stick instead of just shooting you right now. This right here is a numbering gun. I swiped it from the Spoof floor. What I can do with this is brand you and your little brother there with whatever number you want. In exchange, you give me the stick and we go our separate ways."

Julian tried to swallow but his throat was frozen.

Any number he wanted . . .

He could be a Nine. Rocky could be a Nine. They would never have to burn again. They would get every refund and grant and rebate the state offered. They could fix everything. They would be outside the system.

All he had to do was hand over one little data stick.

Nicholas's grin was wild and primeval, like a bloodthirsty wolf looking up from a fresh kill. "Boy, I'd sure like to get one of those nice apartments downtown in the Nine District."

Julian shook his head. "But maybe the life score . . . maybe it's going to come down anyway, once these Attison Project files get out there."

Nicholas nodded. "Perhaps," he said. "Or perhaps they just clean up that project, delete all records, blame some bad apples, and then get back to work. The only thing we can say for certain is that if I give you guys these legitimate Nines right now, however this Attison Project shakes out, it wouldn't matter to you. You'd be free of the system, no matter what."

Julian swallowed.

"Why? Why do you care what number I am?"

Nicholas made a tsk-tsking sound with his tongue as he shook his head.

"The simple fact is that I have trust issues, you see. If you know about my number, then the only way I can live with that is if I know you have a fake number, too. That way, we're both liars."

"You're sick," Julian said. Nicholas twirled the numbering gun on his finger.

"Did I ever tell you about a little phrase I live by, Julian?" Nicholas asked. "You grab life by the neck and you choke it to death."

Julian nodded. "You did," he said flatly.

"Ah," Nicholas said. "Sometimes I repeat myself. It's mildly embarrassing."

Rocky squeezed his arm. Julian looked down into his little brother's big eyes. They were filled with fear. What world was he was going to walk out into when they finally escaped this godforsaken parking lot? A world where their mother and father were both gone? Where they were both low on the totem pole, with nothing else going for them except a hope that people would *maybe* hear the truth and then *maybe* decide to do the right thing?

Julian took the data stick from his pocket.

You grab life by the neck . . .

And he handed it to Nicholas, who snatched it quickly, grinning wildly.

. . . and you choke it to death.

"You win, Nicholas. You always win."

Nicholas pocketed the data stick along with the pistol. He then flicked a switch on the numbering gun, and it hummed to life.

There was no more darkness for Julian to push away tonight. It had all been drained out of him and whipped into a storm of pestilence that had roared through the Attison Camp.

There was nothing else left for him to look at now.

Nothing left to see.

Nicholas put the numbering gun to Julian's neck. He could feel it vibrating. He could feel its heat.

"Do it," Julian said.

There was a hot prick on his flesh as the new chip was injected. Nicholas pulled the gun away, and then with the back of his hand, he gingerly touched Julian's neck on the site of his new tattoo.

"Looks good."

"Now Rocky, too," Julian said.

Rocky winced as Nicholas put the gun to his neck—on the opposite side of his One.

"You'll want to get that One removed once you make it back to town," Nicholas said. "I know a guy if you need a recommendation."

Julian didn't respond. He leaned down next to his little brother, and looked him square in the face. "It's going to be okay," Julian said, trying to convince himself of the same thing.

"Or find someone yourself, I don't care," Nicholas said as he pulled the trigger.

Rocky flinched as the number was seared on, and the chip injected. Julian pulled him into his chest and hugged him. "It's going to be okay."

"You made the right choice," Nicholas said as he tore his robe off and tossed it onto the ground. He was wearing the academy school blazer underneath. The blue one.

He tucked the numbering gun into his inside pocket, then turned to look at his reflection in the window of a bus. He straightened his hair.

"I can go back to the receiving center and find my own way out," he said. "No one is going to suspect me, the son of the Lake director, the unfortunate kid who fell and got hurt in this big terrorist fracas thing, and has to be rushed home now. But . . ." He looked them up and down. "I don't know about you two."

Julian grabbed Rocky's hand.

"We'll find our own way," he said.

"Good luck."

Julian led Rocky across the parking lot, to the edge of the forest. He could feel Nicholas watching him from behind as they disappeared into the tree line.

"Julian," Nicholas said. "Another thing."

But Julian would not turn around. There was nothing else that boy could say now that he wanted to hear.

He grabbed Rocky's hand, and the two of them disappeared into the trees.

Julian and Rocky walked all night until they reached Lake Road, where he tore his robe off and stuffed it in a tree stump—the jumpsuit underneath was dark and would help hide him if they stuck to the shadows. They followed the road, keeping to the tree line wherever possible and hiding whenever the siren of an emergency vehicle screamed by. When Rocky grew tired, Julian hoisted him up onto his back and carried him.

Eventually, they made it to Poplar Heights, and they stuck to the alleys from there as the morning light broke over the day. He led them to the alley behind Bardo Books. A group of Lake cats scattered away from them when they entered.

Julian looked up at the fire escapes, searching for that black cat with the white eye patch, but couldn't make it out among the glint of alien eyes staring back at him.

He led his little brother down the steps to the basement entrance. He pounded and pounded on the door until finally the woman in the rectangle glasses opened it and peeked outside.

"We don't do this anymore," she said, looking over the two disheveled orphans. "You need to find somewhere else."

"I'm sorry," Julian said. "But there is no somewhere else for us anymore."

She looked at them for a long moment. But then she opened the door and led them inside.

CHAPTER 45

AH, YES. THERE'S THAT DELICIOUS BITTERNESS.

Two members of the house staff carried in a tray containing a carafe of freshly brewed coffee. They set it down before Nicholas, who sat reclining in his father's chair with his feet up on the desk. He watched them as they poured a steaming cup. He held it close, savoring the aroma, as the staff gathered the tray and left, shooting each other little nervous glances.

Were they worried they wouldn't have jobs tomorrow?

Or, perhaps, it was the Councilmen who were making them nervous.

Two of the highest-elevated members of the Council of the Awakened were sitting at a table in the back of the room, leafing through stacks of his father's documents. Their two security officers stood behind them, their hands folded behind their backs.

"Would you gentlemen like some coffee?" Nicholas asked.

They declined.

The Councilmen were dressed in simple dark suits. They were here on business. Business they hoped to conclude swiftly and with minimal unpleasantness.

Nicholas sipped from his coffee and scrolled through the headlines on his father's computer. News of the Attison Project leak out of Lakeshore was everywhere. Flashing banners on every news site and social media outlet reminded readers that life scores had been suspended across the country and all extinguishment clinics were shut down everywhere, including in the Lake Superior States. "Do not die," the banners proclaimed. "The risk of failing to be reborn, while low, is not worth it."

Effects had quickly rippled out across the world.

Lakes across Europe had been shut and seized by the military as unrest spread even more virulently across the continent. There were legitimate fears of governments falling now. Of perhaps another Great War looming.

In the opinion pages, experts declared that the "Lake Question" was temporary and would soon be solved. Some columnists championed the direct intervention of the Council to assume control from the obviously corrupt Department of the Lakes, while others lamented that bringing the Council into bureaucratic affairs did not portend well for the independence of any of the scientific inquiries assembled to investigate and fix the problem of the Lakes eroding. The Councilmen were politicians, after all, not scientists. Others wondered about the economic consequences: Would nurses be laid off, bus drivers, actuaries?

Yes, yes, yes, all big stuff, serious stuff, but . . .

He scrolled further, and found what he was looking for.

An exposé asking the most important question in this whole matter: "Who was Nicholas Hawksley, the leaker of the Attison Project files and the hero from the unassuming county of Lakeshore who brought the entire system to its knees?"

Nicholas grinned as he saw they had used his good academy portrait: the one with the perfect part in his hair.

Who is Nicholas Hawksley?

Nicholas had to suppress his smile, as there was a commotion outside. The Councilmen rose from their seats, and the guards made their way to the entrance.

Nicholas's father entered, the servants trailing behind him.

When he saw the Councilmen, he set his luggage on the floor and sighed.

"I suppose it's my time," David said.

The skinnier of the two Councilmen, named Rousseau, stood and gestured to security, who stepped beside David, pulling his arms behind his back and cuffing him.

"We're sorry, Director Hawksley. But we never endorsed your actions."

David shook his head with contempt.

"You knew. You all knew."

The Councilmen looked back at him with silent, stony glares.

"You tasked me with an answer to the overuse of the Lakes, and an answer I provided," David said. "And this is how you repay me?"

Councilman Rousseau frowned. "We needed an answer that was more politically palatable."

David looked over at Nicholas. They made eye contact for a long, painful moment.

"Nicholas," he said. "How could you? You're my son. I protected you."

"Yes," Nicholas said, setting his cup down, "but you never gave me a choice in the matter. You gave me goals and expectations, and pressure . . . God, the pressure." He shook his head and clucked his tongue. "But you never thought to ask me what I wanted. I never wanted to follow in your footsteps. I just wanted to impress you.

"And when I discovered this project of yours . . . I realized that the version of me who wanted to impress you all this time? Well, that version of me is dead now."

David glared at Nicholas. "You blame me for your ambition?"

Nicholas's eye twitched, a fleeting pinprick of anger.

"I blame you for everything."

The Councilmen stepped between them.

"We have to let the process take its course now," said the one called Councilman Gerson.

"How could you do this to me?" David shouted to Nicholas as the guards pushed him out the door. "Your own family!"

Nicholas sipped his coffee.

The Councilmen packed up David's files and, together with security, they escorted him out of the room.

Ahh.

Bitter and black.

He put his feet back up on his father's desk.

It didn't get any better than this.

The next day at the academy, afternoon classes were cancelled for a special assembly.

Nicholas sat on the stage in the gymnasium. Headmaster Denton had the podium, and beside him sat a chubby woman with short hair and a severe expression. There was also a gallery of news reporters lined up in front of the bleachers, near where the old Burners' section used to be. The academy's entire student body filled out the seats.

With two notable exceptions, Nicholas realized as he scanned the crowd.

"I have several important announcements for you today," Denton said at the podium, his voice scratchy, his lips visibly dry and parched.

"First, in accordance with the new rules from the Council of the Awakened, the academy is suspending its life score. Extinguishments are no longer endorsed or condoned by the academy."

He coughed loudly, clearing his throat.

"Second," he continued. "This illicit Burners Society has been shut down. And the leaders of the club, Franklin Overton and Constance Zandt, have been assigned to community service in a project to re-home all the unfortunate souls in Retro Row. It is a fitting and just punishment."

Denton looked out at the crowd and sighed.

"Finally, I am stepping down as the headmaster of the academy. It has been my great honor to have seen so many of you grow and thrive in your many lives."

There were some murmurs of surprise, and muted elation, from the student body.

"I introduce to you Headmistress Perigree."

He stepped aside, and the chubby woman stepped up to the podium.

She introduced herself and explained that the academic year was going to continue as planned, minus any emphasis on the life score, of course. Then she turned to Nicholas.

"Now, I think we should all take a moment to commend the selfless actions of one of our own academy members. A brave soul who dared to stand up for what is right. He single-handedly transformed the world, and he should be an example to all of us."

She gestured for him to stand. "Nicholas Hawksley."

She turned to the crowd. "Let us applaud this young man." Slowly, reluctantly, the crowd began to clap.

"Where would any of us be now without Nicholas Hawksley?"

Nicholas stood, basking, as the flashes of the cameras popped around him. Among the dazzle of the lights and the cheers he saw one figure slink out of the crowd to the exit.

Julian.

Halfway out the door, he turned to look at Nicholas.

Nicholas nodded to him.

Could you be bigger than me one day, Julian?

He grinned and waved for the cameras.

Not anymore, friend.

CHAPTER 46

JULIAN LOOKED UP FROM HIS DESK AND OUT THE WINDOW
of his new apartment. Fat snowflakes drifted through the air. He
was still getting used to this view of the Lakeshore skyline. Lake
Tower stood out among the buildings, like a giant exclamation
point.

Looking at the Tower, Nicholas's shit-eating grin flashed into
Julian's mind.

Nicholas's eyes, wild with perverse morbidity, that night
in the van as they approached the Tower . . . Those eyes—that
grin—of *the hero* of Lakeshore . . .

And here Julian sat, in this apartment, this new life, this new
number, this *Nine* . . .

He had to turn away from the window.

In fact, he was done for the night. He closed his notebook

up. He felt ready to take the exams now. Ready to put in an application to Azura University. The advisers at his new school, Perennial Prep, had assured him that he had a real shot now—especially since he would probably be the only Nine applying.

He went over to Rocky's side of the table. Rocky was halfway through a mathematics worksheet. He helped his little brother complete it, and then it was time for bed. Julian watched, feeling responsible and parental, as Rocky brushed his teeth, and then stood in the bedroom doorway as he crawled under the covers.

"Tomorrow's Saturday," Julian said. "You know what that means?"

Their weekly video game tournament was going to proceed as scheduled.

"You're going down in flames," Rocky said, and laughed.

"Not likely," Julian said. He made sure to catch a glimpse of Rocky's Nine—the digit was a dark smudge on his little brother's neck, contorting as he flexed while wrestling with the covers.

Checking Rocky's number was a new habit—Julian found himself repeatedly verifying it against reality.

Young Rocky would never—*never*—have to know what it's like to crawl, disoriented, out of the Lake and into a new life.

"'Night, kid," Julian said.

"'Night," Rocky replied.

Julian turned off the lights and returned to the table in the living room.

They had three rooms. A big kitchen. A great view. Julian would sometimes run his hands along the tile, like how he would check Rocky's life number—a reminder to himself that this was real.

It was.

It was theirs.

A world of multitudes.

He just wished his mother and father were here to see this.

His father was gone, though they could find no record of his permadeath. In the past few weeks, the Council, making a big show of their sudden empathy, had scoured the Row and brought all the retros into shelters, where they were identified—but Julian's father was not among them. Either he never emerged from the Lake again after his final, doomed extinguishment—a victim of its changing nature—or his permadeath was inflicted by the nurses just as they had done to Julian's mother, and the record of it was destroyed in a final, desperate cover-up.

Either way, he was gone. Like Julian's mother.

And yet, in a way, they were still here.

They were alive again every time Julian saw his brother's Nine: that was his mother, living on in that number. Their father too: together, they created Julian and Rocky, and tried to shelter them from the worst of the world, but it was Julian who completed what they started—he had kept them going.

His mother also came to him when he caught a glimpse of himself in the mirror, and saw his eyes. He would think of hers. Two deep, understanding pools, their colors shifting in his memory, but still there.

Still there.

This thought sparked a kind of pure and unadulterated elation, a joy like he hadn't experienced in years. It was a joy of having a memory. To be able to recall moments long past, and people long gone. To bring things back and *relive* them. That was the kind of "rebirth" that felt right and natural. The kind of rebirth that had a place in the world.

Johanna, the proprietor of Bardo Books, had helped set him up with a lawyer—a big, fuzzy man with a Seven and wet eyes in a swelteringly heated downtown office—to negotiate a rebate check for being so high-numbered. She had someone clean up Rocky's old One, and she also helped them acquire an apartment in the Nine District. More crucially, she helped ensure Julian had guardianship over Rocky—which seemed to go through easier than anyone expected, probably because the courts were overwhelmed with litigation stemming from the Attison Project.

There was a letter from Johanna on the table in front of him, beside his study guide. Julian tore it open. The message it contained was short and simple: someone needed to meet with him tonight.

Once he was sure Rocky was asleep, Julian slipped out of the apartment.

He drove out from downtown, through Lakeshore, and into Poplar Heights.

He parked in front of Bardo Books and walked the narrow side street to the alley behind it. A dusting of snow covered the asphalt behind the store.

There were no cats tonight.

But there was Cody.

She had cut her hair and dyed it black. Her bangs were cropped short and it framed her face in an angular shape. Though he hadn't seen or heard from her since the break-in at the Lake, this was unmistakably Cody, her freckles bright in the flush of her face from the cold air. She had a dark scarf wrapped around her neck, hiding her number.

She looked older. Julian felt like he was seeing her for the first time. Cody as she really was, all along—the Cody that she willed into the universe. Confident and defiant and in charge, the renegade daughter. He felt his cheeks redden—he didn't belong here with her. He never did.

She gave Julian a small wave as he approached her.

"Do you know why they call it Bardo Books?" she asked.

Julian shook his head no.

"The Bardo is the Tibetan concept of purgatory," she said. "It seemed fitting at the time for a group of people who want to stop all extinguishments so we could live our lives any way we pleased." She chuckled slightly.

"But the more I think about it, the more the connotations seem a little too negative to me. Like, does that suggest we would be trapped in a perpetual kind of limbo?" She shook her head. "Mankind was meant to have only one life. That's how the world used to be for millions and millions of years."

Julian nodded. "I like your hair," he said.

She allowed herself a small smile, but she was obviously fighting to repress it.

"I wanted you to know that everyone got out safe. All the kids from Cat's Cradle, from Attison Camp, and even Robbie and Cassie have stuck with us," she said. "Or Molly, as you knew her."

"Where?" Julian asked.

That faint outline of a smile vanished from her lips.

"I can't tell you that," she said.

She glanced at the Nine on his neck, then looked away quickly.

"I understand why you did what you did. But . . ."

Julian nodded. "I get it."

"I also asked you here," Cody said, looking away, "to say goodbye."

Julian exhaled, a sense of melancholy cutting through him like the chill of the Lakeshore winter. Snowflakes drifted down around them.

"The Council is looking for us," she said. "Even if they accept Nicholas Hawksley as the public face of the leak, they know there were others behind the break-in. And they're not going to let us just exist outside their control."

"So, you're leaving," Julian said.

She nodded, frowning slightly, dimpling her freckled cheeks.

"We have reports that burnings are already resuming in the Lake Superior States on a more aggressive schedule. Things might seem better now, but they're actually only going to get worse. There are still food shortages. Droughts and crop failures. That hasn't changed. But somehow I think the Council will only care about protecting their own power over anything else."

Julian nodded. "You will be safe about things, right?"

She stepped close to him. She grabbed his face and kissed him on the cheek.

"You betcha," she said.

Julian pulled her in close and hugged her. She embraced him back, squeezing his head against her face. It was warm in the cold air. As he held her close, Julian saw something out of the corner of his eye.

It was that cat . . .

It was sitting there, in the snow, staring at him, its tail swishing through the night.

His heart skipped its beat.

"Cody . . . ," he said, pulling away from her.

He was suddenly overcome with an odd feeling. Like he was weightless again. Like he was tumbling from Lake Tower.

"Do you see the cat?"

"Cat?" Cody said. She turned around.

"I don't see anything," she said, stepping away from him.

Julian squinted his eyes shut, and rubbed them until the dizzying sensation faded. Until he was on solid ground again. Until he was himself again.

He opened his eyes. The world was fuzzy, but he blinked it back into focus, and as he did, he saw Cody slipping away.

"Goodbye, Mr. Julian," Cody said, disappearing down the alley.

Julian stood for a moment as the snow fell, watching her figure vanish into the night.

Then he turned around, looking for the cat.

But it wasn't there.

Nor were there any tracks.

Only a dusting of snow, undisturbed and gleaming in the moonlight.

ACKNOWLEDGMENTS

Thank you to my agent, Jim McCarthy, for your wisdom and patience, and for your faith in this project. I'm extremely grateful to have you in my corner.

Without my editor, Kristen Pettit, this book would not exist. Thank you for bringing out the best in this story. Your incisive editing and keen sense of narrative were a massive inspiration. I hope to have even a fraction of your skill rub off and follow me to my next book.

Thanks also to the entire team at Harper Collins for bringing this book to life. Thanks to the arresting cover art from Sarah Kaufman and Craig Shields, and thanks to Elizabeth Lynch for the patience and jacket copy (and apologies for having to read my handwriting).

Philippa Donovan—I owe you my deepest gratitude. Your

insight into the business of books, and into this book in particular, and on writing in general (and life in general) has been invaluable to me. Let's just say, I owe you one.

Thank you, Zach Cox, for your encouragement and early reads, and thank you, David Alpert, for taking a chance on me years ago in the first place. Thanks to Elizabeth Lo for the insightful feedback (and infinite patience), even after the millionth draft. Thanks also to Yalun Tu, for several lives' worth of narrative discussions, and Isabel Marden, who helped me envision the teachings of the Temple of the Nine. Thank you to Brenda Hsueh for discussions about Malthusian perils. Thanks to my parents for keeping the place well-stocked with books when I was a kid. Thanks to Eric Puestow and Katie Doering for the hospitality and the house. Thanks also to Travis Hines, Sarah Fung, Adam White, Evan Greenspoon, Wendy Park, Jon Stocking, and Tim Szetela for all the advice and help and friendship over the years.